Sisters of Mercy

Millie Curtis

Avid Readers Publishing Group
Lakewood, California

Sisters of Mercy

Avid Readers Publishing Group

http://www.avidreaderspg.com

ISBN-13: 978-1-61286-372-6

Printed in the United States

Author's Note

In 1861 when the Civil War began in the United States of America, some forward thinking people realized that there had to be a way to take care of the sick and wounded soldiers.

This novel deals only with the Eastern battles of the Civil War. It is about the women who worked as nurses with the United States Sanitary Commission (forerunner of the American Red Cross). The U.S. Sanitary Commission was a private organization formed for the purpose of caring for both Union and Confederate soldiers.

Although the Commission was sanctioned by President Lincoln, and worked in tandem with the government's Medical Department, there was no government funding. It was an organization run on donations and public funding. It was disbanded in May of 1866.

The author has taken stories from diaries recorded by some of these women nurses and intertwined them with the fictitious Mary Sullivan. The names of notable public figures, dates of battles and historical information are as accurate as could be researched.

Acknowledgements

Many thanks to Amy Nishimoto, Catherine Owens, Rebecca Moran, Curtis Nishimoto, Elizabeth Blye and Fred Curtis for helping me finish this novel.

Photos by Elizabeth Blye and Amy Nishimoto

Chapter 1

In 1861 the United States of America was in turmoil.

When I resigned my coveted teaching position to become a volunteer in the New York Woman's Association of Relief, my parents were shocked.

My name is Mary Sullivan. I am writing this memoir from my experiences during the Civil War. They are so ingrained in my memory I doubt they will ever fade. To this day I have nightmares. Nightmares filled with the screams and pleading of the suffering soldiers.

As I am writing this for posterity, it seems logical that I should relate what led up to the war. After all, I am a teacher.

The primary cause was trade. The industrial North wanted government regulations regarding the buying and selling of goods. The agricultural South wanted free trade to sell and buy their goods at any time. The two institutions and cultures were so different a compromise could not be reached, and war was declared between the states.

As the war went on not only was trade the bone of contention, abolition of slavery became a prime cause. It is interesting to note that President Lincoln's Emancipation Proclamation was declared effective, January 1, 1863, almost two years into the war. And, the wording appears only to free the slaves in the Confederacy: *all held as slaves within any state or part of a designated site where the people are in rebellion...*

South Carolina had already seceded from the Union on December 20, 1860. It was the attack on the Union's Fort Sumter, off the coast of South Carolina, in April of 1861 that was the action that precipitated the War of Rebellion.

According to our local paper, *The Albany Bee*, the government expected this insurrection to be quelled quickly.

However, three days later President Lincoln called for 75,000 volunteers from state militias to serve three months to bolster the guard of the government in Washington, D.C.

The states of Maryland and Virginia had many Confederate sympathizers and due to location, posed a bigger threat to the country's capital.

In the North patriotism ran high. I wrote a letter to my cousin, Abby, in New York City. Her return missives were what caused me to act.

Her first letter told that she, her three sisters and my Aunt Martha, had joined the New York Woman's Association of Relief to make preparations for the militias going to Washington.

She went on to explain: shortly after Fort Sumter fell, Elizabeth Blackwell, the first female degreed medical doctor in the country, foresaw medical care would be needed. President Lincoln called for troops, but no adequate preparations had been made for the influx of 75,000 men.

There was no official soldiers' hospital. Most nurses were men, some of them recovering patients. Others, both men and women came from the lower walks of life: drunks, prostitutes, charwomen.

Having trained at Old Blockley Almshouse and Hospital in Philadelphia, Dr. Blackwell had witnessed the deplorable care given patients at that hospital, and at Bellevue in New York City. Her feeling was that women in good standing should be nurses. Something had to be done.

Dr. Blackwell called a meeting of a small group of prominent people which became the Central Relief Committee. They agreed with Dr. Blackwell regarding the need for female nurses.

Therefore, a larger meeting was held at Cooper Union, a massive hall on Cooper Square in Manhattan. At this meeting the New York Woman's Organization of Relief replaced the Central Relief Committee. A board was chosen consisting of 12 men and 12 women. Louisa Lee Schuyler was appointed president.

Two needs were immediate: the need to look after the comfort of the soldiers and the need for training nurses. Dr. Blackwell interviewed scores of women volunteers. One hundred honorable women were chosen to become army nurses. They were to be trained for three months under the physicians at Bellevue.

All of that information came in Abby's first letter. The second one made my decision. She wrote that she and her sisters had watched the different militia groups from Massachusetts, Rhode Island,

and Pennsylvania march through the city headed for Washington. Her only brother, my cousin Charley, had joined the 164th NY Regiment and was assigned to headquarters as an aide-de-camp. What a perfect set-up for my cousins to get first-hand information.

Abby described how she and her older sister, Jenny, were on their way to pay a call to a lady when they saw a crowd gathering at the Brevoort House, a hotel on their street where Mrs. Anderson was staying. Her husband, Major Robert Anderson, had been in charge of Fort Sumter.

Abby explained how the cousins waited with the gathering until Major Anderson came to the doorway of the hotel, bowed a few times in strict military fashion, and the crowd cheered. Abby described him as a man of short stature, middle-aged, average-looking, grey hair, wrinkles, and a proud bearing.

As I read Abby's letter the thought came to me that if women were rallying to the cause there was no reason for me not to join my cousins. My teaching term at a small community outside Albany, New York would end in May. I was young, unmarried, and without further obligations. Without hesitation I submitted my letter of resignation to the school directors.

They were not pleased with the prospect of finding a replacement, and they cautioned me not to be hasty with my decision. They said they expected this rebellion would be over soon. What were they thinking? At that time it was almost two months after Fort Sumter fell and Washington was in pure bedlam. I thought this group of men had their heads in the sand. Of course, I kept my thoughts to myself.

My parents were not understanding when I broke the news of my plans to them. My father's words still echo in my ears. "Have you lost your mind, Mary?"

"No, Father. Abby says much work needs to be done. I can stay at their house. I feel it is my duty."

Their faces held such pinched expressions I tried to lessen their anxiety. "I have given this much thought. I realize what I am giving up. When this is over, I can return to teaching."

That statement wasn't even considered. "You are putting yourself in a dangerous position. How safe will you be in New York City? A young woman traveling alone. It's unheard of!" Father protested, his usual quiet voice becoming a crescendo.

Mother stood wringing her hands. "Mary, dear. Think of your pension. You will need it down the road."

Mother was a worrier.

I am not sure how I would have reacted if Father had forbidden me to go. After all, they had seen to my education at the Albany Normal School at a sacrifice to themselves. Father was only a bank teller. And, I was still living under their roof, although I did surrender some of my wages each month.

I ignored their protests with my mind on preparations and, God help me, a sense of excitement for the journey. I had not been to New York City nor seen my cousins for a long time even though Abby and I had remained staunch pen pals. Financially, her family was far better off than mine. Aunt Martha, my mother's sister, had married well. Her husband, a shipping financier, had died in a tragic boat accident leaving her to raise four girls and one boy. He had left the family monetarily sound and a pillar of society in the city. Despite the disparity in lifestyle and social status, Abby and I had always been more like sisters. We had spent a week in the summer at each other's homes until I went to the teachers' school.

Chapter 2

When it was time for me to depart, my parents were resolved to the fact I was leaving my comfortable surroundings, although they still weren't comfortable with my going. I promised to write, telling them perhaps the insurrection would end before school started again in September.

As I look back, I realize how unprepared I was for what was to come.

Father drove me to the train station in our buggy with Mother along for the sendoff. She was in tears when I waved to them from the window in the train car. They both looked so sad it brought a lump to my throat. But I knew I had to go, even though I was completely unaware of what lay ahead.

The trip from Albany along the Hudson River was beautiful that time of year. There were other passengers in the rail car: mostly men, two couples, a few small families. I was fortunate there was not a passenger next to me so I had more room. I had chosen to wear a full ruffled petticoat under my long light-blue muslin dress instead of a hoop. It would not be pleasant to be packed in like a sardine. Besides, I only wore hoops for Sunday services or an outing with friends.

The sun was bright, the trees fresh for a new season, and pristine farmland sported baby animals; all were positive signs the world is meant to go on despite the threat of war brewing within our own country.

It took some time, but I finally relaxed and sat back to enjoy the trip.

Mother insisted I take some buttered soda crackers with me. It was good that she did as my stomach was not up to breakfast. I munched on the crackers as I rode.

Abby had written directions telling me of the spot to leave the train saving me a ride into the main New York Central station. Although her family lived in the city, it was a big place and not always easy to navigate around the different horse-drawn vehicles. Plus, there were pockets in the city that spelled danger for unchaperoned young women.

I felt a pang of anxiousness when the train began to slow. Questions ran through my mind: Was I doing the right thing? Should I have heeded my parents' warnings? Was I going to be a help or a hindrance? Abby said they were helping with medical supplies. I knew little about anything to do with medicine.

The train slowed to a stop and I was glad to leave the noisy, smelly, smoky rail car. The conductor gave me a hand as I descended the metal steps. With a sense of relief I saw my three cousins hurrying toward me.

"Mary," Abby called waving her hand-kerchief and rushing ahead of the others. Throwing her arms around me she gave me a big welcome hug. "Charley will retrieve your luggage from the depot platform for you."

Jenny came next. She took both my hands, smiled in her mild, quiet way and said, "It is so good to see you, Cousin. We are happy you have come."

Charley, dressed in a blue uniform, had developed into a fine-looking young man instead of the gawky teenager I had last seen. He gave a military bow. "Welcome, Cousin Mary," he said in an adult voice before he went to the luggage platform.

I was so gladly received, I felt comfortable with my decision.

Abby and Jenny wore grand hoops, fine dresses with long sleeves and high necks, and beribboned bonnets. They had not changed much from the last time I had seen them. Jenny was still slim and delicate. She wore glasses, which made her brown eyes appear larger. Her long honey-colored hair was parted in the middle, pulled back in a bun. Although a year older than Abby, Jenny had always allowed her younger sister to be noticed.

Abby was spritely and very much at ease with herself. Whereas the hooped skirts helped Jenny's slimness, Abby was amply endowed and the full skirt caused her to look pounds heavier. She had always had a comely face and ready smile. Abby's hair was chestnut-brown worn parted in the middle and neatly tucked under the wine-colored bonnet that matched her dress.

These were my society cousins. I felt like the country bumpkin coming to the big city in my blue cotton dress and navy straw hat. No one seemed to mind. I wore my dark hair in a long braid. Perhaps I was more like Jenny in that I held a quiet disposition. Perhaps I loved to be with Abby because she was so full of life and spoke her mind. Our birthdays were a month apart.

A handsome open carriage with black leather seats waited. The driver took my small trunk from Charley and loaded it onto the back of the carriage. We were off to Brevoort Street.

It was a pleasant day as I recall. I noticed the citizens of the city seemed to be going about their daily business. What I also noticed were the Stars and Stripes flying high, banners on balconies, and many women wearing cockades with colors of the flag on their hats and bonnets.

The country's colors reminded me that we were close to all-out war with our Southern brothers. I sat next to Abby facing Charley and Jenny on the cushioned seat of the topless carriage.

Abby looked over at me. "Mary, so much has happened within a month, I'm not sure where to begin. Life has been a whirlwind. Do you get much news from the Albany paper?"

"I have been so busy with the end of school and preparing for this trip that I've left the newspaper up to Father. He gives me a daily run down. I am guilty of not paying full attention."

"Do you know about the newly formed United States Sanitary Commission?"

"Please tell me," I suggested knowing Abby was eager to give me the details.

"Well, this is how it came about. There were many relief organizations popping up in the Northern states."

"That should be good," I said.

"If it had worked," she replied. "Men were coming from all different states and their women wanted to see they were cared for. Those silly women loaded up all kinds of jams, jellies, pickles, canned meat, vegetables, and so forth. They loaded them all together with clothing, books, stationery and other needs…"

"Their hearts were in the right place, Abby," came a mild admonition from Jenny.

Abby shrugged a shoulder, "Perhaps their hearts were, but their brains weren't," answered Abby. "Poorly canned foods exploded, glass jars broke, food rotted spoiling the other cargo. The railroads were left with a stinking mess. The railroad heads complained to the government." Abby took a deep breath before she continued.

"Something had to be done. Dr. Henry Bellows, a Unitarian minister from here and member of our New York board, thought a national central relief organization should be formed."

"That sounds reasonable," I surmised.

"It was," Abby agreed. "Members of the board decided to go to Washington to plead their case. Of course, no women members on the board were invited."

"They are notable men, Abby," injected Jenny.

Abby gave a wave of dismissal. "Anyway, Dr. Bellows and three physicians went to Washington

11

last week. June 9th to be exact. They met with the Secretary of War, Simon Cameron, and the Surgeon General of the Army, Clement Finley."

"They must have been notable men if they were received by those department heads," I said.

"I suppose," said Abby. "The outcome of that meeting was to appoint a board to head up a central relief organization, which is called the United States Sanitary Commission."

Finally, Abby was to the point of her explanation. I spoke my thought aloud. "One place to bring all the relief organizations of the Northern states is a wise decision."

Abby nodded. "I agree. Naturally, the national board is all male, but they did appoint our Louisa Lee Schuyler to organize the East and Mary Livermore is organizing the Northwest out of Chicago."

"Does the government fund this Sanitary Commission?" I asked.

Abby shook her head, "President Lincoln approved of it, but it is still a private entity and is dependent on public and private donations."

"None of this has been easy," informed Jenny. "There has been much opposition to women nurses and those in the relief. War is no place for women is the sentiment."

I smiled at the thought. "I believe Father would feel the same. But, it appears there is a great need for women's help."

"No doubt," Abby was back in full swing. "Unfortunately, those men on the board appointed

Dorothea Dix to be the Supervisor of Army Nurses. I don't know why they chose that old woman when Dr. Blackwell was clearly the better choice."

Jenny spoke again with a mild reprimand, "Miss Dix is a well-respected Social Reformer and strong leader, Abby. I understand she is President Lincoln's choice."

"Someone must have twisted his arm," said a disgruntled Abby.

"Mother would not appreciate hearing you talk like that," cautioned Jenny. "Oh look, Mary," she changed the subject. "We're passing the Brevoort House where Major and Mrs. Anderson are staying. Charley has been in conference with the major."

Charley, who had remained silent to this point, corrected, "Not face to face, Cousin Mary. I attended as an aide to my superior."

I looked in the direction Jenny pointed and saw a large brick building much like many of the other buildings in the city.

Suddenly, I was thrown sideways with jolt of the carriage and we all grabbed the sides.

"Our driver is giving you a taste of the rutted city streets of New York," remarked Charley. "Another welcome to the city."

I smiled at my sandy-haired, blue-eyed cousin, a lad at the end of his teen years. I brought the conversation back to where we had left off. "Is Miss Dix performing well?" I asked.

Abby grimaced. "I guess. I still feel that position should have gone to Dr. Blackwell. However, the male dominated medical profession has not accepted a woman breaking their ranks. I guess the powers-that-be think a sixty-year-old spinster a better choice."

Jenny rolled her eyes and shook her head at her sister's outspoken opinion.

"Would you like to be a nurse, Mary?" asked Jenny.

I shook my head at the thought.

Abby spoke up, "I wanted to be an army nurse until I learned no hoops were allowed. Miss Dix has made some stringent rules."

I was intrigued. "Such as?"

Abby turned her nose in the air. "A woman must be thirty or over, plain looking, dresses brown or black, no adornments, no hoop skirts. Can you imagine?"

Jenny looked at her sister. "I believe Miss Dix is being practical. These women will be working in hospitals with men of all ages."

"Fiddlesticks," said Abby.

"What about the 100 women Dr. Blackwell hand-picked?" I inquired.

"They are to be the army nurses working in the hospitals," replied Jenny. "Our sister, Emily, has been chosen and is in training now. Dr. Blackwell was very careful in her choosing of these women. At this point we in the relief are helping from the home front by packing goods, making bandages and lint."

"But, Emily isn't thirty." I was confused.

Jenny answered, "No, dear cousin. The women Dr. Blackwell chose were picked before Miss

Dix became in charge, although, Mrs. Schuyler, the president of our relief organization, told us she had received a letter from Miss Dix, even before she had been named Superintendent of Army Nurses as to what she considered proper qualifications.

"Miss Dix is short-sighted," said Abby. "Under her leadership none of us would be accepted. One has to be an old woman of thirty."

We were nearing their house. "I am not sure I am going to be of help," I confessed. "I know nothing about making medical supplies."

"You'll learn," said Charley. "Mother insists we drag out that bandage roller with scraps of material and we all, neighbors included, must pitch in. I try to spend as much time as I can at the military office to escape."

They all laughed. "It isn't quite that drastic, Mary," said Jenny.

However light-hearted the moment, the thought of making bandages and lint, whatever that was, caused me to wonder if I was up to the task.

The carriage stopped in front of the three story grand brick house that was the Morgan house. Charley hopped out and gave each of us a hand as we left the carriage, and the driver went around the carriage to retrieve my small trunk.

Charley paid the driver and hoisted my luggage to his shoulder. He was quite the gentleman, thought I.

The door opened as we walked up the brick sidewalk to the stoop. Aunt Martha appeared in her hooped dress of navy grenadine. Aunt Martha was of average height and size with dark-brown hair and brown eyes that glistened. Her stature spoke of her status in the social world. How very different she was from her sister, my mother, who cherished her quiet way of life, and whose big outing would be a church social.

With a genuine smile, the gracious lady put her arms around me. "Our dear, Mary. You are here at last. We have all been looking forward to your arrival."

"Thank you for allowing me to come."

She ushered me into the house. "I'm sure you are tired after that train ride, but before you go to freshen up and rest, you must tell me how things are with your mother and father."

Just my aunt and I sat in the tall-ceilinged parlor, which was just as I had remembered. Twin globe lamps sat on two mahogany end tables with a tan leather divan setting between them. Two tall windows, draped in green velvet, sat on either side of a red brick fireplace. Tapestried chairs made a comfortable conversation spot. A wool area rug of muted colors made the room pleasant. Aunt Martha sat next to me on the divan.

After a quiet knock at the parlor door, I was startled when Florence came into the room, and more startled to see that she was expecting a baby. I stood up to greet her.

My older cousin took my hand in hers. "It is so nice to see you, Mary. Mother told me you were coming. I arrived last week. My husband is with the militia in Washington so Mother insisted that I come and stay here until our baby arrives."

"Congratulations," I managed to say over the surprise that no doubt showed on my face.

"I am on my way up to my room for a nap, but I wanted to greet you before I took my leave."

Florence turned and left the room where I resumed my seat next to Aunt Martha.

"It's wonderful that you will be welcoming a grandchild. Mother will be pleased to hear."

"I wish these were happier times, but a new baby always brings a smile. Now, you must tell me how your parents received the news that you would be coming here to help."

I felt I should be honest. "They were not pleased at first. For me, it was a difficult decision to give up my position at the school."

Aunt Martha took my hand in hers. "Of course. I can understand the difficulties for the three of you."

I sighed. "In the long run I believe they are resolved to the fact I am going to do my part if this unrest continues."

Aunt Martha nodded. "These are challenging times, Mary. We never know from one day to the next what is going to happen."

"Father agrees with that," I said. "And you know Mother is a worrier."

A wan smile appeared. "This may be a time for worry, but we are going to put the unhappy thoughts away for now. You will be in the room next to Abby's. It's the same room you've used when you have visited in the past."

"Oh, thank you. I love that cozy room, especially with the door that opens into Abby's room. We used to sneak back and forth when we were supposed to be asleep."

Aunt Martha laughed. "Florence used to tell me how you and Abby giggled through the night and sneaked down to the kitchen for cookies and milk. I guess being the oldest girl she thought it was her duty to tell on you."

My eyes widened. "You never reprimanded us."

"Young girls need to think they're getting away with something. It was harmless so there was no need to let on that I was on to your little pranks."

I laughed aloud. "We did have fun."

My kind aunt patted my hand before she stood. "You go on up and freshen up. I have sent Abby and Jenny to the butcher shop for tonight's dinner, and I need to check in on a lady down the street. You have time for a quick nap before the girls return."

I was on my feet. "A quick nap sounds heavenly," I replied and left to go upstairs.

I settled into my cozy room quite efficiently. Charley had taken my trunk and placed it under the window. It had a flat top and was sturdy so I could use it as a window seat whenever I chose. The window faced Brevoort Street and had a view of Fifth Avenue where I could watch the comings and goings of New Yorkers.

I placed my stationery, pen and bottle of ink on the small oak desk and put the few books I had brought on a shelf over the desk. I had an oil lamp for evenings, but I had the feeling that when evening came I would not have the energy to read.

I had brought one other day dress, two skirts, two waists and an extra set of underpinnings. My woolen shawl hung next to the dress, and I placed an umbrella in a tall vase that sat next to the door. My gloves I placed in my hat and laid it on another shelf above the twin oak bed. I was in heaven because the mattress and pillow were stuffed with down. Aunt Martha hired servants to cook, do laundry, clean the house and empty the chamber pots. Yes, I decided I would be most comfortable.

A nap was what I needed and I awoke with a gnawing stomach that reminded me I had hardly eaten anything except a few soda crackers. I was ready for the supper that would be served in a couple of hours.

As Charley had predicted, after a supper of beef roast and vegetables with dessert of an applesauce cake, Aunt Martha had the bandage roller plus a barrel of scrap material brought into the parlor.

Abby had elected to go to a performance by the New York Philharmonic with her cousins. She invited me to go, but as I had not brought any dress clothes, I declined. Also, I was still tired from the trip from home.

"Abigail, where are your manners? It is impolite to leave Mary behind." Aunt Martha was not pleased.

I didn't want Abby to get in trouble so I said, "Abby invited me to go but I declined. I am most happy to spend the evening with the rest of you. Abby may not get the chance to attend another concert."

Aunt Martha hesitated before she answered, "You are very kind, Mary, and I fear you may be right. Still, Abby should not be running off when she has company."

"I prefer to stay here and learn bandage and lint making."

"You see, Mother? Mary doesn't care if I go," Abby said without a hint of regret.

Jenny and I helped Abby into her evening clothes. Her gown was rose-colored satin with short sleeves and a low neckline. She wore Aunt Martha's cameo necklace and an ornate hair comb of silver.

The corset she wore had been a chore to lace up as tight as she wanted, but between Jenny and I we managed to get it almost right. "I don't see how you're going to breathe," I said.

"It matters not how I breathe but how I look," answered Abby.

"I hope you're not going to bust a gusset in the process," I remarked. That caused Jenny to laugh so hard she fell over on the bed. I plopped down beside her joining in her laughter.

Abby looked down at us. "It isn't that funny."

Jenny and I looked at each other and laughed harder.

"Get off that bed and sprinkle some toilet water on my petticoats," Abby ordered.

We scrambled off the bed and went to do her bidding. Abby was a picture of loveliness in her hooped gown, her silken hair parted in the middle with coils over each ear. The thought occurred to me that Abby would never fit into Miss Dix's idea of a nurse.

Abby's Morgan cousins arrived both elegantly dressed for a philharmonic concert. I was introduced as, "Do you remember our cousin, Mary?"

I was embarrassed and tried not to let it show. I had never felt comfortable around Harriet and Jane Morgan, who gave the impression of being a few rungs up the ladder above me.

After Abby left, the bandage roller was unveiled. It was metal, about two feet in length with a crank handle. The handle turned the roller that held a strip of material and as the handle cranked the material was pulled into a neat roll on a spindle. In the barrels were muslin, cotton, linen, flannel and wool.

While I watched the bandage rolling process, Jenny came to my side and asked if I would like to make lint. I was enthused watching these diligent women, who had come to help, go about their task. However, I believed Jenny would not pull me away from the bandage rolling process without good cause.

Jenny took some flannel out of the barrel and we sat at a side table. She handed me a sharp kitchen knife like the one she held in her slender hand, and proceeded to scrape the flannel leaving little clouds of fluff. That residue was compressed into balls of lint. She explained that the lint is used to pack wounds, apply ointments, dip into solutions, and whatever else the nurses and doctors find a use for.

That satisfied my wonder about lint. I set about to do as Jenny was doing. After an hour my hand was one big cramp, and I was beginning to get blisters. I vowed to learn how to use the bandage roller.

Abby returned from the concert all agog with her outing. "At the finale, the orchestra struck up *The Star Spangled Banner*. Every soul in the house stood with hands over their hearts. Oh, Mary, it was grand! I so wish you had come."

I smiled and, although my hands hurt from the lint making, I was glad I had missed an evening with Harriet and Jane Morgan.

Chapter 3

The next morning I awoke to the sounds of the city. After dressing in the same dress I wore yesterday, I sat on my trunk and watched from the window. There were all sorts of horse-drawn wagons, carts and carriages. Well-dressed men in dark suits and assorted hats carried an umbrella in one hand and the morning paper in the other on their way to the office. Street vendors, both men and women, carted their wares for the day. It all looked so normal until I saw a transport bearing soldiers on their way to the trains for Washington, which reminded me of the turmoil going on there.

In the transport the men's dress was less than uniform. The militias were from different states and not all dressed alike. They looked less like soldiers and more like hunters or lumbermen headed for the woods. Except for the impressive New York Zouaves, who wore navy blue jackets trimmed with orange, a red and orange sash, loose fitting red trousers and a bright, short-visor Kepi cap trimmed with gold. They were a skilled drill team patterned after the French and most stately in their appearance.

It made me wonder if the Zouaves took a ribbing from the farmers and backwoodsmen in the militias because of their flamboyant dress. According to Abby, who had witnessed their precision drills and expertise with muskets and bayonets, it was doubtful the run-of-the-mill militia man would dare to snicker in the Zouaves presence.

I turned at the quiet knock on my door. "Come in."

Abby edged around the door. "I wasn't sure you were awake. Did you sleep well?"

"I was dead to the world. You look dressed for a day on the town."

"Mother has some important people coming for tea this afternoon, and I need to get some flowers for the table."

"I'd love to go with you. Perhaps I can find a gift for Aunt Martha to thank her for allowing me to come and stay."

"Mary, what a delightful idea. Let's go down for breakfast and we can start out right after we eat."

Abby prided herself on getting the best quality for the price she was willing to pay. She knew the shops as well as most of the owners, so I knew I was in good hands when it came to quality frugal shopping.

It was a pretty June day. We pinned on our hats, double-checked the interiors of our pocketbooks and headed toward 5th Avenue. There was less foot traffic than earlier when people were hurrying to work.

"Mornin' Miss Abby," said a raspy male voice as we passed a newsstand.

Abby stopped. "Good morning, Mr. Grimes."

He leaned forward and rested his thin arms on a pile of magazines. "I hear Miz' Florence's husband has been sent to Washington. It's a mess down there according to my newspapers."

"We're working hard in the Relief to better the conditions. Would you care to make a contribution, Mr. Grimes?" Abby had a pleasant coy way of getting what she wanted.

He stood back and folded his skinny arms against his equally skinny chest. "Can't say as I do. That's for all the uppity people so they can get their names on the social page."

"Why Mr. Grimes, I am surprised at you. Are you calling me uppity?" asked Abby.

His face turned beet red as he dropped his arms then leaned forward again. "I didn't mean you, Miss Abby. I'll tell you what; when you come back by I'll have something for the Relief."

Abby's big smile lit up her face. "Mr. Grimes, that is most considerate, and I know the men will appreciate anything they get. We'll stop on our way back home." She gave a wave of her handkerchief and we were on our way to the shops.

"That poor little old man doesn't look like he can afford anything, Abby. You almost shamed him into it."

Abby looked at me and chuckled. "Don't let him fool you, Mary. Mr. Grimes just runs that stand to find out everyone's business. Instead of Nosy Nellie, I call him Nosy Norman. He owns a liquor and cigar store, run by his son, and his wife oversees their boarding house. He's so tight-fisted

I'll probably have to pry the money out of his hand."

I couldn't help but laugh.

We were passing a millinery shop when I noticed a lovely handkerchief displayed in the window. I stopped to look and Abby came to my side. "Do you think Aunt Martha would like that handkerchief?"

Abby shielded her eyes and peered closer as the sun was casting a shadow.

"Let's go inside and look at it," she suggested.

Inside, the shop was a treasure of hats, gloves, scarves, jewelry and handkerchiefs. I can even recall the comforting scent of lavender that invaded my senses when we entered. There were three booths with leather padded swivel chairs where ladies could admire hats in the three-way mirrors. We were the only customers.

"Good morning, ladies," said a short older woman pulling off an apron. "Please excuse my appearance. I was dyeing some material and lost track of the time. My helper hasn't arrived as she was supposed to. People just aren't as dependable nowadays. How may I help you?"

"I'd like to see the lovely handkerchief displayed in the window," I answered.

"It is lovely, isn't it? It was tatted in France and just arrived two days ago," she said as she lifted it from its display spot.

"Ooh, Mary! It is even prettier than I thought," exclaimed Abby. "Look. The lace edge is layered in red, white and blue."

"Yes," said the milliner fingering the lace. "It is done in the finest of silk thread so it makes a delicate trim to grace the exquisite soft linen."

My mind was beginning to work overtime. Tatted in France, finest silk thread, exquisite linen, it would cost more than I felt I wanted to pay.

Abby stood apart from me. "Miss Anna, my mother will be proud to own it."

Miss Anna squinted at her. "Abby Morgan, is that you? I could tell from the sound of your voice. My vision isn't as good as it once was."

"Yes, Miss Anna." Abby stepped forward where she could be seen. "This is my cousin from Albany, Mary Sullivan. She wants to buy Mother a gift."

Miss Anna became Anna the sales lady. "This is a beautiful and rare piece of work. The price is only two dollars."

I gulped. The consternation must have shown on my face because Abby spoke up, "I'm sure it is worth every penny, but with the impending war and all we do have to watch our funds."

Anna hesitated as she took this into consideration. "Well, your mother has been such a loyal customer, and I know she would appreciate this as a gift, but…"

"Would you consider one dollar?" Abby was quick to say. She turned to me while Anna was mulling over the offer. "What do you think, Mary? Is one dollar too much? We might find something for less at the next shop."

"One dollar will be fine," Anna piped in before I could answer.

I nodded and Anna moved to the counter where she laid the handkerchief in a gold colored box and tied it with a gold ribbon. I was delighted and gladly handed over my one dollar as I said, "Thank you, Miss Anna. I am pleased to have met you."

Anna mustered the best smile she could after losing a dollar. "I know Mrs. Morgan will enjoy this." She called to Abby as we were leaving. "Miss Abby, tell your mother I have some stylish new hats that just arrived."

"Of course I will. Thank you again, Miss Anna," sang Abby.

When we were out on the sidewalk, I said, "You were brave. I would never have asked her to lower the price. I could buy a less fancy one for twenty-five cents. I would have left without buying anything."

"I know how the city works," Abby replied. "Besides, Mother's a good customer of hers so Miss Anna will find a way to make up her loss, although I doubt she is out any money at all."

I smile to myself when I recall that scene as though it were yesterday. I never learned to bargain the way Abby did.

One more block up 5th Avenue was the flower shop. Abby quickened her pace. "This a new shop so let's go in and see what they have to offer."

"Are you going to try to talk them down again? It is a bit embarrassing.'

"Fiddlesticks," said Abby. "They all have some bargaining room."

Abby was right. She bought a bouquet of flowers for less than they were asking, and they gave her a graceful vase free. I waited in the background and tried to be inconspicuous.

Abby waved to the clerk, swishing her hooped skirt as we left. "That was fun," she laughed as we started for home. "They gave me the vase for free when I told them who was coming for tea. The clerk gave me extra cards to give to our guests."

"Is that in good taste? My mother would be mortified," I told her.

She chuckled in her good-natured way. "I shall handle it in a delicate manner."

It was noon when we arrived back at the notable Morgan house on Brevoort Street after collecting ten dollars from Norman Grimes. Abby was elated and could hardly wait to tell Aunt Martha.

Tea was to be served at two o'clock, so Abby and I ate a boiled egg for lunch. It would be a high tea with scones, finger sandwiches and desserts, but we were hungry and one egg wouldn't spoil our appetites.

Abby insisted that I change my plain dress and wear one of Emily's as she was in training to be an army nurse. I loved wearing Emily's dress. It was the color of toast with white cuffs and a lace-trimmed white collar. The dress moved gracefully over the hoop. I still didn't know who was coming for tea. "These must be important people if I have to look like a princess," I said.

"They are," replied Abby as she wound my braid into a coil and fastened it with hairpins before she tied a narrow white ribbon around it. Two streamers hung down and tickled my neck. "Mother will introduce you. We have to hurry down before they arrive."

At two o'clock I was introduced to Mrs. Louisa Lee Schuyler, Mr. Frederick Olmstead, and Dr. Henry Bellows. Indeed they were important. Louisa Schuyler was the president of the NY Relief, Mr. Frederick Olmstead, the head of the Sanitary Commission, and Dr. Henry Bellows who was instrumental in getting the Commission started.

I sat quietly listening to the discussion.

"The government has made no preparations for these men," said Mr. Olmstead. "Right now hospitals are being set up in Washington in every available spot. We have had no altercations with the South and those troops of militias in Washington are sick from dysentery, malaria and pneumonia. The Sanitary Commission is doing what it can by inspecting unsanitary and dietary conditions, but the longer this insurrection goes on the more aid will be needed."

Dr. Bellows spoke, "If this insurrection isn't quelled soon there will be battles all up and down the Atlantic coast."

Mrs. Schuyler summed it up. "That's where the relief comes in. We have formed this Central Relief Association so that we can monitor the goods coming in from all the different Northern states. One central place to get supplies to where they need to be."

"We're willing to do whatever is necessary," Aunt Martha offered.

"Martha, I want you to work closely with me," said Louisa. "We will need to keep an eye on our inventory and coordinate with the individual relief associations so they all aren't sending the same supplies."

Although tea was supposed to be at two o'clock the discussion had begun immediately and the meeting of the minds was more important.

I was starving and figured Abby was also. I saw her nudge Aunt Martha with her knee unseen by the guests.

"We have much to consider," said Aunt Martha. "If you will excuse my manners, rather than wait until we're finished, we can discuss over tea."

"Bravo," said Dr. Bellows. That brought a hearty laugh from everyone and tea was served.

Louisa Schuyler looked at my aunt. "Martha, you have been a big support for the New York Relief, and now that I am also heading up the Eastern relief organizations, I would like to have you take over my position for the New York sector."

"We have discussed this among ourselves, Martha, and you are our choice. It is becoming a huge undertaking for Louisa," informed Dr. Bellows.

I could tell from Aunt Martha's hesitation that she wasn't sure this was something she wanted to take on. After a quiet pause that could be felt in the room, she answered, "I am honored that you think me capable of this, but I do have Charley and the girls, and Florence is expecting her first child…"

"Of course you can, Mother," piped up Abby. "We are all perfectly capable of taking care of ourselves and one another. You are a born organizer."

We all laughed at Abby's outburst. But, we all knew Aunt Martha was known for keeping a tight ship.

"Soon there will be an engagement in Manassas, Virginia. What the outcome will be is unknown except there are bound to be injuries. The aid societies are necessary," said Mr. Olmstead.

"Yes, and who knows what will happen after that," added Dr. Bellows.

I guess that was the push that made Aunt Martha make up her mind. "Of course you are right. I will accept this position and pray this madness ends soon."

The visitors smiled with relief. "Your position will be, Supervisor in Charge," said Dr. Bellows.

"I will be in contact with you soon, Martha," said Mrs. Schuyler. "I must remark on that lovely flower arrangement. It has caught my eye."

"Thank you, Louisa. Abby found a new flower shop," informed Aunt Martha.

"It is a beautiful shop and they gave me extra business cards if you would care to have one."

The three left with gratitude and the business cards. Abby had performed her part of spreading the word as she had promised. I was proud of her.

Chapter 4

Rumors about a battle engagement kept erupting as we continued to reinforce supplies for the Sanitary Commission. It seemed each relief organization set up in towns and cities in the Northern states tried to outdo one another in their generosity.

Aunt Martha oversaw the whole process. She organized the huge warehouse so that supplies could be easily found: shirts, drawers, hats, belts, sheets, pillows, stationery, anything that a soldier might need. She also supervised the record keeping.

Food and medicines were kept in a separate and cooler area of the warehouse. A civilian doctor volunteered to take care of the medicines with help from a trained army nurse. Everyone reported to Aunt Martha and she reported to Louisa Lee Schuyler, who reported to Mr. Olmstead.

Jenny, Abby and I helped with labeling and storing the goods coming into the New York headquarters. It was a daunting task finding space to place articles in their rightful places; I wondered to myself if the Sanitary Commission was overdoing all this relief work.

However, the men in Washington were still getting sick not only with major cases of malaria, dysentery and pneumonia but also cholera, measles and typhoid fever. With cramped unsanitary conditions along with heat and humidity, Washington was a hotbed for spreading disease.

Emily had written from Washington, where she was now stationed, that more and more places were being turned into hospitals. She was working out of the top floor of the U.S. Patent Office still under construction.

She wrote: No sooner than we empty one bed there is another man fill the space. Crude beds have been made out of scaffolding. They are so high I have to stand on the lower one to make the upper. Many patients have pallets on the floor. We work around paint buckets, ladders, piles of lumber and sawdust.

The workers here have fixed up a pulley from the 5th floor down to the first. They haul up barrels of water, food, medicine, and clean linens. We have our own small kitchen with a two burner wood stove where we can prepare their meals such as they are. The men are grateful for whatever we can fix. We try to go around with our jelly and jam pots between feedings to give them nourishment. The coffee pot is a huge enamel monstrosity.

We have a volunteer named, Joseph, who helps us in the kitchen. He is a colored man who lives near here. I don't know how we would manage without him. He's big and strong and a darn good cook. His cheerful attitude and ready smile warms our hearts.

Seeing all of this suffering, it would be easy to get discouraged, pack up my bags and come home. But, I know I am needed here as we are caring for over a hundred men and we are only one of the make-shift hospitals in the city.

I can only imagine what lies ahead of us if we go into all-out war. It is troubling to even let the thought enter my mind. We are all in hopes that this upheaval will end soon so these men can go back to their families.

Aunt Martha set the letter down with a big sigh. "I fear the tempest is just beginning."

That evening after we'd finished rolling bandages, Jenny, Abby and I sat in Abby's room. Florence was asleep in the next room, therefore we kept our discussion just above a whisper.

"The Sanitary Commission is asking for volunteer nurses," said Jenny. "I'm thinking of applying."

"Why would you want to do that?" asked Abby. "I'm sure Mother would rather have you here. Florence's baby is due soon and with Mother so busy she's going to need help."

"You can help, Abby," replied Jenny. "You have no inclinations to become a volunteer nurse."

"How do you know? Perhaps I've changed my mind."

"That's not likely," Jenny answered. "What about you, Mary? We could go together."

I was caught off-guard and hesitated before replying while two sets of eyes honed in on me and waited for my response.

My reply was a hedging around Jenny's question. "From the tone of Emily's letter, it seems they would welcome help. Couldn't we volunteer in some other way? I wonder if we would even be considered because of our ages."

"I assume we are already doing our part by helping Mother," said Abby. "I don't know where you got this foolish notion, Jenny."

"It's not foolish. I'm going to tell Mother and go apply tomorrow."

I'm not sure what came over me, but I surprised myself by saying, "I'll go with you, Jenny."

Abby threw a disgusted look in my direction. "Fiddlesticks! Mother will never allow it."

"Is anyone else hungry?" Jenny whispered with a big smile on her delicate face.

Abby's disappointment was short-lived. "I'm starved. Let's go raid the kitchen."

"I hear you girls," came Florence's voice from the next room. "Please bring me a glass of milk and one of those sour cream cookies if there are any left."

"My first nursing assignment," quipped Jenny.

We laughed aloud.

Chapter 5

Both Jenny and I were accepted as volunteer nurses in the United States Sanitary Commission, although I believe it took some coaxing from Mrs. Schuyler for our acceptance as we were both under the age required. Aunt Martha had influence.

Sanitary Commission nurses also had to meet with Miss Dix, the Superintendent of Army Nurses, who was also overseeing the volunteer Sanitary Commission nurses. She was now living in Washington.

I had been remiss in writing to my parents. I placated my guilt by writing five pages. There was no mention of my impulsive decision of becoming a nurse.

It was the middle of June when Aunt Martha and Abby saw Jenny and me off from New York on a morning train. The fact I had not yet notified my parents of my decision weighed heavy on my mind. Aunt Martha understood as she knew my mother to be the worrier that she was, so she kindly agreed that she would send a note to assure them I was with Jenny and not in harm's way. She had secured a hotel for us and would pay any expenses.

Our spirits were high when we left New York City. Abby had packed us a lunch of cold chicken, cheese, and cornbread. We were to be met in Baltimore by a military escort who would accompany us to Washington and to Miss Dix.

Unfortunately, he never came. Jenny and I did not dare leave the train in Baltimore and hoped the escort would meet us in Washington.

It was late afternoon when we arrived in Washington, and after waiting for an hour in that unfamiliar, damp and dirty city, our military escort never appeared. We decided to find Miss Dix's place on our own. By this time we were both tired and hungry.

Aunt Martha had made arrangements for our room at a hotel only a block from Union Station. After securing the room and leaving our suitcases at the hotel, the clerk gave us directions to Miss Dix's address.

It was five blocks to her street, which we chose to walk, but we had a devil of a time trying to find her townhouse. Not only was it getting dusk, the number of her townhouse had been transposed on our directions. It took us another half hour of walking up and down the street before a maid came out of a house. "I've seen you young ladies walking back and forth. Are you looking for someone? These streets are not always safe after dark."

"We are looking for Miss Dix."

"She lives two doors down."

We thanked her for the information and hurried to our destination.

A housekeeper opened the door and ushered us into a small office lit by an oil lamp. Miss Dix entered shortly after without saying a word of greeting. Jenny and I handed her our cards of introduction. The stately woman, close to sixty years of age, scrutinized us from head to toe. We stood like statues as she circled around each of us. Not a sound was heard except the swishing of her skirt as she moved.

"Hmm," she said and circled around again. "Hmm." She came around to face us. "You're late. I was informed you would be coming earlier."

"We're sorry," I said. "Our escort never showed up and we had to find your place by ourselves."

"Resourceful," she murmured to herself. "How did you get accepted by the board? You are both too young, and you, Miss Morgan, with those glasses; they will hinder your work."

Jenny never flinched. "Oh no, Miss Dix. You are mistaken. These glasses give me clear vision."

"And you, Miss Sullivan. How old are you?"

"Old enough to be a school teacher," I replied.

How unlike me to answer in such an impudent manner, but I found the woman's cold reception irksome.

I saw a faint smile in her eyes, although her face remained unsmiling. After a moment of hesitation, she shook her head and walked back to her desk where she sat down in a chair and began writing.

Jenny shot me a questioning glance. I answered with a slight shrug.

Miss Dix lay down her pen and motioned us to come forward. "Here are your papers. You are to report to this hospital where they will have an army nurse train you for two weeks. Do you have a place to stay this night?"

"Yes," I answered. "The hotel is five blocks away."

"That's fine," she said. It seemed her icy demeanor was melting. "This is a safer part of the city, however, you must hurry while it is still dusk. Stay close together and walk quickly."

"Miss Dix," spoke Jenny. "My sister is an army nurse and is stationed at the U.S. Patent Office Hospital. Is it possible she could train us?"

I thought that an outlandish request, especially coming from the quiet and reserved Jenny.

With a furrowed brow, Miss Dix snatched the papers from our hands, went to her desk, jabbed the pen into the inkwell, and changed the name of the hospital to read U.S. Patent Office.

We broke into wide smiles and thanked her with high enthusiasm. "Be on your way," she said and dismissed us with a wave of her hand.

Chapter 6

The next day, dressed in dark skirts and navy colored cotton waists, we reported to the 5th floor of the patent office where Emily hugged us both. She was about my size and of Jenny's coloring. Her brown eyes came alive. "Jenny! Mary! I was overjoyed when a messenger from Miss Dix said you were coming. I'm surprised Mother allowed you to come. But, all that aside, roll up your sleeves and we'll get started."

I had forgotten Emily had been blessed with abundant energy. Everything was rush, rush. I don't recall Jenny or I having a chance to say a word as we rolled up our sleeves while Emily tucked our pocketbooks away in a safe place.

We tied on the white bib aprons Aunt Martha had given us before Emily took us into the small area outside the kitchen. Nurses were not allowed in the kitchen. We were introduced to Joseph who came to where we stood. He gave us a big smile of welcome. Still, I noticed a small incline of his head as if he, like Miss Dix, thought we shouldn't be here.

It was mid-morning and time for nourishment according to Emily. We were each handed a tray consisting of jelly pots, one spoon and a wet towel.

"We have just become inundated with the 19th Vermont. Their regiment is almost all sick with fever. Each man who is able gets a spoon of jelly. Don't be shocked by the smells and moans that will enter your senses."

"Shouldn't there be more spoons?" Jenny asked in bewilderment.

Emily answered. "No. That's the way it's done here. Utensils are at a premium. You can wipe the spoon off on this wet towel, but the men usually lick it clean. Remember a spoon of jelly to each. Are you ready?"

Jenny made a prune face and we steeled ourselves to enter we knew not what.

Emily opened the heavy door that led into a long, high-ceilinged room filled with make-shift beds, busy people, and a sea of male patients.

The smell was what hit us first. Even though windows were open, the putrid odor was like a blast from the outhouse in hot summer. I saw Jenny cover her mouth as though she was going to throw up. I tried not to breathe through my nose.

Human smells of excrement, vomit and dirty bodies mingled with medicines and cleaning solutions.

Emily seemed immune as we followed her to the right side of the room where men lay on pallets on the floor.

"You can start here and work your way around. If you run low, Joseph will take care of you. I will try to check in with you in an hour." Emily hurried away leaving us standing there.

"Are you all right, Jenny?" At least she was not gagging.

"I think so. Let's pretend we know what we're doing."

After the first few patients, we gained confidence. Those men who could greeted us with a smile and deep thank you. Those who were unresponsive, we just walked by.

Of all the miseries we saw, one young soldier touched my heart and made me question if I could handle this human suffering. He was young, educated, and well spoken, but he had fallen on hard times. He told me he knew he was dying of consumption so he joined the New York Zouaves to be buried in a splendid outfit. I could do nothing for him accept give him an extra spoon of jelly.

The hospital staff had separated the different medical conditions into areas in an attempt to lessen the spread of infection. Because of the unsanitary conditions of the hot and humid city, many were sick with dysentery, lung problems, and festering sores. Some patients were sitting in chairs in the convalescent room, close to going back to their camp. Others would never make it out of the hospital.

Jenny and I kept our eyes and ears open to learn what we could. When we heard a doctor call, "Nurse! Basin!" Jenny and I both turned and saw a probe used for the first time. When the doctor punctured an infected carbuncle, green pus poured out, and Jenny fainted. I gagged. Someone rushed in to put smelling salts under Jenny's nose before giving her a sip of cloudy water.

Once Jenny was back on her feet, she was mortified at having been the center of attention, especially when she heard the surgeon shout, "Get that woman out of here!"

We were told we were through for the day, but to report at six o'clock the next morning. At least we weren't cast out as incompetents.

That evening, Emily came by our hotel room to be sure we were both recovered. Finding us still sane and in relatively good spirits, despite the ordeal of our first day at the hospital, she looked at our comfortable room and commented, "Perhaps I should have become a Sanitary Commission nurse."

Later we saw her cramped room, shared with another nurse. They each had a cot with a straw mattress and pillow, sheet and blanket, and a small trunk at the foot. No dresser, no mirror, no nook for privacy. It appeared the government had not provided for the army nurses any more than it had for the militia men. Women nurses were still frowned upon and the surgeons made it as difficult for them as they could.

Emily had been kind and promised the more we became comfortable with our duties, the easier they would become. I wasn't so sure.

Jenny and I slept soundly and were up at five o'clock the next morning. We put on our same set of skirts and blouses. After a peanut butter sandwich for breakfast, we headed to the U.S. Patent Office determined to make it through another day.

That day we learned to make beds, bathe patients and do small errands to relieve the trained nurses. Some of the crude beds, thrown together from scaffolding, were three high. We had to stand on the second to make the top and we first swept off the mattresses with brooms. Jenny took one side and I took the other. After the fifth day, we both felt more comfortable and less like bumbling idiots.

We also had the hotel pack us a sandwich for dinner. The fare they fed the ladies at the hospital was dirty looking bread, dried applesauce, and black tea. It was the same for the patients except they also had some pork.

A week later, Miss Dix visited to inquire of our progress and suitability as nurses. She insisted on taking us to the dead house. I'm not sure why. Perhaps it was the final test to see if Jenny and I could pass muster. There in the cool basement I saw my young Zouave laid out in his splendid uniform waiting for burial. I swallowed hard and said a silent prayer.

Chapter 7

It was early July when we finished training. We had learned much including splinting and bandaging, which we practiced on each other to be sure the bandages had sharp corners and no wrinkles. We were comfortable with making beds, bathing, taking care of soiled linens, feeding, and making the one hundred men under our care as comfortable as possible. We even scrubbed floors and washed windows as the surgeons ordered.

The army nurses took care of medicine and assisting the doctors, but we watched and learned what we could. A few civilian doctors, who worked under contract, welcomed the nurses while others did their best to make life miserable so the women would go home where they belonged. It was not unheard of for a doctor to berate a nurse or throw something in the heat of rage.

Jenny and I persevered for the two weeks and were declared U. S. Sanitary Commission nurses. Although we had learned much, there was still much more to learn. We were taking care of the ills of too many men camped together in unsanitary conditions.

There was talk of a skirmish coming. Union troops had crossed the Potomac into Virginia. Emily had been sent across the river to work in a hospital set up in an abandoned seminary. Those siding with the South had left in haste leaving everything from open books to women's clothes hanging in a closet. Even Robert E. Lee had moved his family farther south leaving his southern estate in Arlington. He later took command of the Confederate army.

We had not seen nor cared for war wounded. Jenny and I prayed the rumor of a battle was idle talk.

When we returned from our day at the hospital, the clerk at the hotel handed Jenny a letter. It was from Aunt Martha. We hurried up the stairs to our second floor room to open it as we were both hungry for news of home.

The big news was that Florence delivered a robust baby boy. He is named after his father, Johnathan. Florence had recovered and was getting help from a hired woman. Abby had helped a great deal between Florence and the Relief headquarters. She and Aunt Martha planned a trip to Washington for they both "needed a change of scenery" as Aunt Martha put it. Jenny and I jumped up and hugged each other when she read they were coming. The rumor of a battle vanished from our minds. Aunt Martha's letter had rejuvenated us.

Chapter 8

Jenny and I were working at the hospital when Aunt Martha and Abby arrived on the train. They rented a room at the same hotel where Jenny and I were staying.

Days did not drag on when we worked. There was always another mouth to feed, a bed to change, or a mess to clean up. That day, however, when I knew they were coming, seemed to never end as I was so eager to see them.

To Jenny's and my surprise, we found them waiting next to a carriage outside the Patent building. We all hugged right there on the side of the street.

"A carriage to ride in." Jenny was pleased.

I did not remark but I was as glad. My feet were always tired at the end of a working day. My brown laced shoes were not the most comfortable.

"Mother and I did not care to walk the streets of Washington," said Abby. "Do you walk every day?"

"Just like the common people," I answered. "We walked the streets in New York," I reminded her.

"That's true," she agreed. "But New York is a much different city and we walked only the fashionable streets."

"Girls, our driver is waiting," urged Aunt Martha.

The driver was at the rear of the carriage and hurried to give us a hand up when he saw we were ready. I sat next to Abby across from Jenny and her mother.

"You young ladies appear in good health," said Aunt Martha. "I did have my concerns after I granted permission for you to come. Newspaper stories are enough to strike fear into any mother's heart."

Jenny took her mother's hand in hers. "You were so right in sending us, Mother. The needs are great. Tuck any worries away. We're both pleased we're here, aren't we, Mary?"

"That we are," I assured my aunt.

Abby wrinkled her nose. "As soon as we get to the hotel, you can change out of those smelly clothes."

Jenny and I smiled at each other. Had we become as immune to hospital odors as Emily had?

"It's the perfume of life." I was in a light-hearted mood.

They smiled and we sat back to enjoy the ride on the lovely late June afternoon. The heat of the day had subsided. As we rode we talked about their work with the relief and our work with the soldiers.

"I am sorely disappointed that we will not see Emily," lamented Aunt Martha. "She has written that she is well, but has little time to write

49

as often as she would like. I understand one needs a blue card to go across the river."

In the next breath, she announced, "Oh, my goodness. Before I forget, you must change into something suitable as we are having supper at the Willard Hotel with an old friend."

"I have nothing appropriate," was my immediate reply.

"I have my plaid silk, but no hoop," said Jenny.

"Mary, did you pack a dress for Sunday church?" Aunt Martha asked.

"I have only the blue cotton dress I wore when I arrived at your house."

"That will do," she replied.

"Each of you wear two petticoats to look more fashionable," Abby ordered. "And, Mary, I have a lace shawl that you may wear."

"Abigail," Aunt Martha's tone was firm. "Your sister and cousin will be appropriately dressed."

"But you and I will be wearing hoops and I brought my taffeta."

"You can pretend you found us along the street begging for food," I said. Jenny and I laughed aloud. Aunt Martha smiled. Abby pouted, "I don't find that humorous."

"I'm sorry, Abby. All eyes will be on you. With your beautiful shawl, my white gloves, and a wide navy ribbon tied around my straw hat I shall look prim and proper."

Abby chuckled. "Dear Mary, you always look prim and proper. I, for one, am looking forward to a delicious meal. I'm starved."

If I had offended Abby with my attempts at humor, I was forgiven.

We reached the hotel and Jenny and I hurried up to our room to clean up for supper while Abby and Aunt Martha went to change into their fine attire.

"Do we dare wear these petticoats that we have worn all day?" Jenny wondered. "I don't wish to disappoint Abby by wearing only one petticoat."

We slipped off the ones we wore and sniffed them. "I don't think they smell bad," I told her. "We will be wearing a dress and another petticoat over them."

To be on the safe side, we opened the window and shook them around in the evening air. Our petticoats couldn't smell any worse than the odor of Washington on a hot summer night. Then we sprayed rose scented toilet water and pronounced ourselves suitable for the Willard Hotel.

As our carriage took us through the streets, we saw masses of tents covering the grounds. Piles of horse manure and the smell of open latrines caused us to cover our noses when we passed crowded encampments.

"It's no wonder so many men are sick," I remarked.

Aunt Martha held a concerned look. "I will talk with Mrs. Schuyler to see when we can start sending more supplies. From what you girls have

51

told me about the conditions you are working under, it is senseless that our warehouses are full when so much is needed."

Once inside the hotel it was a different scene: leather chairs, brocade drapes, shimmering chandeliers. A waiter showed us to our table where a gentleman was waiting.

He stood as we entered. "Martha, how good to see you."

"Good evening, William. These are my daughters Abigail and Jenny, and this is my niece, Mary Sullivan. This is Mr. Seward."

We all gave a slight curtsy and he a bow of acknowledgement. Two waiters seated us.

"I hope you don't mind, Martha, but I have ordered our meals as I am pinched for time."

"Of course we don't mind. I am very pleased you found the time to dine with us."

"How long will you be in Washington?" he asked.

A waiter brought a bottle of red wine to the table.

"If you young ladies would prefer tea at this time, I will ask for it."

Abby took the lead. "Thank you, sir. I believe a glass of wine will be welcome to all of us."

Aunt Martha informed the gentleman, "We will be here for four days. I have good help at the Relief Headquarters, but I don't care to stay away too long."

"I understand," he said.

"How are Frances and the family?" Aunt Martha inquired.

He smiled, which is the first one I had noticed.

"Frances is visiting in New York. She will be sorry she missed you. The children are doing well."

The man looked familiar to me. Could he be the William Seward who had once been the governor of New York? I had seen pictures of him. However, he would have been twenty years younger at that time. This gentleman seated with us was about sixty with graying hair. Still, I thought him a handsome man.

"What do you think of the Sanitary Commission, William?" Aunt Martha wanted to know.

He didn't hesitate. "I believe it is a worthy cause. I am afraid it will be needed in the near future."

"Why is that?"

"Our army, what there is of it, has had skirmishes along the Ohio River. We have been successful, but the rumor of an encounter closer to Washington, I fear, is more than a rumor. Your relief organizations will do well to keep supplies on hand; this government is not prepared for war."

Aunt Martha glanced over at us before proudly announcing to Mr. Seward, "Jenny and Mary are both Sanitary Commission nurses, and my Emily is serving as an army nurse."

He gave us a genuine smile. "Commendable. And, what about you, Miss Abigail?"

53

Abby brightened. "I am busy helping Mother. I did entertain the idea of becoming a nurse, but Miss Dix will not allow hoops."

We all laughed.

"Mr. Seward," she continued with her winning way, "Mother and I would like to visit Emily while we are here. I have been told we need a blue card to pass over the river. Could that be arranged?"

"Certainly. I'll have one of my staff arrange it."

"Mr. Seward is our Secretary of State," Aunt Martha informed us. "Thank you, William. I do not want to dampen our friendship by asking a favor. Abigail has spoken out of turn."

"Miss Abigail, I'm pleased you asked." He turned his attention back to my aunt. "I would like to be of some assistance while you are here. How is young Charley?"

"He's fine. Serving as an aide-de-camp in the 164th New York. And, Florence has presented me with my first grandchild. Her father would be so pleased."

"I know he would. Charles and I were good friends. Congratulations. Times do change. I just hope they don't change too quickly."

Our meals were wheeled to the table, which interrupted the conversation. I was glad for that.

The waiters in white short jackets and black trousers, who had seated us previously, served us: steak, roasted potatoes, carrots and brussel sprouts. The wine had relaxed my whole being enough that

I forgot the stature of the gentleman at the table. I was never completely comfortable with those in higher positions.

The meal was delicious, the company enjoyable, and the setting elegant. Little did I realize it would be a long time before I would experience that type of an evening again.

Before Aunt Martha left Washington to return to New York, she reminded Jenny and me that we were volunteers and could return home at any time we wished. She had been appalled at the conditions she found in Arlington where Emily was stationed.

She described huge tents holding forty men each with one army nurse assigned to each tent. One surgeon served all eight tents. The conditions were overwhelming to my aunt. "I cannot imagine how Emily can keep her sanity. But, she is housed inside the former seminary, which she describes as a luxury. Can you imagine?"

"Oh, Mother. She has those two charming and handsome orderlies to help her. They almost made me change my mind about becoming a nurse." Then Abby gave us that devilish grin. "Almost but not quite."

That was our Abby. She could always brighten the moment.

Chapter 9

Three weeks later a battle was no longer a rumor. On July 21, 1861, the U. S. Army along with the untrained and undisciplined militias encountered a superior southern Confederate army and limped back to Washington. It is said the defeat was not because the Confederates were so good, but because the Union army was so bad.

The once jubilant Union army that had marched off as to a military picnic, disbanded in disarray.

For all the bravado we had heard days before, eye witness accounts told that they saw Union soldiers throw down their weapons and run from their foes leaving Duryea's Zouaves as the last line of defense.

Congressmen and their ladies out for a day of fun in their carriages and buggies, almost overran each other and the fleeing combatants as they beat a panicked retreat. Their day of entertainment became a day of horror left by cannons, muskets, bayonets, and close to five thousand dead men lying where they once stood.

The whole of the North was shocked at the outcome of the Battle of Bull Run or the Battle of the First Manassas as the South named the Virginia engagement.

President Lincoln was disheartened and took action. Because of the defeat at General Irvin McDowell's hands, and the fact that the volunteer militias could return home in August, he pulled the Departments of Annapolis, Pennsylvania, and Shenandoah together, along with ten thousand new recruits, and formed the Army of the Potomac.

He chose Major General George McClellan to organize and lead the newly formed army. "Little Mac" as he was known was a good organizer, but later proved to lack military strategy. Lincoln wanted him to take the southern capital of Richmond with high hopes of ending the war.

While the Union army was being decked out in wool navy blue uniforms, and formed into a disciplined force, Frederick Olmstead, head of the Sanitary Commission and forward thinking man that he was, petitioned the war department for ships that were sitting idle.

He was granted permission to use them. Eight ships were turned into floating hospitals and one became the supply tender. All would be manned by civilian personnel and supplied by the relief associations.

Chapter 10

The Battle of Bull Run initiated Jenny and me into caring for war wounds. In and around Washington every spot that could be turned into a hospital was. Nurses and volunteers were in demand and supplies were short. It was true that the government was not prepared for war.

At this point, the duty of the U.S. Sanitary Commission was to inspect the camps and hospitals to help cut down on disease. That mission would be enlarged.

On Sunday, Jenny and I attended services at St. John's Episcopal Church after which I wrote a long letter to my parents. I had sent short notes a few times and always made them sound rosy so Mother wouldn't worry about her only child.

It was a sunny and pleasant day. We used the tubs in the hotel laundry room to wash out our work clothes. Aunt Martha had brought each of us a gray grosgrain dress. She had taken a dress of Jenny's and the one of Emily's that I had worn to a dressmaker. The woman had done an admirable job of patterning them so they fit quite nicely. There were no buttons or hooks and eyes to fool with, only a tie at the neck. They were all of one piece and could be thrown over our heads like a nightdress. Tying the bib apron around them gave some shape and the loose sleeves could easily be rolled up. They would prove to be a boon as time went on.

While we were washing our skirts and waists, Jenny stopped and looked at me. "Mary, I have the most unsettling feeling that those who marched off in confidence are in trouble."

I stopped sloshing my clothes and looked over at her. "Why do you say that?"

"I don't know. It's a feeling I have."

I understood what she meant. There was a quiet to Washington after all the singing, flower throwing and political hoopla that had preceded the thirteen hour parade to Manassas.

Nevertheless I tried to reassure her. "You saw thousands of men marching away. We must have faith that this will be the end of it so we can return home in a few weeks."

"I know you're right. Still…"

We went back to our task at hand and hung the clothes on the drying line behind the hotel. Sure that our clothes would dry quickly in the July sun, we spent the rest of the afternoon darning, polishing our shoes, and mending what needed to be repaired.

By suppertime we had retrieved our wash and were both satisfied with what we had accomplished. Tomorrow would begin another sixty- hour week at the hospital.

After a hotel supper of vegetable soup and roast beef sandwich, we retired to our room for a good night's sleep.

It was almost dawn when we were awakened by loud rumblings of horses, wagons and shouting voices all mingled together.

Jenny and I awoke with a start and rushed to the window. I shall never forget the scene below us. Army wagons were streaming down the street pulled by lathered horses and full of wounded men. Following were bedraggled silent troops, saddled but riderless horses, all soaked by rain that had fallen. They had tramped the agonizing thirty miles from Manassas. Some were limping, some with make-shift bandages and others so tired they fell to the side of the street.

Then we heard shouts from mounted officers ordering the men to fall into ranks and get to their quarters. We watched as some struggled to their feet and others unable to rise from sheer exhaustion.

Jenny let out a gasp and began to cry. I fought back the tears as I hugged her and we turned away from the window.

"What are we going to do, Mary?"

I handed her a handkerchief to wipe her tearstained face. "What can we do? We will report to the hospital as we are supposed to and follow their orders as we have been doing."

"But we know nothing about taking care of musket ball or bayonet injuries. Mary they look so defeated. Do you think we are in danger of the Confederates overtaking Washington?"

Of course we could have been. However, I didn't want to think of that possibility. Jenny was frightened so I didn't have the luxury of crumbling to my own emotions. "We will go to the hospital early. That way we will know what we are up against. There is no need for senseless worry."

Jenny blew her nose. "I'm sorry I broke down. It was such a shock to see those poor soldiers."

I dreaded the thought of what we would find at the hospital, and the thought did cross my mind that my delicate cousin may not be able to carry on. I pushed those thoughts aside.

Chapter 11

It was no use to try to go back to bed because we couldn't sleep, so we dressed for work. We had learned to keep peanut butter, jelly and soda crackers in our room. A cup of tea would have been welcome but we had no way of heating water, and the hotel dining room was not open that early. Jenny and I ate our peanut butter and jelly crackers and left our room.

The hospital was in chaos when we reached it in the dawning light. Injured soldiers lay on the ground outside waiting for someone to tend to their wounds. We dared not to stop and quickly walked past into the hospital.

A soldier blocked our entrance. "You are to wait here for orders."

"We are not army nurses. We are with the Sanitary Commission," I informed him.

"Makes no difference. My orders are to stop anyone coming in."

"That's ridiculous," said Jenny. "We know where to report as we have volunteered here for weeks. And," she pointed to the yard, "it appears they will need our help even more."

Jenny did surprise me at times.

"Still don't make no difference. I got to follow my orders."

At that point a surgeon, whom I had seen before, was taking steps two at a time on those leading up to the building. He looked at us and said, "What are you two standing here for? Follow me!"

The soldier didn't even question the man. Did the sentry only stop females?

We climbed the stairs behind the doctor to our ward and found the convalescent room had turned into a surgical ward filled with suffering soldiers.

There was no time to react to the scene. Jenny was hauled away by another surgeon and I remained with Dr. S. I didn't particularly like him, but I did appreciate his skills. He had a German last name I could never pronounce to his satisfaction. Therefore, I called him Dr. S. He seemed to prefer that to my mispronouncing his name.

I felt in a tizzy. My whole insides were shaking and my heart was pounding. I just followed him as he checked the wounds of twenty men and made the decision as to who needed his help the quickest.

He ordered me to get water, rags, bandages, lint, alcohol and chloroform, which I brought all back in a big basket with a bucket of water. While I was gone, he had opened his own surgical instruments that he had placed in a deep tray. "Pour in enough alcohol to cover them. I did as I was told while he cut away tattered clothing and dirty blood soaked bandages from the injured leg. These the doctor kicked under the cot.

I gasped when I saw the slash from knee to ankle. I had seen knife cuts before but nothing like

63

this. The soldier was in agony. Dr. S. cleaned the area with wet rags. "Soak a rag in the chloroform and put it under his nose. That'll help some," ordered the surgeon. As I placed the chloroform rag under the man's nose, the surgeon waited for the chloroform to take effect before he poured alcohol into the wound and began sewing layer by layer of that splayed flesh.

I wasn't sure how long I was supposed to hold the rag under the man's nose, but I was sure the surgeon would holler at me if I didn't do it right. When I felt the man relax, I took the rag away. Dr. S. cleaned the wounded area with blue mass, a mercurial preparation. "Apply petroleum jelly, line it with lint and bandage the part," he told me. The surgeon cleaned his instruments and went on to the next man while I bandaged. That's the way the day went on. I filled holes left by musket balls, cleaned cuts from shrapnel, and bandaged shattered limbs all day long. I thought about those bandages we had rolled for Aunt Martha and knew they wouldn't last long at this rate. We didn't stop to eat. Dr. S. was a diligent physician and taught me how to care for the wounds of war. Although I didn't care for his abrupt manner, as time went on I realized how fortunate I was to have been trained under his guidance.

It was late evening before we finished. The surgeon left after the last patient was treated without saying thank you or goodbye. That was Dr. S. If I could have worked with him for the rest of the war, I would have been grateful.

When I finished the last bandage and left water at a soldier's side, I went in search of Jenny.

I found her on the ward where we were used to working, looking frazzled. Her apron was a bloody mess as was mine. We took them off and rolled them into a ball to carry back to the hotel.

Jenny wiped her glasses then pulled some stringy hair from her face and wrapped it around an ear. "I've got to eat before I fall over. The dining room is going to be closed when we get to the hotel."

"Is Joseph still around? Maybe he can give us something from the kitchen."

We went to the kitchen area and called his name but got no answer. Against the rules or not, Jenny and I went in. There was warm pork on the stove and a pot of strong coffee. We washed our hands in a basin of water before we cut bread from a dirty looking loaf, sliced the pork, poured two cups of coffee and went to the small dining area to sit and eat.

As we sat there another volunteer nurse we had seen before and were told was with the Christian Commission, went into the kitchen and poured herself a mug of coffee before she joined us. "You young ladies have worked hard." The woman looked to be in her thirties. She had an athletic build and wore her dark hair straight and ear-length. "I'm Sara," she said.

I don't remember even giving our names. "We have had a frightful day. There are so many maimed soldiers I pray to God there will be no more battles," I said.

"I was at the Bull Run," she said to both of us.

Jenny and I looked at each other with dismay. Perhaps she needed to get the incident in words because she didn't hesitate before beginning her story:

"I was working in the hospital in Alexandria when we got the orders to march. There were only two days of preparation. All those emaciated men we had been tending in the field hospitals were loaded into ambulances and hauled back to Washington.

I went on horseback with my preacher and his wife I called Mrs. B. It was a gay, boisterous army of thousands that left Washington with singing and regimental bands playing, banners flying. The first night we stayed in Fairfax. The day had been hot and we were not used to riding all day in the hot sun. I believe Mrs. B. and I and a colonel's wife were the only females to reach Fairfax that evening. Fires were laid and supper commenced after there was looting of whatever the soldiers could find contrary to orders. But there was no preparation to feed this great group of men. I heard a shot and not long after there were steaks cooking. The field had one less grazing cow."

She took a sip of coffee while Jenny and I sat mesmerized.

"The next day by orders of the army surgeons we helped set up hospitals in every building suitable in Centreville. Mrs. B. and I went around the huge encampments that evening and found soldiers writing by the light of the fire, reading their Bibles, and many sound asleep on the ground in their blankets, exhausted from the long hot summer march from Washington.

The next day I cannot describe the horrors of battle that met our eyes as we did our best to care for the fallen."

She covered her eyes as if to block out the horrors she had witnessed, took another sip of the coffee and continued on.

"At one point Mrs. B. sent me to Centreville, about seven miles distant, to procure more supplies. When I returned she came riding toward me with about fifty canteens dangling from the pommel of her saddle. 'The men are parched.' Mr. B. came with us and we rode to a spring to fill the canteens while Minnie-balls flew around us. This went on for three hours until the Rebels took over the spring. We were ordered to return to Centreville and leave the wounded where they lay.

Mrs. B. and I made it back to the stone church in Centreville where we saw stacks of dead bodies and heaps of discarded human legs and arms. While we were working word came to us that the army had left for Washington. Not wanting to believe this was possible I set out and went back to Bull Run and to see for myself. When I reached the place I found the whole area deserted. I walked around thinking they had changed positions but the guns and artillery that had pounded our ears all day were silent. In the hazy light, as it was getting dusk and threatened rain, I saw a figure sitting by a campfire. As I got nearer I recognized a woman who had been a washerwoman for the army. I also recognized that she had gone insane. Try as I might I could not convince her to go with me. I turned toward Centreville and had gone not a quarter of a mile before I saw cavalry riding up to her. Not knowing whether they were our cavalry or the Rebels I needed to get out of sight. I was near a fence where great heaps of brush were piled and crawled under one. I was not long concealed before I heard horses, then voices. The first was that of the woman. 'She can tell you. I know she can.' Then a male voice, 'Old woman, you had better not be playing a game or I'll shoot you.' I realized they must have seen me. The woman began to cry and drops of rain began to fall. 'Mount up,' came an order. They rode off taking the woman with them."

Sara stopped and took a deep breath. By now her coffee was cold but she took a sip anyway. Jenny and I just sat and stared waiting for her to continue.

"I made my way back to Centreville in the early morning only to find wounded men abandoned at the stone church. Everything was gone including my horse. 'Ma'am you must go before the Rebels come or they will take you prisoner, too.' But how could I leave them. I quickly gathered up what I could to leave water within the reach of those who could and gave water to those who couldn't. It was a dark day and raining torrents. It was afternoon before I finished what I could do for the men. 'You must go,' the soldiers implored me, and I knew the enemy would be coming. Before I got to the door a young soldier with thighs crushed asked me to open a gold locket he held. On one side of the locket was a picture of a beautiful young woman holding an infant, on the other side her name and address in Massachusetts. The dying soldier pressed the locket to his lips while tears filled his eyes. With fearful dread, I heard the clatter of hooves and knew I had to flee. I grabbed the locket from his hand and went out the back door knowing I could not leave by the street. I made my way cross-lots and came out on the Fairfax road about a mile from Centreville. I was blessed by the unforgiving rain and dark of late afternoon. It was noon the next day before I reached my house in Alexandria with scratches from the brush, torn clothing and my shoes worn off my feet."

We sat for a moment absorbing the tale when we both asked in unison, "What happened to the locket?"

Sara smiled. "I mailed it to the address with a note that her husband had sent her a kiss and his love. The sad young widow sent a reply that she had received the cherished locket and thanked me for what I had done."

Scarcely had she finished her story when the army matron of the hospital came by. "Who gave you permission to get that food?"

"No one," I was vexed. "We have worked all day and we have earned it."

She didn't allow the stern look to fade or reprimand for my boldness, but said, "Of course you did. Be here early tomorrow."

Jenny and I talked about our day all the way to the hotel and all evening before we dropped into bed. Her day had been much like mine, although she had worked with three different surgeons. The first threw up his hands and left shortly after he saw the conditions around the ward; plenty of injuries and everything in short supply.

As the Sanitary Commission's role was limited to inspect the camps and hospitals, Jenny decided to send a telegram to her mother telling her that we desperately needed more aid from the Sanitary Commission. I was proud of my cousin and a tad guilty with myself for doubting she could hold up to the daily strain.

I'm not sure how well I slept that night. All those horrible wounds and the cries of the wounded crept into my dreams.

The telegraph office was open twenty-four hours a day because of the war situation. The next morning we stopped on our way to the hospital where Jenny sent the telegram to Aunt Martha. Although it was not within her power to send the goods, she could talk to Mrs. Schuyler and Mr. Olmstead for permission.

We knew about the outfitting of the boats for hospital ships, but we thought there still should be enough supplies to help in the hospitals.

At the Patent Office where our hospital was located, to our surprise, we found many civilian volunteers to assist. Some helped by running errands and some helped with comforting the patients. It meant a lot to the men to have someone sitting at their side, especially the gravely wounded who might never return home. Letters were written, books read, faces fanned and listening to the soldiers' stories were all performed by the good men and women of Washington who came to help.

Perhaps Jenny's telegram started a flow of events. In September we learned that U.S. Sanitary Commission supply depots had been set up in Boston, Philadelphia, New York, Washington, Cincinnati and Wheeling. Did this mean more involvement from the Sanitary Commission? We hoped so.

Chapter 12

We had a reprieve from wounded coming in until October when the battles of Edward's Ferry, Dranesville, and Ball's Bluff took place in Virginia.

Ball's Bluff was the debacle of those engagements. Three regiments had been sent to ferry across the Potomac near Leesburg. Only half of those men survived.

That engagement sent Congress into an uproar. They demanded answers as to whose orders sent those regiments. However, they got none from the War Department or Major General McClellan, who had issued the orders. As they received no answers, Congress imprisoned General Stone, who was in command at Ball's Bluff. General Stone was freed six months later and cleared of any misconduct.

It appears the military sticks together.

At the U.S. Patent Hospital things had settled into a convalescent phase when in came an influx of wounds from the October battles. Both Jenny and I felt confident about our splinting and bandaging and cleaning grotesque wounds.

The Sanitary Commission was sending more supplies so we had plenty of clean shirts, drawers and bedding for our men. A diet kitchen had been set up, which was a god-send. No longer did the sick have to eat pork and dirty-looking bread. We had fruit, lemonade, cider, apple juice, vegetables, meats, and dairy products.

We mashed the foods for those who needed it, cut up the foods for those who had lost a hand or an arm, and fed those who could not feed themselves. In the kitchen, drinking water was boiled and set to cool as the water in Washington was the seat of many diseases.

By November we began to see more patients being released. Some went back to their companies, some went home, still others only made it to the dead house.

Jenny and I continued to live at the hotel with Aunt Martha paying the bill. She would not hear of us living in cramped quarters or sleeping on pallets in the hospital as others did.

At her insistence we were to take some time from our labors and return to New York. Since all was quiet in Washington, we saw no reason not to take a well-deserved rest. After all, we were volunteers.

Chapter 13

Christmas in New York City is always a spirit-lifting time. Jenny and I left the cares of the Patent hospital behind us as we boarded the train.

The morning was drizzling rain. Each of us had an umbrella, but our ankle boots would get wet in spite of having polished them with saddle soap. Our excitement with leaving overcame any nuisances of the day.

Jenny carried only a traveling bag as most of her belongings were still at her home. I packed my suitcase with necessities. We left the hotel and took a horse-drawn taxi to Union Station. Aunt Martha had sent us tickets so we were saved the burden of standing in the ticket line.

The early morning train was crowded. We found a seat together and made ourselves as comfortable as possible in the uncomfortable seats and watched as other passengers came aboard.

"I'm sorry, Jenny. I didn't even think to ask if you wanted to sit by the window."

"I'm perfectly happy right her next to the aisle. The rattle of the window is annoying and they're drafty."

I smiled over at her. "I don't mind the rattle, and I'll take the draftiness instead of the passengers pushing their way through the aisle at each stop."

She chuckled. "I guess we're even."

"Let's get off the train when it stops in Baltimore. I'll want to stretch my legs," I suggested.

"Do you think it's safe?"

"This part of the country seems to have settled down. They won't allow us to get off the train if it isn't safe."

She shrugged. "I suppose not. I guess we'll find out when we get there."

Our trip went well. We were allowed into the station in Baltimore without incident. We ate in the railcar. When we stepped off the train in late evening and found Cousin Charley waiting for us with a rented carriage we were glad. The evening was as drizzling as the morning had been.

He looked dapper in his Union blue uniform peeking out under the unbuttoned canvas overcoat as he maintained his military bearing. "You ladies look well," he said as he helped us into the carriage. "Perhaps a bit tired."

"I hoped it wouldn't show," said Jenny. "We are tired, aren't we Mary?"

"Cousin Charles, you have no idea of what we have been through since we left. If we only look tired and not ten years older that's a gift."

He laughed aloud. "I'm sure Abby will be the judge of that and not hesitate to make her observations known. Mother is excited to have you come. She has the house decorated and has promised not to bring out the bandage roller while you're here."

I let out a sigh. "Thank goodness for that. It will be nice to get away from the maimed and dying."

The three of us grew silent as we looked out at the streets of New York. Wrought iron fences were decked out in boughs, wreaths and colorful red and green bows, people bustling about. If there was upheaval in the country, it was not evident on the faces of the New Yorkers.

8 Brevoort Street had never looked as welcoming as it did that evening. Candles were lit in every window, a cheery wreath hung on the door and inside a blazing fire warmed the parlor. Apples, cinnamon and ginger filled the air. There would surely be apple pie for supper.

Abby and Aunt Martha were waiting for us in the large foyer. We were hugged as though we had been away for years. A maid came to take our coats and umbrellas while Cousin Charley took our bags upstairs.

"Let's go sit in the parlor until supper is ready," suggested Aunt Martha. "You two look like you could use some nourishment."

"I think you need a complete redoing," said Abby. "Your kind of volunteering is taking its toll. Both of you should consider staying here and helping with the Relief."

"Do we look that worn?" asked Jenny.

"Of course not," Abby was quick to reply. "But you can use some rejuvenation. That's the reason I have signed us all up for the Christmas Ball."

Jenny and I looked at each other. The last thing we wanted was to spend a whole evening on our feet.

"It'll be grand," Abby was enthused. "All the notables will be there including military officers who are in town for some kind of important meeting."

"Why aren't they meeting in Washington?" That sounded more sensible to me.

"Mary, you know Washington can't compare to New York. They need respite also and things will be quiet until the spring."

I am not sure how Abby managed to get her information, but she always seemed up to date.

"How do you know that?" I was not sure of her accuracy.

"I have my ways."

Aunt Martha spoke up. "Abigail." When Aunt Martha used Abby's given name, I knew she was bothered, "You don't know that is sure. It is strictly rumor and you are not to spread rumors. Your newspaper friend looks to rile the populace."

"Mother, you know Gerald gets his information from those in charge."

"Yes, those in charge of the newspaper. It is purely speculation. Until that information comes from a positive source, you are not to repeat it."

"Fiddlesticks," Abby murmured.

"Enough of this talk," said Aunt Martha. "You young ladies are home for Christmas. We shall put all the unpleasantness away and have nothing but joyful days while you are here."

Abby hopped up from her chair. "I agree." Abby's disgruntled mood was short-lived. "We are going to go Christmas shopping and we are each going to buy new gowns for the ball."

I knew better than to protest, at least not at that time.

"I have saved the best news until now," Aunt Martha said. "Johnathan has been given a four-day furlough and so has Emily. They will be arriving on the 23rd. Can you imagine how thrilled they will be to see baby Johnathan for the first time? Oh, we are going to do up this Christmas right."

To add to our gleeful state the maid announced supper was ready. I was starved.

Jenny and I relished the food after the many distasteful meals we had eaten. It was a luxury: chicken, potatoes, gravy, cabbage salad, delicious bread, beans and apple pie.

When we retired for the evening, I snuggled under the warm covers and hoped for a good night's sleep without the visions of mangled limbs, musket ball wounds, and bloody dying men.

Chapter 14

I was disappointed that my parents wouldn't take the train from Albany. Aunt Martha had offered tickets as a Christmas gift. If they had accepted, we could all have been together. Mother wrote she worried that something dreadful would happen, and I'm sure Father would not accept train tickets as a gift. It would put a damper on his pride. I knew he would gladly buy the tickets, but I also suspect it wasn't worth putting up with Mother's anxiety.

Perhaps I should have made the effort to go to them. However, I had to watch my pennies. I was tired and spending Christmas in New York City with my optimistic cousins outweighed sitting at home in my parents' parlor while Mother read passages from the King James version of the Bible.

Abby was kind. Jenny and I were allowed to sleep as long as we wanted without her begging us to get up and go shopping. It was around ten o'clock when we wandered down to the kitchen.

Breakfast was long over but the cook prepared oatmeal, bacon and bread she had toasted on the wood stove. She made a fresh pot of coffee, which Jenny and I languished over. Even the coffee at the hotel never tasted fresh.

Abby burst into the kitchen while we were daydreaming. "I see you two sleepyheads are finally up."

"You're ruining our reverie," I said.

"Phooey. I'll have a cup of coffee with you as I tell you what I have lined up for today."

Jenny and I groaned.

Abby accepted the cup of coffee the cook handed to her and took a seat at the table with us.

"What's the weather outside?" asked Jenny. "I'm not going out if it's cold and windy."

"I went to the warehouse with Mother. There is no wind. The sky is overcast, but it isn't raining and it isn't that cold. Your long cape will be plenty to keep you warm."

"You're not saying that because you want us to go shopping?" said Jenny.

Abby acted appalled, "You would doubt my word, dear sister?"

Jenny raised an eyebrow. "I have known you to stretch the truth to your advantage."

I smiled at them both. It was good to be back with the good-natured bickering of sisters who deeply cared for each other.

"We're going to Macy's Dry Goods on 6th Avenue and Lord & Taylor on Catherine Street." Abby was back in full form. "We can buy our ball gowns and whatever else we need for the Christmas Ball."

"I don't plan on buying a new gown," I informed her.

Abby's eyes opened wide. "You're not going to wear that blue cotton dress of yours are you?"

"No. I thought perhaps Emily will lend me one of her gowns. If not, I don't mind sitting at home."

Abby was indignant. "Mary Sullivan! You will not sit at home when you can be enjoying the fete of the season."

Jenny spoke up. "Of course Emily will lend you one of hers. She can only wear one at a time, and I know she isn't going to take them back to her army hospital."

Abby softened. "I suppose you're right. You're going to buy a new one, aren't you, Jenny?"

"Only if I find one prettier than my green striped silk."

"Oh, I forgot how pretty that gown is. You haven't worn it but once that I remember," said Abby.

"That was to Charley's graduation party. No one will remember it as I am not one to stand out in a crowd."

It was true that Jenny was not one to turn a man's head, but she was a sweet and compassionate person.

I wasn't a raving beauty, either, and my retiring personality didn't cause the male gender to flock to my side. We couldn't all be like Abby.

"It's settled then." Abby hopped up from her chair. "I will buy a new gown and the two of you can look for whatever you need to look for."

Her enthusiasm jolted us into movement. We left the table to prepare for a day on the town.

The weather was crisp and dry. We were warm in our long cloaks, wool gloves and bonnets. We decided to walk to the department stores instead of waiting for a street car. Crossing streets meant maneuvering around horse dung, but if it wasn't fresh, it didn't smell in the cold air. As all conveyances were drawn by horses or mules everyone knew to be aware of the pitfalls. The city hired men whose job it was to clean up the streets. As we dodged the piles it appeared they didn't hire enough.

We passed women in hooped dresses, capes and cloaks and men in stovepipe hats as we made our way to Macy's Dry Goods department store.

It seemed a winter wonderland as we stepped inside. Ribbon trimmed greenery of pine-scented boughs and wreaths were plentiful. We went up the stairs to the second floor as I was in need of a new chemise and set of drawers.

The store was busy. We decided to separate and buy our goods and meet at the top of the stairs in thirty minutes. Abby wanted to get to Lord & Taylor before all the pretty gowns were sold.

I bought a set of plain drawers with snaps at the waist but the chemises were too fancy with lace and embroidered roses and cost more than I wanted to pay. As I owned two chemises, I decided to try to repair the one with holes that had worn through from too much laundering with harsh soap.

On my way to the clerk I saw a pair of knee socks and bought them for Jenny. A well-dressed woman wore a chemise, corset, stockings, drawers and petticoat. Unbeknownst to Abby, Jenny and I had done away with the corset and stockings and wore socks for our work at the hospital. We needed ease of movement. Who could see what was beneath our skirts?

At Lord & Taylor the Christmas atmosphere was all about. Abby bought a lovely red velvet gown decorated with tiny white bows. The contrast with her dark hair was striking.

We separated again to do Christmas shopping. I bought boxes of ribbon candy for everyone. For Aunt Martha I bought a box of chocolates. They were expensive but she had done so much for me I wanted to give her something special.

It was almost five o'clock before we returned back to the Morgan house. Street gaslights were lit to aid us in the winter darkness that was descending.

Inside the warmth of the house and lit candles welcomed us home. Supper was ready to be served. We left our bundles in the hall, hung our cloaks on a coat tree and made our weary way to the dining room. All was well at 8 Brevoort Street.

Chapter 15

The evening of the Christmas Ball Abby came into my room. "The woman is here to do our hair." We were both dressed in our chemise, corset, stockings and drawers. Emily had loaned me a corset and a gown. With the low cut and trim waist of the evening gown, a corset to cinch the waist and elevate the bosom was necessary regardless of how uncomfortable it was.

"A woman to do our hair?" That was news to me.

"Certainly, we must look our best. Everyone who is anyone is going to be there."

"They don't know me, Abby."

She gave a shrug of her shoulder. "That makes no difference. You are a guest of the Morgan family and people will be watching."

I wondered if Abby was going to go through her life wondering if others were watching. However, I was not from a notable family and I assume it was important to keep your guard up lest tongues might wag.

Perhaps I was guilty of the same. As a teacher there were certain expectations and guidelines to follow. Stepping off the path meant jeopardizing my position. Is that the reason I preferred to stay in the background, always conscious not to buck the system? At age twenty-two I was still toeing the mark.

We had to throw on our robes and go to the kitchen where the hair woman was heating curling irons on the wood stove. She laid the long prong of the iron on the hot plates of the stove and the wood handle with burn marks rested on the side away from the heat.

I watched as she took an iron, touched her finger to her tongue then touched her finger to the iron to hear it sizzle. "If it's too hot it'll singe the hair, if it isn't hot enough it will not curl," she explained.

Jenny was first. When the woman finished, Jenny looked like she had grown a few inches. Her hair was piled up atop her head in regal fashion, held in place by silver combs. Teasing tendrils framed her fine-boned face. It was the first time I thought she was attractive. Her usual style of a tight bun made her look drawn. When she put on her glasses, the thick lenses made her eyes look like saucers. The magic disappeared.

I was next. No one ever fooled with my hair and the touch was foreign as the woman combed and ran her fingers through it. "You have thick, heavy hair, miss. I am going to braid it similar to the French style."

I wasn't sure what that was but I was at her mercy.

"The reason I am not going to touch the iron to your hair is that the curl won't last in the evening damp air."

I knew that to be a fact. My hair drooped in the humid air while Abby's curled tighter.

I still am not sure how the hair woman braided it differently, but I too, looked transformed. The braids were crisscrossed in the back and held in place by hairpins and an elegant gold comb.

The woman had done Abby's silky brown hair many times. She worked quickly until she produced a mass of tight ringlets and placed red velvet bows on each side of her head.

When we were fully dressed, the plain Mary Sullivan had disappeared into a glowing ball gown and fancy hairdo. We gathered in the hall when it was time to leave: Abby in her red velvet, Jenny in green striped silk, I in Emily's gold plaid taffeta, Aunt Martha in a purple silk trimmed in white, Emily in yellow satin, Florence in silk copper print. Both Charley and Johnathan were in their Union blue.

We must have looked the color of the rainbow in our billowing hooped dresses and smelled like a flower garden with the different scents of toilet water.

Abby was so excited she clucked like a mother hen as she scrutinized each person to be sure everything was perfect. A general inspecting his troops, I thought.

The maid, who was going to watch over baby Johnathan, announced the Hansom cabs had arrived. We wore long dark cloaks and white gloves. Bonnets were ignored. Cold ears were better than ruining our freshly coifed hair. Charley and we three rode together in one cab while Aunt Martha, Emily, Florence and Johnathan rode in the other.

The noble soldiers helped us up the steps into the cabs. Each driver remained in his seat at the back holding the long reins to the sleek black horses harnessed at the front.

We were packed in so tight I could see Abby's and Jenny's laced drawers and boots sticking out from under the hoops that sprang up as they sat crowded together. Charley and I sat opposite, which gave me a few inches of room. I felt like Cinderella going off to the king's ball.

There was a light dusting of snow on the myriad of steps illuminated with gas lights leading up to the great hall. Young men in red uniforms were stationed at the foot of the steps to lend an arm to the ladies. I was grateful for the assistance as I had to hold my dress just above the toes of my boots with one hand and feared I might slip on the snowy steps. There was a doorman at the entrance. Our escorts gave a bow and were off to aid the next attendees.

Crystal gasoliers hung from the ceiling of the immense decorated ballroom. Oil-fueled sconces were generously placed on the walls and candelabrum lit on the serving tables. As I took in the grandeur, it was then I understood Abby's excitement. Christmas was in the air and everyone was in a merry mood. I pushed the sorry conditions of the war from my mind.

There was an area reserved for our party with two small round tables draped in white linen tablecloths. Green wax candles in crystal holders were set in the middle of the table and four chairs at each. A young man hurried over to wipe them off lest we smudge our white gloves. White gloves must be impeccable. Aunt Martha's white gloves were sewn in black thread, a custom to show that she was widowed.

Johnathan and Charles brought china cups of wassail. After the cold ride in the Hansom, the hot mulled cider warmed our insides.

I surveyed the beautiful gowns and snappy dressed gentlemen as they moved about. There were plenty of army officers attending and looking sharp in their uniforms just as Johnathan and Charley did. What a lavish display of finery to behold. Abby was right to be sure we were all perfectly appointed.

The tables were far enough away from the staged musicians that we could still converse. We were given dance cards with instructions as to what each dance would be.

Abby's dance card was almost full within the first half hour as young and middle-aged gentlemen came by to greet the Morgan family. Jenny and I were less fortunate. Abby went with her first dance partner to talk to a group of friends.

The orchestra struck up the first tune taking Florence and Johnathan onto the dance floor. Charley gravitated to a group of young soldiers. Emily and Aunt Martha had left their table to make the rounds of people she knew and those who might benefit the Sanitary Commission.

Jenny and I remained at the table until a bespeckled young man, whom Jenny knew, asked if she would care to dance. "I'm sorry," she said. "That will leave my cousin alone. Perhaps another time."

"Jenny, dance with the young man. I am quite satisfied to sit and watch."

"I should wait until Mother returns."

I was sure she wanted to dance and there might not be another chance. "Jenny, for heaven's sake go and enjoy yourself."

She rose as if uncertain to continue until I nudged her with my foot. The young man offered his arm and they went swirling off with the rest.

I was perfectly content by myself, as I rated the ability of the different dancers in my mind. When Jenny returned she thanked the young man and took her seat.

"You looked like you were having a good time," I remarked.

"The little weasel tries to corner me at every dance. I don't think he can get another girl to wrestle around the floor with him."

I chuckled. "He seems to like you."

"It's just because I'm nice to him. I wanted to dance at least one number. You notice no one else has asked me."

"That was only the first dance," I reminded her.

"Yes, but I'm sure all of Abby's friends have their dance cards full."

"We're here to have a good time. If we have to sit like wallflowers, we can still enjoy watching others and listening to the music."

"I hope Mother doesn't see us here by ourselves or she'll try to drum up some partners. I'll drag Charley out on the floor before that happens."

By now the orchestra was well into its second number.

She took off her glasses and rubbed her eyes. "I wish I could leave these off."

She was attractive not wearing them. "Why don't you? They must hinder your dancing."

"They do. I'm blind as a bat without them. Everything is fuzzy. I'd have to grope my way back to the table." She picked up her glasses and held them to her eyes. "Now I can see Abby."

She turned to peer around the room. "Oh, my goodness, Mary. Do I see two soldiers headed in our direction?"

I looked up from where I sat. "Maybe there is someone behind us."

"I don't think so," she replied as she set her glasses back on the table.

The two in Union blue stopped at our table. "Good evening ladies."

I didn't want anyone feeling sorry for the two of us. Especially young men we didn't know. The thought struck that Charley may have put them up to it. That was even a worse possibility.

"You ladies are not dancing?"

"Obviously," I said.

"I'm Lieutenant Daniel Phillips and my friend, Lieutenant Ted Stevens."

They gave a military bow in unison.

"Do you not dance?" Lieutenant Phillips asked.

"Not without a partner," I replied. My abruptness did not seem to scare them off.

Lieutenant Phillips was the spokesman. "Well, I'm not much of a dancer, and it appears all these in attendance are familiar with each other and the different styles."

Both Lieutenant Stevens and Jenny had been quiet until she was quick to say, "I love to dance. I know all that are printed on my dance card." My quiet reserved Jenny had surprised me again.

"Are all dances taken?" Lieutenant Stevens asked her.

Without a hint of embarrassment, she told him, "They are all open."

"Then, Miss…"

"Morgan, Jenny Morgan."

Lieutenant Stevens of average height, stocky build, ruddy complexion, red-blond hair and blue eyes said, "Then Miss Jenny Morgan, would you care to dance?"

Jenny was on her feet in a flash. I noticed she left her glasses on the table.

She smiled and answered, "I would like nothing better." Lieutenant Ted Stevens offered his arm to my demure cousin and they were off.

"May I sit?" Lieutenant Phillips asked. He was a few inches taller than Ted Stevens, slimmer with black hair and clean shaven face.

"Yes, you may. I apologize if I sounded short."

He lowered himself into the chair next to me that Jenny had occupied.

I decided to be cordial. "I'm Mary Sullivan from near Albany."

"It's nice to meet you Miss Sullivan. Ted loves to dance. We noticed you two lovely ladies and decided to press our luck."

My inner thoughts began to work. He said lovely not lonely and Charley hadn't sent them. Someone sitting at this table would make me look less conspicuous. My initial antipathy was melting. He had soft brown eyes and a pleasant smile. "Are you from New York, lieutenant?"

He shook his head. I'm from Vermont. My colonel is here from Washington for a conference. I came as his aide. Ted's the same. He's from Michigan."

I had to smile. "So we are all strangers except for those we came with. You are not a dancer?"

He chuckled. "I enjoy the reels and waltzes. The fast numbers cause too much heat in this uniform."

I grinned. "We enjoy the same dances."

The ice was broken. I told him I was a teacher and my cousin and I had joined the Sanitary Commission nurses. Also, that we were taking a respite from a hospital in Washington.

He had left his job as a secretary/bookkeeper to join up. He became an aide as many of the soldiers had little schooling.

The orchestra struck up a waltz. "Miss Sullivan. Would you care to waltz with me?"

"Yes, I would."

"Good. I would not like to miss *The Blue Danube*."

I can still feel the strong arm that went around my waist as he led me to the ballroom floor. I had danced with different gentlemen, but his touch sent a ripple of pleasure through me that I had never experienced before. When he took me in his grasp and we started to dance, I felt I would swoon. He could waltz like a feather drifting in the wind. We floated around the room and I hoped the music would never stop. My arms were bare and although the wool of his uniform rubbed my skin, I didn't care.

But the dance did come to an end and he led me back to the table.

"I haven't had that much pleasure in a long time, Miss Mary Sullivan. You are a grand waltz partner."

The pleasure wasn't all his. "I can say the same for you."

"They have cold drink. Would you like to have one?"

"Yes I would."

Jenny's escort brought her back to our table where she took her previous seat. I wanted Lieutenant Phillips to return while the chair on my left was still unoccupied.

"Your friend has gone for some cool refreshment," I informed them.

"That sounds perfect to me. What do you say, Miss Jenny?"

"I am all for something cool."

Off went Lieutenant Ted Stevens in the direction of the refreshment area.

Jenny was all smiles. "Oh, Mary. He is a wonderful dancer. He may be big but he is light on his feet."

"You left your glasses on the table," I reminded her.

"I did it on purpose. I was afraid he wouldn't ask me to dance if I was wearing them. I was glad to hold onto his arm, or I may have stumbled back here."

Before the two lieutenants returned the orchestra took a short break. Abby was escorted to our table where she took the seat to my left that I hoped Lieutenant Phillips would occupy. She pulled a folded fan from her reticule and fanned her face. "Did I see you two waltzing about with a couple of our soldiers?"

Jenny and I nodded.

"I'm sure they are lonely and missing being home. It's good you two were free to make them feel welcome," she surmised.

Abby had a way with words and there it was. Two lonely soldiers with two lonely wallflowers.

The lieutenants returned with our drinks. They both stood. I made introductions and secretly hoped the good-looking Lieutenant Phillips wasn't captivated by my vivacious cousin. Abby offered a winsome smile. "I am always glad to meet soldiers from our upright army," Abby said.

"We have brought the young ladies a refreshing repast as you can see," Daniel Phillips said. "Would you care for a glass, Miss Abby?"

"Oh, Lieutenant. That would be welcome. I am almost spent from all the dancing. I believe I have only one space left on my dance card."

Did I see my flirtatious cousin bat her eyes?

Charley happened by at that moment. "I see you have met my sisters and my cousin," he said to Ted and Daniel.

"It has been our pleasure. I was about to get Miss Abby a refreshment."

Charley didn't hesitate. "Come with me, Abby. I have someone I'd like you to meet. We'll grab a glass of punch on our way. That is if you will all excuse us."

We had no objection. I could have kissed Cousin Charles.

The lieutenants, Jenny and I sat at the table with our lemon-flavored drinks.

As the night went on Ted Stevens and Daniel Phillips never left our sides. Ted and Jenny danced every dance while Daniel and I stuck to the slower pace. It was an evening I shall never forget.

Chapter 16

That Christmas of 1861 was one of the happiest I have spent. Aunt Martha invited Ted, Daniel and Charley's friend for Christmas. The day before we had packed boxes and baskets of food and clothing for the less fortunate Aunt Martha knew from her charitable work.

Johnathan and Florence took the baby to Johnathan's parents' house outside the city to spend the day.

Ted and Daniel arrived late Christmas morning with Charley's friend, Edward, another soldier and the person Charley was eager to have Abby meet the night of the ball. He was not just a soldier but a Major and from a prominent family in Philadelphia.

By now we were all on a first name basis. The three soldiers looked resplendent in their uniforms as the maid answered their knock and we hurried into the hall to greet them. Daniel gave me a warm smile and my heart danced a few beats. Hesitant to track wet snow into the house they remained standing on a rug by the door.

Aunt Martha appeared and quickly sized up the situation. "Come in gentlemen. You may slip off your shoes. We don't care if you are in sock feet." Neither did she care to have wet snow tracked onto the wood floor.

"We all made sure there were no holes in them," quipped Ted causing us to chuckle and relax as they took off their shoes and we went into the parlor. The blazing fire in the fireplace warmed the room.

Aunt Martha told them, "This morning, we are taking these baskets and boxes to distribute. We can use your help and strength to get them loaded onto the wagon that will be arriving shortly."

She left no room for refusal. I admired my Aunt Martha.

"We're happy to help," said Daniel. "It doesn't hurt to see soldiers turning a good deed. There are places where we aren't popular."

"True," Edward enjoined. "But we have made a pact not to talk about politics or the war. This is Christmas."

We all clapped our hands and set to work sorting the gift baskets.

"Where is Emily?" asked Abby. "Isn't she going to help?"

Aunt Martha was busy overseeing the operation. "Emily has to return on the morning train. She's writing some letters and putting her things in order. She'll be at Christmas dinner. By then, we'll all be begging for food."

Abby, Jenny and I wore only day dresses and petticoats. Aunt Martha remained in a fashionable hooped black wool. She had given us the addresses and names of those who were to receive the gifts. The driver of the wagon was familiar with that part of the city for which we were grateful.

Aunt Martha handed the same list to the driver that she had given to us. The six of us crowded into the back of the wagon after it was loaded and sat on dry straw covering the bed. Daniel sat next to me. "Will you be warm enough?" he asked.

"Aunt Martha made sure we brought our lap blankets." I had a warm coat that went to my ankles, wool mittens and a wool winter hat that covered my ears. Daniel wore leather gloves, military hat and overcoat, and a navy wool scarf around his neck. I thought he looked grand.

New York City was quiet which allowed us to take in the sights that were usually crowded with busy people and horse-drawn vehicles. It seemed we were mesmerized by the stillness of the city. Only the clip-clop of the horses and crunch of the wagon wheels were heard as we rode along the snowy streets.

The driver drove into the squalid part of the city. I felt uneasy. Perhaps I shifted in my seat. As if Daniel had sensed my disquiet he reached under the lap robe and gave my hand a gentle squeeze. I looked over at him and smiled.

The families were happy with the packages we gave them. Even the dull eyes of the undernourished children seemed to light up with joy. Overworked, underpaid and eking out a living most remained thankful and offered a 'God bless you' as we delivered the needed goods.

Our soldiers assisted us back into the wagon where we again sat on straw covering the bed. We had more room but still Daniel sat close to me and

I noticed it was the same with Jenny's and Abby's partners. I liked Daniel's attention, and I was not a bit unhappy that Abby was focused on her officer friend.

Dinner was ready when we returned from delivering the gifts. The table looked elegant with china, silver and crystal. The buffet held ham, roast beef, chicken, a variety of breads, squash, potatoes, carrots and cabbage salad. After consuming that delicious meal we had our choice of baked custard, apple cobbler, cherry pie or coconut cake. There were eight of us around the large dining room table filled with conversation, laughter and Christmas cheer.

After dinner we retired to the parlor. We had opened gifts after church services the night before. Aunt Martha surprised the visiting soldiers with a box of hard candies, dried fruit, and nuts. Charley asked me to play the harpsicord for the singing of Christmas carols.

Charley had a lovely tenor voice and sang a solo of *O Holy Night*. We finished the singing and Daniel came to sit beside me on the bench as I was folding up the music pieces. "I want to see you when you are back in Washington," he said in a quiet voice.

"I would like that."

"Do you know when you will be going back?"

"I believe it will be when Jenny is ready. After the start of the new year probably."

He took the music books from my hand and laid them on top of the harpsicord before he took a piece of paper from his pocket. "Here is my address. Please send me a note as to when you will arrive. If I'm free I'll meet you at Union Station."

I nodded as I took the paper from him.

Daniel Phillips took both my hands in his. They were warm and strong, "Promise?"

I felt a bit dazed. But I was able to mask my feelings and replied, "Promise."

This lieutenant from Vermont had completely disarmed me. Me... the stoic, prim and proper Mary Sullivan.

Chapter 17

On January 3, 1862 Jenny and I boarded the train in New York City dressed in our long cloaks, bonnets and wool gloves to return to our volunteer duties in Washington, D.C.

It was not without deep soul searching that we decided to go back to the hospital. However, the war in the East was still quiet and we prayed that was a good omen. Perhaps a peaceful settlement could be reached soon.

Once again Aunt Martha and Abby saw us off before they resumed their duties at the Sanitary Commission warehouse. Abby said she was definitely coming to Washington to see "her major"; the first time I had ever heard her use those possessive words toward a suitor.

Emily and Johnathan had returned to Washington a week before. Charley was still stationed in New York although he was sure he would get orders to leave for Washington. Why, I wasn't sure.

Jenny and I conversed little on our trip back. We could enjoy each other's company without the glib chatter. I had mixed feelings. Perhaps she did too, but we had both talked at length and decided to return. I thought about seeing Daniel. It was a pleasant thought as I was as eager to see him again as I was sure Jenny held the same expectation about seeing Ted Stevens. However, we remained cautious knowing that they were soldiers and away from their native states. Who knew what the spring would bring. I didn't want to think about it.

Jenny looked over at me and smiled as we neared D.C. "Do you think Ted and Daniel will meet us at Union Station?"

"Daniel said he would if he is free."

"I'm a little on edge. Ted and I had such a good time at Christmas I have to wonder if he will have second thoughts about seeing me again."

"Perhaps they both will." Was that terse reply to prepare myself? Gird my loins as the Bible says?

Jenny had no response to my flippant reply. "I wish I still had that fancy hairdo and didn't have to wear these glasses." She turned her head and looked out the window across the aisle.

I was sorry for my shortness, but I could not bring myself to apologize because we both needed to face the prospect that Ted or Daniel or both had a change of heart after they returned.

The train pulled into the cavernous Union Station in the late evening. Our excitement and edginess disappeared quickly as we scanned around the murky shadows and saw neither Ted nor Daniel there to greet us. We looked at each other. She shrugged a shoulder.

"Let's go up and see if there is a taxi we can take to the hotel," I suggested.

"Yes," she agreed, "I don't think it's wise to walk to a streetcar stop." Idle conversation. Anyone who knew us would be able to hear the crestfallen tone in our voices.

We carried our cases and two large tote bags of whatever Aunt Martha could stuff in and was sure we needed. There were three horse-drawn taxis waiting. I gave one driver the address of the hotel where we were staying and he motioned us to another taxi. "He's goin' that route," he said.

We went over to the next enclosed buggy. The driver hopped off his seat. "I'll load those bundles in for you young ladies. First trip to our fair city?"

I shook my head. "We're returning from the Christmas holidays. We are both Sanitary Commission nurses at the U.S. Patent Hospital."

Jenny and I climbed in and sat side by side while he resumed his driver's position and chucked to the horse to move on. At the hotel he insisted on carrying our luggage inside. When I tried to pay him he refused. "The trip's on me. God bless you young ladies for the work you do." That was the second time in a week we were wished blessings from above. I hoped the Good Lord was listening.

A porter came to carry our bags. "Miss Morgan, the clerk says there is a message for you at the desk."

Jenny hurried to the desk to get the message. She opened it immediately while the young porter and I waited. Her worried expression turned into a wide smile as she hustled back to us. "It's from Ted," she said.

We walked up the stairs to the second floor. The porter opened the door for us and took our luggage inside before he handed us the key. "It's nice to have you ladies back," he said.

"Thank you." I answered and handed him a ten cent piece for his help.

As soon as he closed the door, I could hardly wait before I asked, "What does Ted say?"

"He says he is sorry he couldn't be at the station because of a late night meeting, but he will get in touch with me as soon as he can."

"Oh, Jenny. That's wonderful."

We were removing our bonnets and cloaks. "Yes, it is. I was so concerned."

She didn't mention Daniel and neither did I. We got to work emptying the large tote bags and it was like Christmas all over again. Dear Aunt Martha had packed soap, tooth powder, handkerchiefs, toilet water, nuts, candies, soda crackers, peanut butter, strawberry jam and tea. In the very bottom was another simple dress in the same pattern as the gray one she had given us earlier for hospital work. This one was brown with a brown apron to match.

"Why do you think she sent a brown apron?" Jenny mused.

"She probably saw the stains on our white ones."

"Do you think Miss Dix is going to approve?"

I chuckled. "They're drab enough. She may insist everyone wear one."

It was then Jenny took a serious tone. "I'm sorry Ted didn't mention Daniel. Perhaps they haven't been able to communicate with each other."

"I don't know. We both had our doubts before we even left New York. Time has a way of changing things. I am disappointed, but I never get my hopes up so high that I will fall flat."

Jenny confessed. "Mary, I try to be as brave as you but I fail. I think I would have flopped down and cried myself to sleep if I hadn't heard from Ted."

I offered a weak smile. The way I felt I may have done that very thing.

We set about getting ready to report for work at the hospital the next day. We decided to wear our new brown dresses and aprons taking a bit of New York and a happy Christmas to face the grind of hospital work. Although I was tired from the train ride and no word from Daniel, it was not a restful sleep.

Chapter 18

At the hospital we found the Sanitary Commission had instituted a Diet Kitchen, a welcome addition to the health of the soldiers. Even though Major General McClellan had been organizing the Army of the Potomac into military order since November, the sanitary conditions in Washington had not improved to a satisfactory level.

The soldiers in the hospital were still suffering from dysentery, lung conditions, cholera and typhoid fever. Most of those injured at the Battle of Bull Run, six months ago, had been transferred to hospitals in New York or Philadelphia. Others were lucky enough to be discharged home where some of them would be plagued by infirmities for the rest of their lives.

A soldier's pay was $13.00 a month, attractive to many young men. The militias who had come to defend Washington at President Lincoln's request last April had fulfilled their obligation. By the first of August those who had families and farms and jobs returned to their native states. Even with those depletions, the army was increasing in numbers.

What had also changed when we resumed our duties at the U.S. Patent Hospital was that nurses were now allowed to go into the kitchen. Joseph kept the coffee pot on and cooked up the meals, but I felt like a bird let out of its cage when I could give extra nutrition where it was needed: peanut butter on a soda cracker, an extra spoon of jelly, a drink of cider, apple butter on a piece of bread.

Jenny and I boiled eggs and kept them in a basket hidden from view. We fed them to our soldiers with discretionary pleasure. We were concerned that the matron of the hospital would question an increase in the orders for eggs, but either she turned her head or the extra we used were not enough to tip the balance. After all, how can one decide how many eggs are needed to feed a hospital full of sick men?

Jenny was like a different person. Ted Stevens had brought her out of her quiet ways. She kidded with the soldiers and took on her duties with a new burst of energy. I envied her.

For two weeks she and Ted spent as much of their free time together as was possible. I was invited at times but declined the invitation. Apparently, Ted didn't talk about Daniel. Jenny didn't offer and I didn't ask. I was down-hearted about the absent Lieutenant Daniel Phillips but did my best to not let it show.

One Saturday afternoon when Ted and Jenny had gone skating, I was coming in from a trip to the library. "Mary." I knew at once the owner of that voice. It was as if the room stood still as I stopped without turning around. There was a movement of air before I felt him at my side. "Mary, I've been waiting for you."

I clutched the books I had borrowed with a tight grip. I couldn't look at him for fear I would burst into tears. In a raspy whisper I murmured, "Hello, Daniel."

"Will you come and sit with me so we can talk?"

I still couldn't raise my eyes to look at him; all I could do was nod my head. I knew I had to compose myself as I felt my heart thumping in my chest.

He took my elbow and guided me to an alcove where two tan leather chairs faced each other. My eyes remained downcast looking with a blank stare at the books that lay in my lap.

He leaned forward and covered my gloved hands in his, "Mary, there was no way I could get a message to you. Even Ted didn't know where I was. My colonel had been summoned to a secret meeting and insisted I go to take notes for him."

It was then I could raise my eyes to meet his. "I thought you had changed your mind about seeing me, Daniel."

"I was sure you would feel that way and I am sorry, but I had no other choice. Am I forgiven?"

I felt my body relax and smiled at the tight look on his face. "There is nothing to forgive. You told me that you would meet me at the station if you were free, nothing more." Wasn't I the noble one?

He leaned back in the chair. "It didn't bother you that I didn't contact you? You didn't ask Jenny to ask Ted? I'm sure they have been seeing each other."

I was not about to reveal my inner feelings so I replied, "I didn't ask and Jenny didn't say." Then I added, "I am glad to hear it was not your choice and I am pleased that you're here."

These words brought a wide relieved smile to his pleasing face. "Would you like to go out for a walk?"

"I'd love to. First I have to take these books up to my room. Actually, Jenny and I share a room on the second floor. I'll be a few minutes."

Daniel was out of his chair and gave me a hand to rise. "I'm not going anywhere until you return."

I felt his eyes watch as I walked away. There was no slouch to my shoulders as I mounted the steps to the upper floor. In my room I placed the books on my bed and hurried to change into a more suitable outfit as I had worn the shapeless brown dress Aunt Martha had given me at Christmas. I put on a tan wool cardigan over a white waist and slipped on a brown wool skirt. We were going for a walk and regardless of the winter sun it was a chilly day. I replaced my wool cap with the navy velvet bonnet I had worn on the train. I didn't want to keep Daniel waiting, so I hurried out the door and down the stairs to the lobby where he was waiting.

His smile was warm as he held out his hand. "That was quick, Mary Sullivan."

I knew there was a twinkle in my eye as I replied, "Lieutenant Phillips, the Irish are not known for dragging their feet when there's merriment about."

We both laughed as he took my arm and we walked out into the chilly damp air of Washington. At that moment all seemed right with the world.

Chapter 19

Saturday evenings and Sundays were usually free times for the four of us. There were tea rooms, dance halls, saloons, and small restaurants springing up all over Washington. Some catered to the officers and government people, others hoped to capture the soldiers' pay.

Ted Stevens knew every spot that offered dancing. I don't think he and Jenny missed a Saturday night dance. Daniel and I preferred the plays and concerts, but we also joined them a few times. The fact that Daniel and Ted both were aides for officers, army horses and buggies were available to them.

On Sundays the four of us went to church services and then to a small restaurant for brunch. Ted and Jenny were crazy about ice skating. While they skated Daniel and I took a ride or walked and talked. We were satisfied to be together arm in arm.

Our room was close to the back stairs of the hotel. If we were back from our Sunday early enough we let Ted and Daniel in the back door of the hotel and snuck them into our room to play cards. We were acting like teenagers but we didn't care. We cherished those times.

It was late February while Daniel and I were out for a ride in the cold air when he said, "Mary there is going to be big trouble. It will soon be all the news. Lincoln has ordered McClellan to take Richmond. Preparations are being made."

I looked at him with wide eyes. "Oh, Daniel. No. I don't want to hear that. I don't want to think of more battles, more lost men, more shattered lives. I want this awful time to end."

He drove the buggy into a copse of trees and took me in his arms. "As do I. This is the result of the meetings I attended in secret with my colonel. We have to save the Union. Isn't that what we want? If we can take Richmond the superiors feel it will end the conflict."

Daniel's arms were always a comfort yet I felt myself go limp in those strong arms and broke into loud sobs. Whatever feeling overcame me, I couldn't stop my blubbering. Daniel just held me until I stopped the uncontrollable tears.

Through my shaky voice I said, "I saw the effects of Bull Run. I don't want to see any more carnage, and I know there will be. I'm afraid for you and Ted and all the men."

I pulled from his arms and fished around in my pocketbook for a handkerchief. He pulled one from his pocket and began to wipe my tear-stained face.

This act of kindness touched my heart, and while he was dabbing he apologized, "Maybe I shouldn't have told you. I'm sorry."

I sat composing myself after the sudden flood of unexpected sadness. I shook my head.

"No, you were right to tell me. I don't know why the news seemed to smack me in the face."

We sat quietly side by side with his arm around my shoulders until I felt in charge of my emotions. "All better?" he asked. I nodded.

By then I had my handkerchief and blew my nose. "Do you know when this will happen or what it means to you and Ted?"

"Ted and I will get orders when all arrangements are made."

"Mary, when this is all over I'd like to have you come to Vermont to meet my family."

Why didn't this surprise me? I looked over at him with my red swollen eyes. "I'd like that very much."

And then he kissed me with warm gentle lips, held me close and we sat there neither speaking a word for the longest time. I wanted to stay there forever. I didn't want to think of any more shot-to-pieces young men and boys. "I am so afraid of what's to come, Daniel, so afraid for everyone."

He tipped my head up and kissed me again. "Let's not think too far ahead. For now we are together, we'll meet up with Ted and Jenny and go on as though none of this conversation had ever taken place."

"Does Ted know about this?"

"At this time it's strictly rumor. He will soon. We'll meet up with them and enjoy a nice warm supper at the hotel."

I dabbed at the corner of my eyes. "Do I look bad? I don't want them to know I've been crying."

His arm was still around me and he squeezed gently. "They'll think it's the cold air that's made you rosy." And, he thrilled me once more with his kiss. I wanted us both to float away. "Are you ready, Mary Sullivan? I don't want Ted and Jenny turned into icicles."

I kissed his cold cheek. "I'm all better."

When we got to the skating rink they were waiting. "It's about time," said Ted as he helped Jenny into the back seat of the buggy. "Our feet are numb."

"That's what happens when you go ice skating," answered Daniel. "Bundle yourselves up in that army blanket." He looked over at me and winked.

If either of them noticed I had been crying, they never mentioned it. But then, they were so wrapped up in themselves I'm not sure what they noticed of others.

We had supper at the hotel, and I did my best to hide what Daniel had told me even though it lingered uncomfortably in the back of my mind. When Jenny and I went to our room, she asked, "Did Daniel say something that upset you?"

"You noticed I had been crying?"

"No. I sensed something wasn't right."

I offered a weak smile to my dear cousin. "Daniel asked me to meet his Vermont family after this war business is all settled. Tears of joy."

Jenny gave me a hug. "I am happy for you. Daniel must have serious thoughts."

"Quite serious," I replied.

Chapter 20

Near the end of February Cousin Charles was transferred to Washington with his regiment. He was allowed to travel separately from the troop so Aunt Martha and Abby rode the train with him. Abby wanted to see "her major" to whom she had communicated by letter. Aunt Martha wouldn't allow her to come unchaperoned. Once again they stayed in a room in our hotel.

We were happy to see them. Aunt Martha brought all sorts of treats and necessities including rose toilet water and face cream. She fitted Jenny and me out with several new aprons and another shapeless dress. Now we had three work dresses: gray, navy and brown. I believe we were far better dressed than many of the volunteer nurses. Most of the aprons were heavy cotton but there were also a couple of canvas. All held deep front pockets, which Jenny and I were happy about as we could conceal tidbits for our soldiers. Aunt Martha had brought us a gallon tub of gingersnaps. We saved those for our favorite patients.

For the ten days they were here, Jenny and I kept our work routine at the hospital while Aunt Martha and Abby attended dinners and meetings related to the Sanitary Commission. All of Abby's free time was spent with Edward, but Daniel and Ted were kept busy.

Two days before they were to return to New York, Jenny and I were in Aunt Martha's room when Abby announced there was to be an officers' banquet the next evening and we were all invited.

Jenny and I looked at each other. "We haven't heard of this," Jenny said to Abby.

Abby flicked a white speck off her pretty green velvet dress. "It's true. Edward told me. It's to lift the morale of the officers."

"Why does their morale need lifting?" I asked.

"Edward says they soon will be taking Richmond."

"Abigail, you should not be spreading rumors," chided Aunt Martha.

Abby was nonchalant. "But it's true. Mother. Edward is close to McClellan and privy to all of what's discussed. Why do you think Charley's regiment has been called to come here? The army will be in need of replacements."

The minute I heard that I felt my heart begin a staccato beat. Would Daniel be leaving?

Aunt Martha's jaw was set firm. "Edward should not be telling what he's heard in private."

"Oh, fiddlesticks," said Abby. "He only told me."

"And you told us," reprimanded Jenny. "You can be a blabbermouth, Abby."

I was open-mouthed for I had not heard the sisters speak to each other in such a way. Was Jenny as alarmed as I?

Aunt Martha held up her hand. "Jenny, that's quite enough. Abby, you are not to let this information slip out. If there is to be a banquet to which we are all invited, we must get ourselves in proper order."

We left their room without an apology from either sister. Jenny said as we went to our room, "I shouldn't have been so sharp with Abby. The instant she said the army was going to march I feared for Ted and saw flashes of those who came back from Bull Run."

I put the key in the lock and we entered our room. "I understand." Still I kept silent as to what Daniel had told me. This news had come from Edward. Now there were two knowledgeable men who voiced the same opinion. Abby had not seen what Jenny and I had witnessed, so I wasn't sure if she grasped how serious a "march to Richmond" could be.

Indeed, we attended a lavish banquet with Daniel and Ted as our escorts. Abby went separately with Edward, and Aunt Martha was accompanied by an Episcopal minister and his wife.

We wore the dresses we had worn on travel from New York, which were appropriate for a banquet. Abby was in a hooped black gabardine with white lace at the collar and pearl buttons down the front. She did look elegant. She and Edward were seated near the head table. I thought my cousin Abby a suitable match for General McClellan's wife who was lovely, charming and very much enjoyed the attention. McClellan, himself, was handsome and short in stature, but I do believe his ego made him appear taller.

Daniel was close to me all evening. It was almost as if he felt this would be our last happy time together. After the feast as we walked to the buggy I asked him, "What's wrong, Daniel?"

"I'll be leaving next week."

I didn't answer right away. I just tightened my hold on his arm and willed my voice to be steady, "So they weren't all rumors. The army will be going to take Richmond." I didn't cry because I had been preparing myself for this news. My voice dropped. "Is Ted going?"

"Not as yet. We'll be leaving on the 17th. We're departing by ship for the Virginia Peninsula. It'll make the news this week, I'm sure. I don't know why the papers need to tell the Confederates our every move."

He put his arm around me as a boy brought the buggy to the steps of the banquet hall. We stood there together until Ted and Jenny caught up with us. This time Ted took the driver's seat while Daniel and I snuggled in the back. I didn't want to think of him leaving.

The day before he was to go we spent the whole day together. The March wind was cool, but it was a clear day and the snow had melted. We walked and talked, went to our favorite tea room and stole as many private kisses as we could before it was time for him to go. "I have a deep feeling for you, Mary Sullivan, and once this nasty war is over, I'm going to do something about it."

How I savored those words. "I hope so," I replied. We were standing in a quiet alcove in the hotel lobby. I gave him a white pebble that had been washed smooth from ocean water. I had kept the pretty piece as a memento when I had gone to the ocean with Abby's family. "Perhaps this will be your good luck charm."

He was pleased. "I have nothing to leave with you," he apologized. "I should have brought you something."

"Daniel, you have given me more than I ever dreamed. I shall carry your words in my heart." He kissed me tenderly before we parted. I turned toward the stairs, he turned and left.

Chapter 21

Major General McClellan took about 120,000 men with him by boats from Alexandria, Virginia down to the Virginia Peninsula and headquartered at Fort Monroe. The plan was to capture Yorktown, twenty-six miles from the fort, control the James and York Rivers then fight their way toward Richmond.

Daniel wrote to Mary:

Dearest Mary,

I am at Fort Monroe where we are adequately cared for. The fort is strategically located and we are awaiting orders to proceed to Yorktown. I believe the general is hoping for reinforcements as his intelligence reports a large Confederate army is encamped there.

The weather is cool and the rains heavy. If you are fond of being near water this is the place to be. The air is not clean and fresh as it is in the northern part of the state.

I am not sure what lies ahead but I carry your pretty pebble close. Just to touch it brings an image of your fair face and endearing smile to my mind. This little stone is a great comfort. I am praying this campaign will be the end to this awful war and we can go on with our lives.

I may not get another chance to write for quite some time. Please write to me here at the fort.

As we begin to work toward our goal the mail will be forwarded to us in the field (I hope).

Until we are together again, I remain your loyal and ardent admirer.

Affectionately,
Daniel

It was April when the siege of Yorktown began. The terrain was low swampy land and the rain was relentless. The grand Army of the Potomac became mired in mud. Even the mules were bogged down. To add to the misery, McClellan's intelligence overestimated the strength of the Confederate army and he was reluctant to move without reinforcements.

Frederick Olmstead, head of the U.S. Sanitary Commission, was busy getting the fleet of hospital ships ready. The first to be completely stripped, redone and equipped was the *Daniel Webster,* a small older ship docked at Alexandria. All in all the U.S. Sanitary Commission outfitted about twenty hospital ships for the Eastern area. The Western part of the Commission also had their hospital ships.

In late April when I heard that the hospital boats were to be taken to the peninsula, I volunteered to serve as a nurse. There were two reasons for that decision: one was because I wanted a change from the hospital; the second, most important, because I thought I might meet up with Daniel. I was accepted and was assigned to the *Daniel Webster*. I looked at the name as a good omen.

Jenny decided to stay on at the hospital. Ted was still in Washington, so I didn't begrudge her not signing up with me as I probably would have done the same in her position.

The morning I was to leave she gave me twenty-five dollars. "Take this, Mary. Mother sent it to me to put to good use and I can't think of a better way. I'm not sure what you are going to find and perhaps you will need the money for our soldiers or even for yourself. God bless you for your courage."

I didn't hesitate to take the generous gift for I thought I might need it for our men. I hugged her before I left the room carrying my two tapestry satchels, which I found less cumbersome than a case or trunk. They contained what I considered essential.

The Sanitary Commission had arranged for a buggy to transport me to the boat along with four other volunteer nurses. I was the youngest. Two of them had husbands in the army, one was a widow and the other had been a teacher as I had been. That was where our compatibility stopped as she was stern-faced with a stony personality. Perhaps Miss Dix saw something nurturing in her that I missed.

I was in awe when we boarded the boat. The cabin was set up for surgery. There was an apothecary, a diet kitchen, berths and cots for the soldiers. The mission was to take the soldiers from the battlefield and treat them before they were transported to hospitals in the Washington, New York, Philadelphia and Boston areas.

The Sanitary Commission absorbed all expenses at no cost to the government. The Medical Department of the government with Surgeon General Hammond in charge, was slow to move and short-sighted in providing for their army. Even private surgeons assigned were paid by the Commission.

My next jaw-dropping experience aboard ship was when I learned the surgeon assigned to my boat was no other than Dr. S. with the German name I could never pronounce to his satisfaction. He stood straight as an arrow watching as the other four nurses and I stepped off the gangplank. I was astonished when he looked at me and gave a slight nod of recognition. I felt my face blush and hurried past. There was something about his stature that made me feel inadequate.

Chapter 22

It was early in May when McClellan's army routed the Confederates out of Yorktown, and it was there the army set up a large depot and hospital. Many of the sick had malaria and dysentery from the poor land and weather conditions.

The *Daniel Webster* sailed past Fort Monroe and Yorktown to a field hospital and army supply depot at White House Landing on the Pamunkey River, a branch of the York. It was there I was instructed to stay to attend the wounded before being transported to Yorktown and eventually up North.

White House Plantation had been the home of Martha Custis before she married George Washington. It had been handed down through the family to Robert E. Lee's son Fitz Hugh Lee. The original house had burned down. Only two chimneys remained. Another house had been erected.

The efficiency of the Sanitary Commission was proven as the battles raged on the march to Richmond. Hospital ships were anchored next to each other and connected by gangways. We nurses would sometimes run through three or four boats to tend the wounded. The banks of the wharves were steep and huge planks were laid to get from ship to shore.

The injured soldiers were carried from the battlefield by cart, freight or ambulance then loaded onto stretchers. Men carried the stretchers up the planks to the deck then hoisted the stretchers by pulleys. The injured soldiers were deposited on berths or cots. Sometimes the ships were so crowded it was almost impossible to move around on them. Surgery was performed in the main cabin where there would be a stream of blood running and dismembered arms and legs thrown onto a stack of human limbs.

I served in the field hospital and on the ships, but it was a second corps who transported the men to the hospitals up North. It appeared the army still preferred male nurses. There were surgeons who made it almost unbearable for the women to work. Nurses' tents were placed a distance from the hospital tents, supplies were denied, accommodations sparse. Still, the women persevered and the soldiers were grateful for their help. As the war went on the more accepted the women became to everyone involved.

Some wives followed their men, some came from different relief groups, many from the Christian Commission and others unattached volunteers. All were welcome as we treated the sick and wounded from the battles of: Mechanicsville, Gaines Mill, Ganett's Farm, Peach Orchard, Savage's Station, White Oak, Glendale, and Malvern Hill. We treated everyone who came to us, Union or Confederate, black or white.

I was kept so busy I didn't have time to think of anything but hoping to get some rest. I had three other tent mates, all volunteer nurses. We were fortunate to have a wood floor, but no privacy. Although we lived together our only common bond was caring for the soldiers.

I still had no word from Daniel. I had no word from anyone. Mail was brought from Fort Monroe and each time it arrived I hoped for a letter from someone. Finally, in late May I received a letter from Jenny:

Dear Mary,

I apologize for not writing sooner. We are swamped with the men from the Peninsula Campaign, who tell all kinds of frightening tales. I can only imagine what you are going through.

I am in a hurry and will give you only the information I think you will be happy to hear. Most important is that Ted and I got married. I'm not sure Mother is too pleased with my decision, but as Ted says 'we may only have a short time together so we might as well enjoy what time we have'. That is one thing I love about him. He does not dwell about the future. And, Mary, he loves me with my glasses and all.

Abby is engaged to Edward. When the war is over she wants a lavish wedding and, as Edward is of well-to-do fine breeding, I'm sure she will have it. Mother seems satisfied with that union. I am pleased for my dear sister as she would not be satisfied with anything less.

Charley is still here in Washington, but Johnathan has been sent south. Florence helps Mother and I'm sure does her share of worrying.

Baby Johnathan is growing like a weed and is a joy to them at home.

Emily is stationed at the army hospital in Yorktown. Have you crossed her path?

Mother is busy taking care of the N.Y. Central Relief. Steady donations keep coming in. They must be organized and sent as quickly as possible. The needs are great. No one knows better than you, I suspect.

We are getting more and more volunteers at the hospital. Some I could do without. I found a surgeon taking a bottle of brandy that was meant for the patients. Some of those "doctors" are butchers. I doubt if they have had any medical training at all. But, they are men and seem to get away with their chicanery. There are some who are kind and welcome the nurses' help.

I must close as Ted has this evening free, and I can hardly wait to see him.

I pray for you and Daniel and all the men in harm's way.

Sending my love,
Jenny

I read the letter twice before I tucked it away in my satchel. I hoped Jenny hadn't made a rash decision, but she deserved her happiness. Although I was glad for Jenny, the letter had triggered a melancholy feeling. Would I ever see Daniel again? Was he still alive? That thought brought tears to my eyes which I quickly wiped away, swallowed hard and left the tent to help cook supper for the soldiers.

Chapter 23

June of 1862 was a horrible nightmare. During the Seven Day Battle to take Richmond our Army of the Potomac was depleted by a third. McClellan, always hoping for reinforcements, failed to take Richmond even though his pickets were within four miles of the city. However, Joe Johnston had an army of 95,000 Confederates and General R.E. Lee brought his Northern Army of Virginia to protect Richmond. McClellan's army was in retreat back down the Peninsula.

We were ordered to make a hasty evacuation of our depot at White House Landing. The Rebels were within earshot and booming cannons deafened our ears. It was the women who made sure all the wounded were removed from their hospital tents to the fleet of transport boats. All wounded were loaded on before the boats sailed down the York River. A new army base with 140,000 soldiers was established at Harrison's Landing on the James River.

I went ashore there from the *Daniel Webster.* The conditions were deplorable. We slogged through glue-like mud up to our ankles. The Medical Department of the government was still not equipped to handle their men. A thousand army tents were set up at Harrison's Landing many old, mildewed, and leaky. Newer ones were of the wedge type and bivouac kind with black cloth. Neither was suitable for sick and injured men, especially in the hot sun. The wounded kept coming, far more than the transports could carry to the hospital and headquarters in Yorktown. Overflow were placed in abandoned cabins and shanties. Sometimes as many as seven men were left in an attic without food or water.

I was put back on the *Daniel Webster* at the request of Dr. S. who had just returned from a month's absence. He, like many of the private doctors, had taken a leave. I felt honored that he asked for my assistance, although I was still not comfortable in his presence. He was a remarkable surgeon, but I was always on edge because of his abrupt manner. The more I worked with him, the more I learned to anticipate his needs for surgical instruments. He did so many amputations I believe if I were in a life or death situation I could perform one myself. I was becoming an expert at bandaging the stumps of human limbs.

I remember one time when I was assisting in surgery and standing among human discarded parts, an amputated hand began to curl and pull at the hem of my skirt. I must have jumped or turned pale for Dr. S. looked at me and said, "What's the matter? Go sit!" Then he called to an aide, "Give her brandy." The burning brandy revived me and I took my place at his side once again. I had seen so much horrible mutilation of human bodies I thought I had become immune.

When we were finished with the surgeries he came to me. "You need a rest. Take the next transport to Yorktown and stay there for a week. I'll send an order with you."

"I should stay here. We're short-handed..."

"Do as I say," said Dr. S. and walked away.

The Commission's steamer *Wilson Small* was going to Yorktown the next morning. I packed both satchels and took what I owned. It was not unheard of for items to be stolen in the camp. I was glad to get away. There was jealousy among some of the nurses. They didn't like that I was picked by Dr. S. or that I was going on a furlough. They looked on it as favoritism. Perhaps it was. I didn't care as I had been there the longest. It was not my choice to be singled out by Dr. S.

Jenny had written that Emily was in Yorktown and I prayed I would see her there. Just to see a familiar face would be a blessing. I also prayed there would be some news of Daniel.

When I was ready to board the ship, I wasn't sure I wanted quiet time to allow my mind to conjure up all kinds of ugly images I had seen. Mostly, I didn't want to think of Daniel lying dead in some swampy muck. After all the bloody carnage I had witnessed, I wasn't sure I could will myself to think on the positive side.

The *Wilson Small* was a large steamer and I was afforded my own cubicle. What a luxury. I could not in good conscience hide myself away when there was help needed. I set about tending to the injured being sure they had water, combed their hair, changed clothing, dressed their wounds or just stopped to give them a kind word. The day was overcast, hot and humid, the water choppy, which made it difficult to walk around on the boat. I cannot say it was a pleasant ride to Yorktown.

At Yorktown, I departed the ship with rubbery legs. A steward came and escorted me to a cart that took me to my quarters. It was a single tiny house. The front door opened into a sitting area with two rocking chairs and small table with an oil lamp. A hand-hooked rag rug was on the floor. I opened the other door in that room to find my own bedroom. How glad I was to see a real bed with a down-filled tick. I was used to sleeping on a straw mattress on a cot. The sleeping room held a straight chair, side table and another oil lamp.

Most inhabitants who were native to the area had abandoned the town. I wondered who had occupied this little house. Later I was informed that the place was used for visiting dignitaries or officers' wives.

There were still a few shops open on the narrow streets in the town, and I could walk about as I pleased. Sutlers, storekeepers who followed and sold provisions to the soldiers, had settled in and were experts at getting goods.

Perhaps Dr. S. was right in seeing that I needed a change when I couldn't see it myself. I became selfish those few days because I stayed away from the hospital. I took long walks and discovered a private spot among the pines near the water. It was a peaceful scene watching as ships came and went. That bucolic setting helped me forget that there was war raging and destruction of lives happening at every minute.

Because the U.S. Sanitary Commission was independent from the government, but worked to assist the Medical Department, I was allowed free rein on the army base. The first day I had dinner at the big dining tent and went back to my cozy room to sleep most of the day. When it was suppertime I went back to the same dining place hoping to meet Emily. I saw many army nurses but not Emily. So, I walked back to my tiny place and slept until the next morning. Although I was among many I felt so alone.

The weather was hot, but there was a constant ocean breeze. The house sat under tall pines keeping it protected from the unrelenting sun. I had bought two books from a sutler and spent time reading. There was a little tea shop where I found a quiet nook next to a window overlooking the water, and I savored every sip of my tea. The owner must have bought tea from sutlers or blockade runners for he was well stocked.

It was Sunday morning that I attended church services held on the main base and there I saw Emily. She burst into a wide smile and hugged me with all her might. "Mary! What are you doing here? Mother wrote that you were working on the transports. What a blessing those ships are."

To my surprise she told me both Mr. Olmstead and Miss Dix were visiting the army base. She said Miss Dix was giving the surgeons fits because she had peculiar ideas about diet. She did not approve of meat and wanted all patients fed arrowroot and farina and absolutely no crackers served with gruel. "Them does not go with this." I laughed at Emily's interpretation of the stately spinster.

One day, Mr. Olmstead was at dinner. I gathered my courage as I had met him a year ago at Aunt Martha's. After reintroducing myself, I told him of the sad conditions at Harrison's Landing. He said he recalled meeting me at Aunt Martha's when the Sanitary Commission was first being formed. He said he would send Commission agents to check Harrison's Landing.

I was fortunate not to have to meet with Miss Dix. I'm not sure she would have taken kindly to my furlough from the toils of war nursing.

Before leaving Yorktown I helped other Sanitary Commission nurses set up the steamboat *Knickerbocker,* another big ship of the Commission's. The story was that a sutler was leaving and gave a four burner stove and a cart full of tins of goods to the cause. We separated the trash that he had also donated, including bugs and mice. We ended up with the stove and tins of goods.

We filled the linen closets, put the kitchen in order and made up three hundred beds. A pail of soup would feed twenty-five and a loaf of bread would serve five. With the four burners, four pots of soup or stew could be cooking at once.

I looked in vain for a soldier who may have been with Daniel's outfit. I would not let myself believe that I would never hear word of him again. If I knew that he was dead, it would at least have been a finality. It was the uncertainty that plagued my thoughts.

Chapter 24

The time spent in Yorktown had been rejuvenating. I boarded the *Daniel Webster* that had just returned from taking wounded to New York City. It had been cleaned and re-outfitted with medicine, food and linens to carry another load from Harrison's Landing to the main hospital in Yorktown. I had washed and had mended all my clothes. My hair and body felt clean for the first time in two months. I saddle-soaped a new pair of shoes I had purchased with some of the twenty-five dollars Jenny had given me. I also bought a can of lanolin to soothe my work-worn hands.

On the ship were medical students who had come on board when the boat was in New York. I was happy to see them. When we returned to Harrison's Landing perhaps Dr. S. would take one of them on in my place. Perhaps Dr. S. hadn't stayed in that camp with the conditions as they were.

The base had improved a bit. The Pennsylvania Relief had sent hard tack, salt pork, beans and salt junk for the soldiers. Soft bread was an idle promise. Supplies had finally arrived from the Commission and the government so we had medical supplies. I had been given another tent closer to the hospital tents and with only one other occupant. This tent had a wood floor and leaks had

135

been patched. It crossed my mind that this might be another gift from Dr. S. until I discovered that my new tent mate was a woman-of-means from New York. She was in her middle thirties and a widow. Although she had money, she was not of the same social stature as the Morgan family.

Her husband had accumulated his wealth in building and she had worked alongside him: sawing, hammering and "learning the trade" as she put it. "After all, Mary, when this war is over I'll have to make a living for myself. The money won't last forever." Then she laughed. "Maybe I won't either."

Annie surprised me with what she could do. She was of a nice build, taller than most women, quite attractive with dark hair and coal black eyes; a woman far ahead of the time. What I liked most about Annie was her cheerful disposition. It was spirit-lifting to be around her. I had not gotten close to anyone since I'd left Jenny in Washington.

The early July days were hot and humid. Annie cut holes in our tent and put in netting. She left the flap so we could cover the nets when it rained, which was less than the terrible spring rains. Now it was the dust and dirt that covered everything. I cleaned dirt and filth from my new shoes hoping to keep them usable.

If a cot needed fixing Annie fixed it. She built a table for our cooking pots and a cupboard for our supplies to keep out the vermin. She and I tended the hospital tent set up for those with typhoid fever and those who needed liquid food.

We made greasy bean soup with fat salt pork and soaked hard tack in the liquid made with salt junk. I often wondered what kind of animal was in that junk meat but it was welcomed by the patients. We had an orderly and a medical student to help us take care of the forty men in the tent, which meant duty day and night. We served beef tea, milk punch and lemonade both day and night. The water was never clear so we boiled what we could to give to the soldiers. Of course, soldiers who were not sick drank that cloudy water and many eventually came down with all the intestinal problems of the camp.

As the days got hotter the humidity increased and the bugs multiplied. We were plagued with mosquitos, flies, ants, fleas and gnats. At times we strained the tea to get the ants out of it.

One day a soldier came into my tent and asked if I would take care of his wound. He raised his shirt and I saw a gaping wound as big as a teacup filled with worms, big round worms with black heads and bulging eyes. Immediate nausea. I had him lay on a cot. I set about trying to pull out the wiggling mass of worms with an instrument when a surgeon came walking through the tent. "That's too much for you," he said. He took a bottle of chloroform out of his bag and poured it into the wound. The ugly worms stopped their wiggling. "Now you can clean it out and give him a new shirt." Which I did. I believe the soldier was transported to Yorktown but I never saw him again.

It was not unusual to see men infested with head lice that crawled onto their eyebrows or into their beards. We used kerosene to kill them and mercury solution for intestinal worms, which were also plentiful. I got used to the wounds infested with maggots but I never saw another with those awful, ugly, black-headed worms.

The surgeon in charge had done a fine job of organizing the men as to their conditions. The goal was to either get the men back into condition for returning to their corps, get them to Yorktown for further recuperation, or send them to the Northern hospitals. The volunteers and army nurses were invaluable.

During this Peninsula Campaign we had visits from government agents and government officials. Did they turn a blind eye to what was happening? The battles had left thousands either dead or incapable of living a normal life. Even President Lincoln had come to the Landing to confer with General McClellan. I did not see him but Annie got a glimpse of him in a black suit, stovepipe hat, and riding a horse next to the general, flanked by his officers and bodyguards. "You couldn't mistake him," said Annie. "He was head and shoulders taller than 'Little Mac'."

I asked soldiers both Yankee and Confederate, "Why did you join the army?" The Yankees said, "To save the Union." The Confederates said, "I went with the state."

Chapter 25

When Annie and I had some down time we talked. Her husband had been killed in an accident. "I needed something to take my mind off being alone, so I became a volunteer. We had a good marriage, worked together and I missed him terribly. I had no interest in sitting in my home dwelling on the unfairness of life."

I told her about Daniel and that I had no word of him, that I had written to him at Fort Monroe but got no answer. "We were not promised to each other, but I was sure those were his intentions. He wanted me to meet his family in Vermont, Annie. Don't you think he had serious thoughts?"

She laughed. "It sounds that way to me." Then she took a serious tone. "If he got your letters maybe he couldn't answer. It's possible they never reached him. What if you hear that he is dead? We're losing so many."

"That's my biggest fear. I don't know. Maybe I should have kept writing. What if he ends up losing an arm or leg or is blinded, or horribly scarred, or crazy like some have become? How would I handle that? I think he would feel that I was only saying yes to marriage because of sympathy. That scares me, too. What if I did?"

"Would you?"

"I don't know. We only had a short time together, which in truth means I don't know him that well."

Annie shrugged a shoulder. "You seem to know him well enough. What are his plans after the war? Is he going back to Vermont, doing what he did before?"

I had to think. "I don't recall him ever mentioning that. He did ask if I was going to return to teaching."

"Are you?" she asked.

I tossed the question around in my mind before I answered, "I don't know. Volunteering with the Commission has opened up a whole new world."

"Maybe it's that way with Daniel. Life is short, Mary. We need to make the most of what we can. Stop thinking so much." Then she added, "And, it could be that your Daniel is right here in this camp. There are thousands of soldiers and not all are wounded. We are only a small part of this place."

I snickered. "You sound like Ted Stevens. My cousin knew him the same amount of time I knew Daniel and they're married."

"Smart girl," she replied.

I told Annie about my parents, teaching school, and my close relatives in New York City. Annie knew of the Morgan family, but she had grown up in the lesser part of the city and so had her husband. Their wealth came from hard work.

I backtracked on our conversation. "About teaching, Annie. I guess that would be the smart move to make. It's all I know. I'm fortunate because there aren't many respectable positions open for women."

"Not unless you marry someone with money and prestige. Then you could throw yourself into serving tea and doing charitable work."

I made a prune face at her. "My Aunt Martha is very good at that, and I rather like the pomp that goes with it."

Annie roared with laughter. "Well, Miss Mary, it's time to get that mush started for our ailing men. How much pomp can you put in that?"

I assumed a haughty air. "I shall find a silver spoon to serve it."

Annie laughed again, threw her arm around my shoulder. We left the hot tent to begin our task at the outdoor fireplace.

That evening I checked the medical supplies as Dr. S. was still here and there were surgeries to perform tomorrow. The Seven Days Battle had ended. Still our ambulance corps went into the field and brought back dead and wounded who were on the brink of death.

On one of the soldiers I recognized a patch that was one Daniel wore. He was filthy from dirt and gunpowder; his face almost blackened. The young soldier's hair stuck out in all directions pasted with dirt and sweat, and his uniform was molded to his body from the damp Virginia clay soil. His eyes were closed. He was barely breathing. I knelt by his stretcher and leaned near his ear. "Do you know Daniel Phillips?" I said in a quiet voice. I caught a slight flicker of his eyelids. "Is he alive?" Again I noticed a slight movement. My heart was beating a quick cadence. Was it just his subconscious responding to a voice? Was he trying to tell me something? I got to my feet and rushed to get him water. When I got back he was dead. Men came and laid him with the others. I sat on the ground and cried.

Back in the tent Annie was sound asleep. I lay down on my cot with my eyes wide open. There were pickets outside the big camp and I heard distant shots through the night. Was it friendly fire? The hospital tents were closest to the river for quicker evacuation if need be. After the abandonment of White House Landing, I did not want to think of need for escape again.

Chapter 26

I received two letters, one from Abby and one from Jenny. Abby wrote of her efforts to comfort soldiers who were sent back for recuperation. She, Florence and two neighbors had decided to treat the two hundred convalescing soldiers at the hospital on Bedloe Island to a joyous Fourth of July picnic.

They took a tug boat filled with ice cream, cake, wine, tea, flags, flowers, and a chest of forty quarts of milk and butter. When they reached the island they found only forty men as the day before others had been ordered back into service and sent to Fort Monroe. Abby thought each man left in the hospital had at least a quart of ice cream each, a good slice of cake, and a glass of Catawba wine. A singer went from tent to tent singing patriotic songs and hymns, and when they left the patients gave them cheers and overwhelming thanks. As an afterthought, she wondered if the soldiers might get sick from overindulgence and then the ladies would be blamed.

She also wrote of going to a hospital to read and write letters for the soldiers. It was a hot July day so she took a fan. While she was fanning an ailing soldier the surgeon-in-charge came by and said, "Who gave you permission to bring that fan in here?" Abby told him no one. The surgeon left and came back with Miss Dix. "No one gave permission to bring in that fan. You must leave at once!" Miss Dix told me. I looked that old woman in the eye and replied, "My carriage does not arrive for an hour and I do not plan to wait in the hot sun."

She stayed right where she was and continued to fan the soldier and kept volunteering at the hospital.

Her letter made me smile as I could picture my cousin floating about with her attractive ways, raising the spirts of the injured men and being confident in her actions.

Jenny's letter was not as uplifting. She had left Washington to work in the Portsmouth Grove Hospital in Rhode Island. Ted's regiment had been called up and she did not want to stay in Washington.

The woman chosen to take the directorship of the hospital in Rhode Island was a friend of Aunt Martha's and had requested Jenny's help.

Jenny wrote: I am happy here although I miss Ted so very much. Have you any word from Daniel? I don't know if Ted will meet up with him. I am somewhat comforted by the fact that they are close to their colonels whom, I assume, may have some protection from the front lines. News reports lead us to believe that the major encounters on the Peninsula are over and the Confederate armies are moving in the northern direction.

Mary, why don't you give up there and come to work in the hospital here? We have just received two hundred and ninety men from Fort Monroe and

Fredericksburg on the *Daniel Webster*, the boat you sailed on. The ship could not get close to the pier so boats were rowed out and the men brought ashore. They were all in good humor. Most likely to be out of the conflicts.

The hospital is ready for four hundred and fifty soldiers: clean beds, clean sheets, clean clothes. We have good stores and they are welcome to the jelly, peaches, oranges, pickles and everything we have.

The surgeon-in-charge is kind, which is more than I can say for many of the surgeons. Please think about coming, Mary. You have done so much under the worst conditions.

As I sat in the blazing August sun and sweltering humidity of Harrison's Landing I considered what she had asked. Perhaps I had done my part. Perhaps the war would end this year. Cooler days in the North sounded enticing. As the days went on the hope of news about Daniel grew dim.

My reverie was short-lived. Annie returned after installing new side boards on a wagon that had been damaged by coming too close to a tree. Her face was beet red and she slumped onto a bench.

I brought her a glass of water. The water that was never cold and always cloudy. "You look awful," I said as I handed her the glass.

"I feel awful. I'm not going to be able to help with supper."

"You should see a doctor," I suggested.

She shook her head. "They'll want to take off my leg. They seem to think that cures everything."

"I'm serious, Annie. This place is full of disease. Maybe you've caught something."

She shook her head again. "No. I'm going in and lie down."

I had already started the supper for our men, so I went to find an orderly or someone who could help me take care of the feeding if Annie wasn't available. From the looks of her, she wasn't, and I began to get concerned. I soaked a rag in a mixture of alcohol and water, went into the tent and placed the rag on her forehead. She was burning with fever. I went in search of Dr. S. and found him in his tent writing. "Dr. S., my tentmate is very sick. Can you come to see her?"

He didn't look up from his writing. "What's her problem?"

"She's burning with fever."

"I have to finish this. Go on back. I'll come by."

I didn't dare ask him how soon, so I turned and left and went back to preparing supper for the soldiers in our hospital tent. An orderly and medical student had found an aide to help with feeding.

I took off Annie's dress and left her in her chemise and drawers and sponged her with the water solution. By then Annie was not coherent. Where was Dr. S?

An hour later he came by. "A swamp fever of some kind. Maybe malaria? Get her on the next ship going to Yorktown." Off he went. I left the feeding to the three men who were helping, loaded up Annie's belongings and went to the wharf to inquire as to which ship would be sailing next. It was the *Wilson Small*. Back at the hospital I asked an ambulance driver to take her to the boat. He came with his horse-drawn ambulance with another helper and put her on a stretcher. Annie was shaking with fever and chills so I wrapped her in her blanket. "See that she is well taken care of and ask the ship's surgeon to see her immediately." The attendants said they would. I kissed Annie's hot cheek as she was taken away.

My spirits were at low ebb, but there were those who needed my help. I was not allowed the luxury to feel sorry for myself.

The next day Dr. S. called me aside. I thought he was going to ask me about Annie. However, he asked nothing of her and in his abrupt way asked, "Why aren't you married?" This man was a puzzle.

I was taken aback but quickly recovered and answered, "No one has ever asked me."

"What are you going to do after the war?"

"I am a teacher."

"I'm leaving this hell hole tomorrow as my contract is up. We make a good team." He thrust a paper at me. "Here is my address if you are interested in working with me."

Dr. S. left me standing there open-mouthed as I tucked the paper into my apron pocket. I believe that is the closest Dr. S. ever came to a compliment. Yet, I was confused as to what he meant. Did he suggest I leave this volunteer position now? Was he talking about after the war? Was this an open invitation for whenever I decided to consider his offer? The man left me guessing.

Chapter 27

Annie was gone and Dr. S. was gone. I decided it was time for me to go. Harrison's Landing was due to be evacuated soon. One of my selfish bones took over, and I sailed to Yorktown on the boat *Knickerbocker.* I had no desire to help tear down the camp at Harrison's Landing. I had done that chore when we fled White House Landing.

When I got to Yorktown I inquired about Annie to find she had been taken to a hospital in New York City. The doctor confirmed she had malaria. Although it was a condition that might be recurring throughout her life I felt comfort in knowing she was alive. I had known too many who had died of camp fever.

Emily had been transferred to Alexandria. These past grueling months had taken their toll leaving me depressed and exhausted. I would go on to New York and up to Albany to spend a week with my parents away from the hospitals, soldiers and sickness.

When I arrived in Washington, before taking a train to New York City, it was August 30th, the last day of the Second Battle of Bull Run. The injured were already pouring into the hospitals in and around the city.

I was told Emily was working in the Baptist Hospital in Alexandria. I secured a pass determined to see her so I could report to Aunt Martha when I continued north. I boarded a boat on the Potomac. We passed forts on both sides of the river, the Washington Naval Yard, the Arsenal and the Insane Asylum. The hills and valleys were filled with the snowy white tents of soldiers.

Alexandria looked dingy, gloomy and dilapidated. I closed my eyes to the depressing sight with the thought of seeing a familiar face once again.

Emily was at the hospital and had little time, but she hugged me mightily. "How good to see you, Mary. We are becoming inundated with the soldiers from Bull Run. Have you come to help?"

"No," I replied. "I am going north for a week at least."

"Are you ill?"

"Not physically, but I have seen so much death and destruction I'm not sure I can handle any more right now." I felt my throat choke up but held back tears.

"Perhaps I have some news for you. Wounded from Daniel's regiment are being housed at the Southern M. E. Church on Washington Street. Maybe someone there knows of him."

"I threw my arms around her. Oh, Emily, that's the most encouraging words I've heard since April."

"Don't set your hopes too high, Mary. It is only a possibility. Will you see my family in New York?"

"Yes."

"Please tell them that I am well but much too busy to write."

"Of course I will." We hugged again. I kissed her cheek and left the Baptist Hospital with a lighter step.

At the Southern M. E. Hospital I found a sentry at the door pacing back and forth with a musket over his shoulder. I showed him my pass and he allowed me entrance.

There was a soldier at a desk whom I told of my mission. "Let me check the rolls first, he may be here. Is he wounded?"

"I don't know. If I can speak with someone from his outfit I would be obliged."

The soldier wore glasses and put his ledger close to the oil lamp on his desk. He ran his finger down the names and turned the page. "This shows a Daniel Phillips. I can take you to him."

I felt my heart jump and tried to calm my anxiety telling myself it may not be the same Daniel.

He led me past cots of groaning men and stopped at a cot where a bearded soldier lay in his undershirt, uniform trousers and boots. With closed eyes, puffy face, bandaged head and splinted left arm, the soldier looked pitiful. Was this Daniel? I stayed by his cot and the escorting soldier went back to his task. The man lay so still I wasn't sure he was conscious. He was gaunt in the torso but he was alive. I leaned down and whispered in his ear, "Daniel?"

His eyelids fluttered. I whispered again, "Daniel."

This time his eyelids flickered and he slowly opened his eyes; they were the same brown eyes that I remembered but they had lost their warmth. "Oh, Daniel. It is you!" I kissed his hot cheek and grasped his clammy hand. "I have been so worried." Then the tears ran down my cheeks and I couldn't stop them.

His voice was hoarse, "Mary? Oh, my dear Mary. Why didn't you write?"

Through my tears I mumbled, "I did, Daniel. When I got no reply I went with the mercy ships down the peninsula hoping to meet up with you. I am on my way to New York to spend a week away from the blood and gore."

A slight smile emerged. "We have both been to Hell."

"How badly are you hurt?"

"I don't know. It hurts to move. I feel fuzzy," and he drifted back into a stupor.

It took over an hour but I did find the surgeon to ask of Daniel's injuries and if he could be moved. "I dug a ball out of his skull. He can't be moved yet. Maybe in a couple of days if there aren't further problems."

I told him that I was a volunteer nurse and that I was leaving for New York the next morning. "Cancel your ticket and find a room. He can't go anyplace. They're coming in by the wagon load. You can help us out until your soldier is ready to go."

"Does that mean he will be released?"

"As far as I'm concerned all in good time," said the surgeon. "Of course, you'll have to clear it with his commanding officer."

"Where will I find him?"

"How would I know? Maybe he didn't make it out of Bull Run." He shook his head. "Senseless war." He walked away.

I went back to Daniel's side and took his good hand in mine. He opened his eyes. "Daniel, I need to know your commanding officer's name. The surgeon says I can help out around here until you can travel, but I have to have permission from your commander."

It was difficult for him to talk so I gave him a sip of water. "Colonel Dowd. Don't leave."

"I will sit with you for a while, but I will have to find a room for the night. I'll try to find your colonel in the morning."

The answer must have satisfied him because he was back in his drowsy state. After an hour of sitting at his side, I kissed his cheek and left the hospital in search of a room.

I had enough money for a few days thanks to Jenny's gift of twenty-five dollars of which I had been frugal. There were no rooms. Alexandria was not safe for a woman alone once dusk set in, so I did the only thing that sounded reasonable. I went back to the Baptist Church hospital to find Emily. She knew of a corner of the church that was used for storage. We moved crates and boxes around, and I ended up sleeping on a crate with a blanket and pillow she had brought to me. The cubbyhole of a room had a lock on the door giving me a feeling of security.

The next morning I arose early and tiptoed out of my illegal shelter. My quest was to find Colonel Dowd. The whole place was in a chaotic state. Perhaps tomorrow would be better. I went to the hospital after noon to sit with Daniel. He didn't look any better than he did the day before. At least someone had removed his boots and put him in a flannel shirt and flannel drawers.

The fact that I had spent the whole morning unable to locate Colonel Dowd did not distress me greatly as I knew Daniel could not be moved for a few days. What did bother me was trying to find a place to stay at night. I couldn't put Emily in jeopardy again.

However, my good fortune was still working for me thanks to the good Lord above. Colonel Dowd came to the hospital to check on his men. I stood when he came to Daniel's cot. He looked at me and smiled. "You must be Mary," he said.

I was stunned for a moment. "Yes, I am. Mary Sullivan."

"Daniel is my close aide and I have heard him mention you. He was concerned. You are a volunteer nurse, are you not?" He looked worn out but maintained his military bearing.

"Yes, sir, with the Sanitary Commission. I left Fort Monroe and am on my way to New York to spend a week away from the madness."

He nodded. "It is that. So you were also on the Peninsula. We were in all the battles and Daniel was a ready and dependable soldier. The wounds he has suffered are by accident."

I tried to keep my voice steady. "Accident? They were not inflicted in battle?"

He lowered his voice and explained, "We were returning to Washington when a gun misfired and the ball struck him in the head. I believe he broke his arm when he fell. The doctor on board did not want to operate as the water was choppy making the boat too unsteady. We were a day out. When we landed I saw to it that he was cared for right away." His eyes were sad as he shook his head, "It all seems so senseless."

I stood letting the information settle before I asked in a hushed voice, "What has the surgeon told you, sir? He has not been forthcoming with me, although he said Daniel could leave when he is ready…with your permission of course."

He looked down at Daniel and then back at me and whispered, "The doctor says it is touch and go."

We both stood silent. Then he asked, "Are you going on to New York?"

I shook my head. "I prefer to stay here, but there are no rooms. I am going back over to Washington where I believe I can find a hotel room."

"I can be of service in that area. There is a house here for visiting officers' wives. There is no reason you can't stay there. I will clear the path for you. I think it is most important to have you with Daniel."

I was overjoyed. "Colonel Dowd, that is most thoughtful and generous of you. I accept without an ounce of hesitation."

He leaned down and took Daniel's hand. "How are you doing soldier?"

Daniel did not open his yes but a hoarse whisper came out. "Fine, sir."

"Mary is here to stay with you until you are back to your old self."

He stood up and took my hand. "Take good care of him, Miss Sullivan. He is like a son to me."

The colonel gave me the address of where I was to stay before he turned to leave. I watched him go. It was then I understood Daniel's admiration for his superior.

Chapter 28

The red brick house designated for the officers' wives was only two blocks from the Southern M.E. Hospital. It was the end of August and the warm, humid days were still with us but less intense than on the Peninsula, and the evenings cooled off.

I had my own room at the home. What a luxury after all the times I had slept on straw or husks or the bare ground. I wondered if I looked worn from my days on the Peninsula. I felt ten years older. I had done my best to wear a wide-brimmed hat for protection from the sun. My hands had lost their smoothness and my face felt rough. Perhaps it was a blessing that Daniel's vision was hazy.

I was up early. I had an actual bath the evening before and slept on a down mattress. These little niceties that people take for granted. Even the water was clearer. It brought to mind all of the poor suffering men who cried out for water and the river water we had to give them. I didn't want to think about it.

Dressed in my navy hospital dress and canvas apron I was prepared to work at the hospital. I chose the canvas apron because I was sure I would be called to help in surgery. The heavier material was more protection from the bloody messes. A breakfast was waiting consisting of apple muffins, apple juice and coffee. I tucked a molasses cookie into a handkerchief and put it in my pocket. I wasn't sure when I would have time to eat. It was six o'clock and no one else was in the dining room. A cup of coffee without the sound of cannons or gunfire or insects buzzing about was a glorious quiet.

My walk to the hospital was enjoyable in the cool of the morning. I showed my pass to the sentry and went immediately to Daniel's bedside. His face was still puffy and flushed. There was dark bruising around his eyes under the redness, but his hand was not clammy. I bent down and kissed his cheek.

He didn't open his eyes but whispered, "Mary?"

"I'm here, Daniel. I'll be here all day. I must help in the hospital because there are many who need help. I will come to see you as often as I can." Then I held his hand to my lips and said a prayer that he would get better.

Leaving his side, I went in search of the surgeon-in-charge. "We'll need help in surgery. Can you work there?"

I nodded. "I have helped with many procedures."

"Well, that's something." He pointed to the back of the hospital. "You'll hear the shrieks and know where to go." He sounded as callous as many of the surgeons in the army.

I didn't want to go. I didn't want to see the loss of limbs, the mutilation, or any butchers passing for surgeons. However, I steeled myself to what lay ahead because of the soldiers. There in the small room, passing as an operating room, was one table. A male army nurse was assisting the one surgeon who wore a mask. I only knew one surgeon who wore a mask during surgery. Could it be? My pulse jumped. The surgeon glanced up when I entered and said, "Get over here and take over with the ether."

Yes, it was Dr. S. the man who had left the war for good. All day long we worked together as a team, each understanding the abilities of the other. If I concentrated on the work we were doing, I could blot out the cries of those in pain. It was almost six o'clock when Dr. S. said he could do no more. I was drained.

While packing up his instruments he asked, "What are you doing here, Miss Sullivan? Did you leave one hell hole to come to another?"

Maybe it was the grueling day, maybe it was Daniel, or maybe I stood up for myself because I answered. "I was on my way to New York for a rest. I thought you had given up, but I see you are back in full swing."

He didn't even look up just kept packing his articles.

I told him about Daniel and asked if he would come and look at him. Dr. S. followed me to his cot and started to unwrap the bandage. Daniel opened his eyes. "That hurts."

Dr. S. looked at me. "At least his sense is intact."

159

It was the first time I had seen the wound. It was nasty looking, swollen and infected. The wound itself was not large but it was deep.

"When was this dressing last changed?"

"I don't know," I replied.

"Sloppy medicine." I heard Dr. S. mutter. "That infection needs to be cleared or he's in for trouble."

Whether Daniel heard and understood I wasn't sure. I knew what the surgeon meant because I had seen many men die from infections. "Get some clean dressings, alcohol, Blue Mass, mercurial ointment."

"I'm not sure where to find them," I answered.

"If you want him alive, you'd better go and find them."

I didn't know the workings of this hospital. I asked a male nurse if there was an evening matron overseeing the hospital. He directed me to the woman, an older army nurse. In as few words as I could I told her what the doctor wanted. She said she would have to consult the surgeon-in-charge. Tomorrow.

"This cannot wait! Dr. S. is with him this minute. Will you come with me to talk to him?" I knew Dr. S. well enough to know that he was short on patience. To my relief she came with me.

When the matron told Dr. S. that she had to check with the head surgeon he was indignant, "My good woman. This man is under your charge and you are responsible for his care. Now get me the supplies I need and be quick about it."

The matron didn't reply. She crooked a finger at me to follow her and we went to the medical supply area. I returned to Daniel's bedside and Dr. S. demonstrated how he wanted the wound cleaned and dressed. "You are to do this twice a day," he ordered me. "If anyone gives you a problem refer them to me. I checked his arm and it doesn't appear to be a major break. I expect it will heal without any disfigurement."

I repeated the steps to the physician, "Clean with alcohol, apply the ointment, pack with lint wet with solution of Blue Mass and bandage."

He nodded. "Where are you staying?" he asked.

"I have a room at a house where the officers' wives stay."

"How far is it?"

"Only two blocks away."

"Say goodbye to your soldier and I'll take you there."

I protested. "It is only two blocks. I can…"

"Do as I say, Miss Sullivan. It's past dusk. You are to be here early to dress this wound. Then we will spend the day together ruining more young men's lives."

He picked up his bag and placed his gray fedora, badly in need of blocking, on his head while I kissed Daniel's inflamed cheek and told him I was leaving. Daniel was back in a stupor.

Dr. S. had his own horse and buggy, which he had hired a boy to watch and care for during the day. I climbed up onto the seat without help while the physician tossed his bag into the small compartment behind the seat.

"We turn right at the next corner," I told him after he got onto the seat and held the reins. "The house is the third one up the street on the left."

A slight tap of the reins and the horse started. The man always seemed to surprise me or leave me guessing. This time it was surprise when he asked, "How is your friend? The one with what I thought was malaria?"

I hadn't given Annie a thought since I arrived in Washington. "My friend, Annie. You were right. It was malaria and she was transferred to a hospital in New York. I hope to see her when I get to the city."

"It appears you will have to put those plans on hold," he said.

I sighed. "All plans have changed. It was only by accident that I found Daniel. I always had my eye out for him on the Peninsula, but we never even knew the other was there."

"Too many soldiers, too many camps, too many battles," he replied.

For once I wasn't uneasy in his company. I was glad he asked about Annie. It showed he cared. Or was it because he was satisfied he'd made the right diagnosis? I was also pleased that he tended to Daniel.

"Miss Sullivan, what are you going to do if your soldier doesn't pull through?"

The remark caused me to shutter. "I don't like to think about that," I answered.

He stopped the buggy in front of the house where I was staying. I picked up my pocketbook and meant to stand but he put his hand on mine and looked right at me. "But you do have to think about it. You need to prepare for that possibility."

I shrugged my shoulders. "I suppose I believe I will continue on to New York as I had planned. I don't know."

He removed his hand and got out of the buggy, came around and helped me down. "The offer to come and work with me is open. Once this crazy war is over I will go back to private practice in Washington."

As kind as I could express myself, I said, "I thank you for the offer and I thank you for driving me home. Dr. S., I am praying earnestly for Daniel's full recovery. I believe the Lord has guided me to this point. What the future holds none of us know."

I caught a slight smile on his face. "You couldn't ask for a better guide and I hope your prayers are rewarded. I shall see you tomorrow."

I walked up the short brick walk to the three steps that led up to the entry before I heard the clip-clop of the horse as Dr. S. drove away. For the first time, the good doctor had shown me the kinder side of his personality.

Once in my room I thought about what he had said. What if Daniel doesn't survive? I know the doctor was trying to be kind, to prepare me for what might be, but I couldn't bear to think about it now. I wouldn't believe the Lord would bring us together once again just to take Daniel away.

Chapter 29

For the next week I dressed Daniel's wound as Dr. S. had told me to and there was improvement. The infection was gone. The wound was still swollen and red but that should settle as it healed. The scarring would be there either as an accidental war souvenir or to cover with his hair.

Colonel Dowd checked on him during that week and was pleased with Daniel's improvement, but I was still unsure of his recovery. He still slept a lot and carried a low fever. When he was awake it was to say a few words and drift back into lethargy.

I told Dr. S. of my reservations about Daniel's condition. He said, "Miss Sullivan, if you were shot in the head and had been through the battles he has been through, don't you think your body would like to take time to recover?"

The doctor had set me straight and relieved some of my concern. I kept helping in surgery as needed and filled in around the hospital as I was told.

I did not like the surgeon-in-charge. I wanted to tell him how fortunate he was that I happened to show up. Of course, I didn't say a word. I prayed Daniel would get better so he could get out of there and so could I.

Also, I didn't want to overstay my welcome at the home meant for officers' wives. Colonel Dowd said there was no hurry for me to leave, however, I did not want to be obliged to anyone. I guess that was sinful pride stepping in.

The next week there was a big change. Dr. S. was pleased with the condition of Daniel's wound and stopped the Blue Mass mercury solution. I cleaned the wounded area with soap and water, applied a thin layer of camphorated ointment, then bandaged. I did this upon arriving at the hospital and leaving in the late afternoon.

Daniel could sit in a chair next to his bed and I could take him for short walks around the room. He had dizziness at times. I enjoyed the walks because he was close by my side. We were not in a private place, so the only other contact we had was holding hands under the cover of the sheet and a quick kiss on his forehead or cheek when I came and went. The bruising of his face had faded to yellow, the puffiness was gone and his brown eyes regained their warmth. The Daniel I remembered was back.

Colonel Dowd came by the next week. I quickly rose from where I was sitting at Daniel's bedside. The colonel nodded a greeting. "Lieutenant Phillips, I have arranged for you to go home to Vermont until your arm is strong enough to hold a musket. Our regiment is pulling out to go to Maryland."

"I'd like to be with you, sir," replied Daniel.

"I know you would. I don't look forward to what we are to meet up there. Your job is to get well, soldier." He shook Daniel's hand.

Then he turned to me. "Miss Sullivan, I assume you can continue on with your plans now that our boy is on the road to recovery." I nodded. "How much longer will you need to stay at the home?"

"Through tomorrow night. That will give me time to make arrangements."

"Certainly," he answered. He gave both of us a military bow and left.

"Well, Mary, do you find that good news?"

I had resumed my seat beside the cot. There was hesitation before I spoke. "I'm not sure. It means we will be separated again. From your conversation it sounds as though you will rejoin your regiment once your arm heals."

"It is my duty if the war continues. Mary, please hand me my haversack."

I pulled the knapsack from under his cot and placed it on the bed. Daniel undid the leather straps. From an inside pocket, he pulled out a small box and handed it to me. I took it and looked at it. "Open it up. It's for you."

With careful fingers I opened the box to find the white pebble I had given him. Now it was attached to a gold chain. He lifted it from the box, motioned me to lean forward, and he fastened it around my neck. "Now we will always be together," he said.

I touched the stone with tears in my eyes. "Oh, Daniel. I will wear it always."

This time I kissed him full on the lips, and he hugged me tight to the applause of the convalescing soldiers near. "We're going to get through this awful war, Mary."

"I pray we do."

Chapter 30

The army was quick in whisking Daniel off to Vermont, no doubt to make the cot available for another wounded soldier. I had his address and he had mine at Aunt Martha's, where I planned to stay for two or three weeks. I had decided not to continue to Albany to visit my parents as I thought the country would be too quiet. I wanted to see my cousin Jenny, who was back in New York, and Abby, who always lifted my spirits.

I took the ferry from Alexandria to Washington and bought a train ticket for New York City. Once settled in the passenger car, I felt a relief to put the past months behind me and settled in for a relaxing trip.

When we reached Baltimore, I left the train to stretch my legs before it continued on. A newsboy was hawking his papers calling out about the big battle at Sharpsburg: "Antietam Creek runs red with blood; many dead, come get your Baltimore Sun!"

I stopped in my tracks. Colonel Dowd had said his regiment was going to Maryland. I bought the newspaper. When I read about the thousands killed and wounded I thought of Daniel and I was glad he wasn't there. But there would be others, many others who needed help. How could I be selfish and turn my back on them? I took the next train to Frederick, Maryland. There would be a relief society there, and I hoped I could get over to Sharpsburg to lend a hand.

After a few inquiries I found the relief association and a line of wagons loaded with supplies from the Sanitary Commission heading for Sharpsburg. They were glad to take me with them. I climbed into a wagon and sat beside another woman. "I don't know what we'll find," she said. "I have heard terrible stories." She, too, had helped as a nurse in Washington.

After all I had seen in the Peninsular wars, I was not prepared for the sight that greeted my eyes when we reached the battlefield on the 19th, two days after the fighting. Dead, some in heaps, and wounded were lying on the grounds in the light rain that was falling. Ambulances, soldiers on foot and on horseback, were scrambling this way and that. It was a huge battlefield, relatively flat to sloping where the cornfields lay in ruins. Hills, woods and ravines led to the creek.

Some of the injured soldiers had found refuge in barns, silos, outhouses, any shelter they could find to rest their painful and exhausted bodies.

Dead men looked stiff like statues. One with an apple in his hand, one about to drink form a cup. Two were in the act of going over a fence, another sitting against a tree with a coffee pot dropped to his lap. I had to cover my eyes. The horror of it all caused my heart to ache.

We were told Clara Barton, a volunteer nurse who now traveled with the Union army since the Battle of Cedar Mountain in Virginia on August 9th, had arrived on the last day of the battle with a wagonload of bandages and supplies and all the bread she could buy along the way.

I had heard of her. She was a woman who had once been a teacher and then worked as a clerk at the U.S. Patent Office before she devoted herself to nursing and providing for the soldiers of the militias in Washington.

We stopped in front of a log house near the Potomac River used as a hospital where thirty men were crowded together. The Sanitary Commission wagons brought: dry goods, medicine, first aid material, dried fruit, bottles of wine and cordials, food, hospital clothing and bales of blankets. My nurse wagon mate and I set about to do what we could. The lamentations from the wounded grew so loud they were deafening. The Irish in their regiment were much louder in their misery than the regiment of Germans. What could we do? We started to sing hymns and the soldiers began to listen. Those who could joined us. Soon the place quieted down as we went about our work.

I spent a week there while soldiers were transported back to Washington or other hospitals or tagged to be buried. The Dunker Church was used for embalming. Union soldiers were buried at the scene of battle while the Confederates were transported for burial in Hagerstown and Frederick, Maryland and in Shepherdstown, Virginia.

As I write this memoir I must make a note that Shepherdstown is now a part of West Virginia.

The government did send supplies, but they didn't arrive until after the Sanitary Commission carried theirs to that insane scene.

There were thousands of injured. Rebel soldiers left behind were cared for the same as for our Union boys. I am not sure whether they were imprisoned or released. During the early years of the war many prisoners were released on both sides.

What remained of both armies retreated south. I continued my travel north.

Chapter 31

Eventually, I ended up at the Morgan house to the welcoming arms of Aunt Martha and my dear cousins.

How wonderful it was to see smiling faces and feel safe. We had much to talk about, but Aunt Martha had set guidelines. We were not to discuss the horrors we had seen.

I learned that Charley and Ted were healthy. That Johnathan had been wounded but was recuperating. Florence and the baby were with him at his parents' place. Aunt Martha said her house was much too busy for a convalescing soldier.

It was close to suppertime when I arrived. The house smelled of candles and the aroma of food. It was then I realized I hadn't eaten since breakfast.

The meal of potatoes, roast beef, green beans and fresh vegetables was heavenly. I was used to gruel and ground food mixtures we had cooked over wood fires and had not eaten a home cooked meal in months.

Jenny told of Ted being back in Washington and that she was hoping to join him. Abby was all agog about Edward and making plans for their wedding once the war was over.

I prayed Edward and our other men would make it through as I had witnessed too many who did not. However, I took into account his standing and suspected he would be kept out of danger. It was one thing to be in the infantry and another to be stationed behind a desk.

Abby was so spirited in her lavish plans that I joined in with the wonders that were to be. It had been a long time since I had felt this carefree.

That night when I snuggled into that comfy bed in the cozy room I thanked God that he had brought me this far. I also prayed for those still suffering and fervently for an end to this bitter war.

After three days of eating, resting and reading, I was getting restless. Aunt Martha, Jenny and Abby spent most of the day at the supply headquarters for the New York Relief. Aunt Martha said that after the Battle of Antietam the supplies of the U. S. Sanitary Commission were depleted, and the donations were not coming in as readily as before.

I knew my friend Annie was in the city somewhere. She had told me the name of her husband's construction company, but I had to wrack my brain to think of it. Brooklyn I remembered. I told Abby about my friend and she made it her quest to find her.

It took two days but Abby tracked down the company and was determined that we would scout it out if it still existed.

Meanwhile, I received a most welcome letter from Daniel:

Dearest Mary,

I am in hopes this letter reaches you at the address you gave me. I assume you are with your

173

family in New York and that they are delighted to have you there. I trust you are resting up.

As for me, I am doing well. The country is so quiet. I still jump at the slightest noise expecting a Minnie ball or shell to land at any moment.

Mother's food is good and I am putting some weight back on. I need to fit back into my uniform. I believe it will be early November when I will be able to return to my outfit. I received a letter from Colonel Dowd that we lost a lot of our regiment at Antietam.

I wish I could see you, Mary. Even though I wasn't pleased about the hole in my head or the broken arm, I believe Providence brought us together.

Please know that I think of you often and anxiously await the time we are together again. Wouldn't it be grand to attend a play or a concert, just the two of us?

I have sealed a kiss for you in this letter.

Affectionately,
Daniel

I read the letter once more and smiled at the thought that he was doing well. So much had happened, I vowed to pen a letter to him when Abby and I returned from wherever we were going to find Annie. A twinge of guilt hit me that I hadn't written to Daniel as soon as I arrived. I did send a note to my parents.

While I was sitting with Daniel's letter in my hand, Abby came into the parlor. She looked vibrant in a day dress of copper and white stripes but she wore only a petticoat instead of a hoop.

"What does Daniel have to say?" she asked.

"That he is improving and hopes to be back with his regiment in November."

"He didn't send any amorous suggestions?"

"He sealed a kiss within."

My cousin rolled her eyes. "How romantic. He is usually so quiet and serious, it must be there are notions hidden underneath."

I gave her a sly answer. "It is the quiet ones you have to watch out for."

Abby laughed and hugged me tight. "Let's go find your friend. I am dressed for Brooklyn."

Abby had hired a trusted driver to take us in a small buggy. She thought a carriage too showy. We sat in the back under the covered roof and the sides were tall enough that two young women alone were less conspicuous.

The driver was familiar with that part of the city and stopped in front of a small house with a sign that said *Garland Builders*. I felt my pulse quicken at the thought of seeing Annie. The driver pulled the buggy to the side of the street and opened the passenger door for us. We walked up the short brick walk and knocked on the door.

"Come right in the door's open," we heard a female voice call and I knew at once we had found my friend.

Abby and I stepped inside. Annie, dressed in overalls, had her back to us, "I'll be with you as soon as I can stuff these papers back on the shelf," she said.

We stood without a word until she turned. "Now, what can...Mary Sullivan!"

"Hello, Annie."

We rushed together and met with a crushing hug.

I stepped back. "This is my cousin..."

"Abby," said Annie as she extended her hand. "I've heard so much about you and your family I feel I know all of you. You are just as becoming as Mary said."

I could tell Abby was pleased. She replied to Annie, "If Mary hadn't told me stories, I admire your fortitude."

"Thanks," Annie answered. "I am the un-conventional woman. Would you like a cup of tea? I have hot water on the stove in the other room." She waved her hand toward another door. "This is my office but I live in there." Annie hung a closed sign in the window of the entry door and turned the lock.

Abby and I followed her into a comfortable room used as a sitting room and kitchen containing: wood stove, sink with an indoor water pump, oak square table, cushioned settee, rocking chair. A braided rug covered the sitting area in front of a pot-bellied stove. On one wall was a book shelf and a painting of Annie with her husband, according to the inscription below it.

Annie pointed to a door. "My bedroom is in there and I have an indoor bathroom that I devised myself. All the comforts for a woman alone." She sighed. "I sold the big house."

The three of us sat at the small table and Annie poured tea. "How did you find me?"

"I have to thank Abby for that. I couldn't remember the name of your husband's business, and I wasn't sure it was still a business. The last time I saw you, I didn't know if you were going to make it out of Yorktown."

Annie laughed. "I didn't either. Your Dr. S. was right in giving me that quinine medicine. I came back and spent another week in the hospital here. So far I am healthy. I eat well and get enough rest. What about you, Mary? When did you leave the Peninsula?"

"In August. They broke up McClellan's camp at Harrison's Landing a couple weeks after I left."

"It gives me the creeps to think about that awful place."

"Annie, when I got to Washington I found Daniel."

Annie's eyes widened. "Still in one piece, I hope."

Abby, who had been quiet to this point, chuckled, "She said she found him with a hole in his head and a broken arm."

I went on to tell Annie of Daniel's injuries, the surprise meeting with Dr. S., and my experience at Antietam.

"What are your plans now?" Annie asked.

"I'm not sure. Daniel is going back to the army. I guess the immediate future depends upon how the war is going and the needs of the soldiers. Dr. S. has also offered me a position in his practice."

"Dr. S.? The man with the charming personality," quipped Annie.

I smiled, "He is an excellent surgeon."

"We are praying for this madness to stop," Abby spoke up. "The Sanitary Commission has dwindled its stores since the Battle of Antietam. If this war doesn't come to an end soon we are going to be in a bad way."

"I remember it was the Commission we depended on while we were on the Peninsula, wasn't it, Mary?' said Annie.

I nodded. "Will you go back to help if it's needed?"

Annie thought for a moment. "I don't know. I'm doing all right at this time."

We stayed another hour after we finished our tea.

"Abby, I'm so happy to have met you and that you had the gumption to find me," said Annie.

"It was my pleasure," replied Abby.

"Mary, if we don't meet again, know that you are always in my thoughts. Those miserable weeks we put in were only bearable because of our friendship. May God go with you."

We three walked to the front door where Annie unlocked and opened it. Abby offered her hand before she stepped out. Annie and I gave a parting hug.

It was the last time I saw her. I was informed she died a year later of a lung infection.

As I write this memoir, I can recall Annie's smile, her voice and her genuine caring that brought me out of the despair I was falling into on the Virginia Peninsula.

Chapter 32

Florence's husband, Johnathan, was well enough to return to his outfit in late October. Now that Jenny had an escort, Aunt Martha allowed her to go to Washington to be with Ted. Florence returned to the Morgan house in New York City with baby Johnathan, who had grown since I had last seen him and was now in the creeping stage. What a joy for the whole family.

I wasn't keen on Jenny being alone in Washington as I knew Ted would have limited down time. Aunt Martha was probably aware of the same, but Jenny was a married woman. She could make her own decisions.

It was October and I was completely revitalized and ready to go back to the Sanitary Commission to help in the hospitals. I knew there would be overloads of convalescing soldiers from that terrible slaughter at Antietam a month ago.

Daniel had written that the doctor said he could return to his regiment in Washington the last week in October as long as he took another week to get his arm in shape.

Again my selfish streak overtook me. I rode back to that city with Johnathan and Jenny. Aunt Martha footed the bill for our stay at the same hotel as she had done before. This time she secured two rooms side by side. She and Abby were going to Washington in November as Mrs. Schuyler had called a meeting of all the eastern relief agents of the Sanitary Commission. She was very concerned about the complacency of the public. Donations were not being readily given and the Sanitary Commission was not going to be as prepared as they had been a year ago. Aunt Martha wanted to be sure she and Abby had a room when they arrived for that meeting.

Double rooms were perfect. If Ted had time off, he and Jenny could use one room and I could the other.

Ted was married so he came and went from the hotel without accusing eyes. It seems that because he brought Daniel it was acceptable for both to come upstairs.

We always conducted ourselves in an honorable manner. If anyone wanted to wag a tongue, I didn't care because I was comfortable with the way in which I conducted my life.

Jenny and I were having a discussion about returning to hospital duty when a knock came on the door. She rose to answer it. There stood Ted Stevens with Daniel Phillips behind him. Jenny folded into Ted's big hug and I sat with my mouth agape.

Daniel walked around the two embraced in each other's arms and pulled me to my feet before he put both arms around me and kissed me soundly.

Ted had kicked the door shut with his foot. He looked at me over Jenny's shoulder and winked.

"Surprised? I found this soldier looking lost so I dragged him along with me."

I hadn't uttered a word, still spellbound entwined in Daniel's arms, his warm brown eyes were lost in mine. He didn't look at Ted when he said, "There was no dragging to it, Stevens. I have been chafing at the bit to get over here since I landed last evening."

"I'm so glad you're here," I said. I raised his dark hair to examine the scalp wound and found wrinkled pink scar tissue and an indentation where the ball had entered. "It looks good. You had a capable surgeon."

Daniel smiled, stepped back and held out both arms. "This one's a bit shorter but it works well." He grabbed me around the waist and pulled me close. How wonderful it was to be held close, to be with Ted and Jenny, to block out the world around us.

We had ten days of bliss. All free time Ted and Daniel had was spent with Jenny and me. Daniel and I did go to a concert by ourselves, took in a play, and took walks around the good parts of the city. The four of us went to a tea room and played games of cards together. But, Ted and Jenny were married, so Daniel and I allowed them as much private time as possible.

At the end of the week, news came that Ted's division would be moving out. Daniel's regiment was being sent as backup to headquarters in Falmouth, Virginia.

General Burnside, now in charge of the Army of the Potomac, planned an assault on Richmond.

The plan was to cross the Rappahannock River in mid-November at Fredericksburg and continue on to the Confederate capital.

Jenny and I kept our eyes on the newspapers. It seemed reporters knew all the plans and thought the information should be available to Union and Rebels alike.

However, bureaucratic matters muddied the waters. Supplies were not sent so pontoon bridges could not be built until mid-December. By then the Confederate generals, Lee and Jackson, had deployed their troops around Fredericksburg. From December 11-15 another bloody battle ensued leaving great casualties for the North, lesser for the South, the Union army retreating, and the Confederate capital safe.

The Sanitary Commission boats were once again needed. Both Jenny and I volunteered. Wounded were taken to Fairfax Seminary Hospital in Alexandria, north of Fredericksburg, and others went farther north to Fairfax Court House where there was a large army hospital.

This was Jenny's first time on the transport ships and she marveled at the organization that was carried out: the placement of the wounded, plenty of stimulants, hot food, plethora of bandages and medical supplies, surgery area and apothecary. We worked long hours tending the injured on the boat. This was a larger ship. We had the extra help of three surgeons as there had not been a major battle since Antietam in September.

We had plenty of supplies, which meant to me that Louisa Lee Schuyler's meeting in

Washington to regenerate the relief societies was successful. Aunt Martha had written that President Lincoln received both the Eastern and Western Commission women leaders. He was described as having a slump to his shoulders and a weary haggard face, appearing as though he carried the weight of the country on his shoulders. Perhaps he was in despair as the Union had lost more battles than it had won.

Daniel wrote that he had remained at the headquarters in Falmouth, but Ted's division had been in the thick of the carnage. Ted was unscathed and again I was glad Daniel was safe.

Chapter 33

In December after the ships had transported the wounded from Fredericksburg, Jenny and I were back in our hotel room. Jenny's complexion was sallow and she had lost weight. There were dark circles under her eyes and she had no appetite. I didn't think it was from the work we had done on the boat or her concern over Ted. I knew Dr. S. had a private practice in Washington and he had given me his address. It was the week of Christmas. Ted and Daniel would be returning within a couple of days. Something had to be done.

"Jenny, will you go to see a surgeon if I make an appointment?" She looked at me with tired eyes. I added, "We talk about going to help in the hospital, but you don't look well."

"I think I just need some rest. The past few weeks have been taxing."

"I know a good surgeon here who can give you something to increase your energy. Maybe you just have tired blood. You want to be looking your best when Ted gets back."

She sighed. "Yes. And, Abby has written that the officers are having a Christmas banquet here in Washington to jack up their spirits."

"If they keep losing battles and killing more men, we won't have any army left. I don't feel like having a banquet. Do you?"

"I don't know. It might lift our spirits, also. You know Abby is eager to see Edward, and we would all be together at Christmas, almost like we were last year."

I had to smile at the memory. That was when I had met Daniel and Jenny had met Ted. I fingered the stone on my neck chain as I frequently did at the sound of Daniel's name, "Happy memories, Jenny."

"Wonderful memories," she answered. "Mary, I don't know what I would do without Ted."

"We're going to see Dr. S. tomorrow. We'll sit in his office until he will see you. Then we're coming back here, rest, and think about our men returning. We could think about a Christmas banquet, but that's for Abby to get excited about."

It was December 21st when Dr. S. examined Jenny. His report was not completely unexpected. He said Jenny was anemic and most likely with child, although it was too early to be positive. What wasn't expected was that he was sure she wasn't strong enough to carry a baby.

Dr. S. was not one to mince words. "Even if you take to your bed, it isn't going to help. You are not in good health. I suggest you forget about this war, go home to New York, build up your stamina."

My heart went out to my cousin. She burst into tears.

"I'm sorry to give you that news, Mrs. Stevens, but with your husband in the army and your volunteering, they are too much of a strain. I believe you need to know what to expect. It is possible that I am wrong."

Jenny wiped her eyes. She sniffed a couple of times then asked, "How many times have you been wrong? I may look weak, but I have a strong constitution."

"Not often wrong." I saw a hint of a smile on the surgeon's face. "It appears you and Miss Sullivan have something in common when it comes to determination." He handed her a prescription. "Take this to the apothecary. It is an iron preparation to build up your blood."

He turned to me. "Did you have a good couple of weeks in New York?"

"Yes, I'm back volunteering. Jenny and I both were on a transport ship after Fredericksburg."

He shook his head. "Senseless war. Are you going to stay in Washington?"

"I am taking one day at a time."

He chuckled. "So am I. My offer is still open. How is your young man?"

I offered a wide smile. "He is back with his regiment. The head wound has healed well and he has full use of his arm."

"That's good. I hope he makes it through the end of this madness."

That was Dr. S., caring and caustic at the same time.

Jenny and I thanked him and left the office. We stopped at the first drug store we came to where the prescription was filled. We bought ham sandwiches along the way and took them to the hotel.

Jenny and I sat on the edge of our beds as we unwrapped our sandwiches and folded up the waxed paper to be used again.

"Mary, I don't know what to tell Mother and Ted. You know Mother will insist that I go back home. Ted will agree and I'll be put to bed as an invalid. What if Dr. S. is wrong? Should I keep this between you and me?"

I sat for a moment. "I think that's something you have to answer for yourself. What would I do in your situation? I would take this medicine and go about as I have for a month. I would give up work at a hospital and limit help to reading or writing letters for the soldiers."

"What about your parents and Daniel?"

I rolled my eyes. "You know my mother. She is the world's champion worrier. She'd question every five minutes if I was all right. As for Daniel, he has enough on his mind rather than to worry about me."

Jenny thought about my words, then said, "Dear cousin, you have answered my question. We are much alike."

I had to be honest with her. "Jenny, if I noticed that you don't look well, your mother is going to notice also."

"I have the answer. I have tired blood and the doctor has given me medicine."

"What if she wants you to go back to New York with her?"

"I shall tell her that I must stay because the doctor wants to see me in another month to check my blood."

I countered her reply, "There are good surgeons in New York. Your mother will want you seen by her personal physician."

Jenny sighed, "Then I shall tell her that after a month, if, I am not better, I will go home."

"Is that the truth?"

Jenny smiled. "I don't know, but it will give me a month's reprieve."

I laughed aloud. "Are you going to eat the other half of that ham sandwich?"

"I couldn't possibly."

"Good," I grabbed up the half. "I'm starved." I sat eating the food when an idea struck. "While you lie down and rest, I'm going out to see if I can buy something to put more color in your cheeks."

"Do I look that bad?"

"The dark circles under your eyes don't complement the grayness of your skin."

She balled up the waxed paper she had folded and threw it at me. "Finish that food and be on your way."

As she curled up on the bed, I put on my cloak, hat, gloves, and golashes to go out into the December air."

Chapter 34

Two days later on December 23rd, Aunt Martha and Abby arrived in Washington. I had bought rouge and face powder for Jenny to liven up her complexion. As long as she wore her glasses the dark circles were less noticeable.

Of course Aunt Martha noticed a change, but attributed it to working too hard. Jenny did tell her she was taking medicine for tired blood. The explanation was accepted without further discussion, much to the relief of Jenny.

Ted and Daniel returned from the Fredericksburg disaster on the same day. That was fortunate as the soldiers from that battle were wintering in Fredericksburg.

When they arrived at the hotel in military dress, Ted had healing scrapes and scratches on his face and hands. Jenny and I fell into their arms so happy to have them back. The sore feelings of defeat were not mentioned.

We had a late supper that evening. Edward joined us as did Major Porter, the son of a friend of Aunt Martha from New York. The dining was cordial, but the gaiety that we usually enjoyed when we were all together was lacking. When we finished our meal at the hotel, the four soldiers left to return to their quarters. We had no private time.

Daniel and I held hands under the cover of the table as I suspected my cousins did.

The next day was the day before Christmas. The joy of the season was escaping us with Jenny's condition and the low morale of the army.

Abby came into our room the next morning. She insisted Jenny and I accompany her in her search for a new dress for the officers' banquet to be held that evening. Aunt Martha was going to meet with someone from the Sanitary Commission. My aunt always combined business with pleasure.

Abby sat beside me on the edge of my bed facing Jenny. "I'm not going traipsing around the streets of Washington while you look for a dress," said Jenny. "I don't know why you didn't bring one from New York."

"Because it was a nuisance to pack one. It's all right if you don't want to go. I know you don't feel well."

"I feel fine," replied Jenny. "I just don't want to go on one of your excursions to find the perfect dress. It's only a banquet."

"Fiddlesticks," said Abby. "I want to look my best for Edward. Don't you want to surprise Ted by wearing something he hasn't seen before?"

"No," answered Jenny. "I'm not trying to impress my husband. He likes me the way I am."

"What about you, Mary? Don't you want a new dress?" asked Abby.

I turned to look at her. "If I find something that catches my eye and agrees with my pocketbook, I might be tempted."

Abby jumped up from the bed. "That's just what I want to hear. Let's get going. You can stay and rest, dear sister, while Mary and I are gone."

"That sounds like heaven to me," replied Jenny as she lay back on her pillow. "Throw that blanket over me before you leave."

Abby went next door into her room to get her cloak, bonnet and gloves. I unfolded the blanket and laid it over Jenny before I put on my outerwear to accompany Abby.

There was no snow but it was cold and damp as Washington can be in the wintertime. My heart wasn't into a shopping trip, but I didn't want to disappoint Abby. Nor did I want to sit around in my hotel room quiet as a mouse so as not to disturb Jenny's nap. I did my best to act enthused.

We had walked only a few blocks before Abby spied a dressmaker's shop. Could I be this fortunate that she would find a dress she liked in the first store we entered?

"There is a festive green brocade in your window," Abby said to the clerk. "Is it for sale?"

The dressmaker smiled, "My dear, that is for display only. Come look at my lovely brocades. I can make a beautiful dress for you."

Abby offered a sweet smile. "I haven't time for a dress to be made. I need it for this evening. That brocade in the window is exactly what I hoped to find. Money is no object."

I stood quietly listening to Abby plead her case and wondering if the dressmaker was going to set an impossible price on the dress.

"I am sorry it's not for sale at any price. I need it for display as there is another week before New Year's Eve and there will be ladies needing ball dresses. Are you attending a ball, my dear?"

Abby shook her head. "No, madam. I am going to an officers' banquet and I need to look my best."

"I understand. You will be lovely in any dress you wear, but I'm sure you want to look special for a certain someone. I have dresses in the next room that may be what you are looking for."

I was observing a master saleslady. I followed Abby and the dressmaker into her fitting room. There was a long rack of dresses in brocade, velvet, silk taffeta, and gabardine. It made me wonder where the woman got such fine material during wartime and was it procured by legitimate means. The fact that the woman wouldn't sell the brocade on display at any price caused me to wonder even more.

Then I remembered people in New York City continued on as though there was no war or scarcity of materials for the well-to-do. Should Washington be any different for the wives of the government officials?

"What do you think of this royal blue velvet?" asked the saleslady. "It would look grand with your coloring. It can be worn with only one petticoat, which would be more suitable for a banquet."

The dressmaker spoke as Abby fingered the material. "Don't you agree that it is a lush velvet?

You must try it on to get the full picture," her sales pitch continued. "I can make small adjustments if needed."

"Go ahead, Abby. Try it on," I encouraged. Abby went into a dressing compartment to peel down to her corset.

"And what of you, miss?" The saleslady asked me. "Are you attending also?" She pulled a shiny deep red satin. The color reminded me of the color of beets. A band of white seeded pearls graced the round neckline with the same bands decorating the fancy elbow length sleeves.

"No thank you," I said. "I'm not looking for a dress."

She gave a gentle shake to the dress. "You see the material glides as you walk and the color shimmers."

Abby called that she was ready to try on the royal blue velvet so the dressmaker went to help her. I stood there with the beautiful dress hanging before me. I touched the satin and felt the smooth material slide through my fingers. I took it from its hanger and held it in front of me.

While I stood dreaming, Abby stepped out of the compartment to view herself in the full length three-way mirror. "Oh, Mary! You must try it on."

"No. I don't need it and I don't plan on buying it."

"For once in your life be more daring. We will all look lovely. Jenny will wear her striped green, I know. We will look festive for Christmas and raise the spirits of our soldiers."

My resolve melted and I tried the dress. The satin was easy to wear and smart looking. Was it me? Daniel might think me too overdone. Did I owe it to myself after going through the Peninsula battles?

Abby broke my train of thought. "You must buy it. Mary. If you don't, I will and then you will have to wear it."

I knew my cousin and knew she would do as she said, whether I wanted it or not. But, I did want the dress. And, I was not going to let her pay for it. So I bought it. Then I wondered if I had made a foolish impulsive decision.

We walked back to the hotel with our dress boxes to get ready for the Christmas Eve banquet that was now only two hours away.

Abby did our hair. She had a knack for fixing different hair styles. We had no iron to make curls, but somehow she was able to wind Jenny's hair in such a way that it gave more life to her face. As for my long braid Abby wound it around and secured it with hairpins. I watched as she parted her hair in the middle, tied white velvet ribbon around each hank of hair and coiled each side around her ears. It was the style of the day. She put a gold comb in Jenny's hair and a pearl beaded comb in mine.

"Where did you get those combs?" I asked.

Abby gave a pleased smile. "I happened to notice them in the dressmaker's shop. Merry Christmas."

"I thought we had an agreement that we would not exchange any presents this year."

"I know, Mary. They are the perfect accent and I wanted to give Jenny a little something to make her feel better."

I was still a bit chagrined. "These are expensive combs. I feel fine. Why did you buy one for me?"

"Because you needed something to dress up your hair. Dab a little of that rouge on your cheeks. You and Jenny can both use some color. I don't know why you two work so hard."

Jenny spoke up, "We haven't worked since we left the transport ships after Fredericksburg."

"I think that left its mark," said Abby. "Hurry and get your things together. The carriage will be coming to take us to the banquet hall. I'll see if Mother is ready."

After Abby left the room, Jenny said, "I think Abby has missed her calling. She's bossy enough to be a general."

It felt good to laugh. "You look very nice, Jenny. How are you feeling?"

"I needed that long nap. Now I plan to get through the dinner. I hope there isn't any odor of food that's going to send my stomach reeling."

"The way your luck is going they'll probably serve fish chowder."

"Don't even mention it. Just the thought of smelly fish puts a lump in my throat."

Dressed in our cloaks, bonnets and gloves, we four women left the hotel to find a carriage waiting. Our soldiers were to meet us in the banquet hall. The streets of Washington were dark and deserted. It didn't feel like the night before Christmas.

The driver pulled the carriage to a stop in front of a long unimpressive brick building big as a warehouse. Gas light lit the path and young soldiers dressed in their finest uniforms and white gloves were on hand to escort each of us to the hall. When we stepped inside our cloaks, bonnets and gloves were taken and we were given a piece of paper with a number to identify our belongings. I tucked the piece of paper into my beaded evening bag.

Our young escorts took us to the table where Ted and Daniel were waiting. Aunt Martha was taken to Major Porter seated closer to the head table, and Abby taken to Edward seated even closer. I assumed the nearer to the head table, the higher the rank of the officer. The place was so organized I had to wonder if General McClellan had been in charge of the banquet. Organization was his forte. Military strategy wasn't.

With military pomp, the young soldiers gave a bow as they handed us off to our waiting partners. As Daniel seated me he leaned and whispered in my ear, "You look ravishing."

I felt my face and neck flush the color of my satin dress. They were words I had never heard relating to me.

Ted had a big smile and was his usual robust self. In a low voice, he said, "It's a bit too stiff for me." I saw Jenny pat his hand as she was seated.

Once everyone had entered and the doors to the hall closed I looked around. The tables held red tablecloths, candles surrounded by sprigs of greenery. The long head table, elevated on a platform, had a white tablecloth. The table held a long centerpiece of holly and berries and red bows. Swags of greenery were draped across the front. I recognized General McClellan and General Burnside with their ladies. Behind them a big American flag hung from the ceiling.

Once the hall quieted General McClellan rose and asked us to stand as he led us in a salute to the flag. Then a small army band played and we sang the National anthem. We sat again and General Burnside welcomed all of us. "We heard the inspiring speeches before you ladies arrived," said Ted. "I'm hungry."

Daniel chuckled. "You're always hungry."

"We can't all be as trim as you, my friend. How are you lovely ladies tonight?"

"Happy to be here," replied Jenny. "Abby and Mary let me have a long nap this afternoon."

"Are you feeling better?" Ted was concerned.

"Oh, much," Jenny lied.

"I went shopping with Abby," I said to change the subject of Jenny's health. "She is such good company."

The young soldier acting as a waiter for our table approached with a tray of cordials and water glasses. Jenny and I both waved away the cordials so Ted and Daniel helped themselves to theirs and ours. It wasn't long after the alcohol was served that the whole room began to loosen up. It was good to feel the stiffness relax even if it was caused by the Devil's brew.

The evening went too quickly. Jenny picked at her food but she kept an upbeat attitude. If she was uncomfortable she did a masterful job of keeping it to herself. The four of us talked and teased and laughed through our three hours together. The evening turned out to be cathartic for everyone. Perhaps the military leaders knew how to lift the morale of their officers after all.

The arrangements for leaving were the same as when we arrived. A carriage awaited to take us four back to the hotel. Our soldiers were allowed to walk us to the carriage. There was enough darkness and a crowd of people that Daniel pulled me close. "We will spend the day together tomorrow. Can we find some private time?"

"We have the entire day until six o'clock when Aunt Martha has arranged for a Christmas meal in the hotel."

He gave a gentle squeeze. "Perfect. I will be there at eight o'clock, and we shall begin our day with breakfast in the hotel."

The trip back was full of conversation about the evening we had just experienced. Even Aunt Martha, although seated with others twenty years her junior, had enjoyed the Christmas Eve of 1862.

On Christmas Day all plans changed. The army decided to send Daniel's regiment back to where the bulk of his corps was spending the winter near Fredericksburg.

Aunt Martha rearranged for dinner at the hotel for noon. At ten o'clock Daniel, Ted and Edward arrived and we all attended church services.

Both Ted and Daniel would be leaving. Edward would remain in Washington. We did our best to keep the spirit of the holiday, but underneath was the sense of loss once again for Jenny and me.

Aunt Martha was not one to let Christmas pass without a present. At the end of the meal she presented all of us with a basket of dried fruit, nuts and oranges all tied up with a pretty green velvet bow. Her gifts brought a smile to everyone and lifted the dejected thoughts of departing soldiers.

Daniel and I had one hour to ourselves. We walked out into the cool of the December air and found a private spot where we could say goodbye oblivious to the weather. He left me with a passionate kiss. "We will be together again," he whispered in my ear.

I was near tears but I held them in. I whispered back, "I wish you didn't have to go."

He stood back and looked at me. "Next week begins a new year. Let's keep our hopes alive that it will bring an end to this craziness."

However, neither of us could have imagined what 1863 would bring.

Chapter 35

On January 1, 1863 President Lincoln issued the Emancipation Proclamation declaring that all slaves in the rebellious states were free. This had been bantered around since September but now it was a decree.

The news was accepted with mixed emotions. Certainly, the agricultural south could not afford to lose their labor. But the majority of the southerners did not own slaves. They worked their small farms and depended on the fruits of their labor to survive. Because of the embargo on the waters, the South was not able to ship cotton or other goods. At this point in the war, the South was already in trouble for procuring supplies.

The North, on the other hand, had a mix of industry and agriculture. It was free to ship goods to and from other countries. Although there were some slaves in the Northern states most of the labor was performed by immigrants coming into the country.

And, people wondered, once the slaves were free, who was going to care for them? Freed slaves would need money, food, and shelter. The government is good at giving orders but not so good at taking care of the problems it causes.

President Lincoln was getting concerned about his depleting army. Those who had served their time went home, and those who didn't want to serve any longer deserted. Plus, support from the public was declining. People were tired of the war.

What was the government to do? In March of 1863 came the first conscription of men for the Northern army. This caused unrest among immigrants as they were eligible to serve but the freed slaves were not. What if immigrants lost their jobs to the freed men?

By now, Jenny was well into her fourth month of pregnancy. I worked at the U.S. Patent Hospital, but Jenny spent most days in the hotel room looking worse every day. Risking Jenny's ire, I took a ride across the river to the Fairfax Court House Hospital where her sister Emily was the head matron.

I found her in her cubby-hole of an office. "I am most concerned about Jenny. I think she needs to go home to be with Aunt Martha. I told her that I would go back with her, but she doesn't want to hear it. She wants to be here in Washington in case Ted is sent back."

Emily was understanding. "Do you think I should have a talk with her? Perhaps I can convince her that she needs to be at home where she can rest under Mother's care."

I was skeptical. "If she will listen," I replied. "Dr. S. does not encourage her that all is well. He tells her this baby is not a sure thing."

"Is she happy?" asked Emily.

"No, she's scared. She doesn't say it, but I know her well enough."

Emily set her jaw firm. "Then I'm sending a telegram to Mother. Either Jenny goes to New York or Mother comes here."

A day later Aunt Martha sent a reply telegram. "The city is in a state of unrest. Dare not leave."

The letter unsettled Jenny. Whether her family's peril was the cause I don't know, but it had a profound effect on her. Two days later she complained of a crampy feeling. I took her to see Dr. S. The minute we stepped into the office she started bleeding. Dr. S. picked Jenny up and carried her to the examining table. "Get her clothes off."

Jenny seemed in a daze, but I did as the doctor ordered after I threw my shawl over a chair.

"She's aborting," said Dr. S. while he was readying instruments. "You'll need to give her some chloroform."

This was different from any surgery I had helped with, so I wasn't sure what to expect. I had never witnessed a baby being born, although I had seen plenty of bloody messes.

Before I could administer chloroform there were a few more painful cramps and the baby arrived in a glob of encapsulated and bloody tissue. The tiny shape, looking much like a seahorse, was formed enough I could see he was male.

"Give her the chloroform," said Dr. S. "I need to scrape out what's left."

I was nervous. I placed the mask over Jenny's nose and mouth, dropped chloroform until her moans stopped.

Dr. S. finished and Jenny was in a deep sleep. "She will have to stay here for a couple of days. Will you stay with her?"

"Of course I will," I answered. "What will I do with the baby?"

"What do you suggest?"

The man should have some idea. I gave an edgy answer. "What do you usually do? I don't know. I think he should be buried. Should Jenny see him?"

Dr. S. glanced at what the basin held. "There's not much to see, but for her I believe it is important. There is a spot in the cemetery where these little ones are buried." The man was human after all.

Once Jenny was awake enough I showed her what remained. She sobbed and I cried along with her. For two days we stayed in a room at Dr. S.'s place. We talked a lot about the past, good memories which seemed to brighten Jenny's outlook. I slept on a sofa and the doctor's housekeeper brought us meals.

When Dr. S. said Jenny was free to go, we took the little box we had lined with lint containing the baptized remains of her baby and walked to the cemetery. The caretaker dug a hole and with gentle care placed the box. "This is our baby graveyard," he said. "We call it a special spot for the angels God wanted early." Jenny whispered a quick prayer as the caretaker put sod over the grave.

We were not too far from our hotel and Jenny, disregarding my concern, wanted to walk.

We walked side by side without saying a word until she spoke, "Maybe it wasn't the right time for a baby to come into the world. When this war is over, Ted and I will be together again and we can bring a child into a safe place. I have been thinking that this baby wasn't to be and is now an angel who can watch over his father."

I must admit this thinking had never occurred to me. However, her words gave me a warm feeling. I put my arm around her. "Do you think you should go home for a while?"

She nodded. "I need to get my strength back. I am no use in the hospitals or to anyone in this condition. Why does life have to be so hard, Mary?"

I had no answer.

Chapter 36

Daniel had written from Falmouth where all was quiet regarding movement of armies. It was his last letter that put me on edge.

Dearest Mary,

I was sorry to hear of Jenny's loss. I am also sorry that you had to be the one to help her through it all. It is good that she is with her family in New York, but you are still in Washington. Do you plan to stay there by yourself or do you have thoughts of returning to New York?

We have spent the winter shaping up the army. We have new recruits from the draft and we have been busy training them, not that they want to be here anymore than I do.

Colonel Dowd has had many meetings, and I believe we will be trying another assault on Richmond with General Hooker now in charge. The president doesn't seem to find a leader among his generals. We have always had wives, cooks and washerwomen following the army, but with General Hooker in charge we have tawdry women in the camp. Perhaps this is a way of lifting the morale of some soldiers. Not for me.

Mary, I am not sure when I will be free to write again. I so enjoy your letters and I look forward to the day when I see you again.

With my deepest affection,
Daniel

I sat in my lonesome hotel room and read the letter once more as I usually did while fingering the pebble I wore around my neck.

It wasn't long after I was contacted by the Sanitary Commission, I was back on the mercy boats.

On April 30, 1863 came the Battle of Chancellorsville. Once again I was on the *Daniel Webster* headed down river on the Potomac from Alexandria.

A hospital was set up at Potomac Creek, south of the Rappahannock River, ten or twelve miles from the battlefield. I went ashore to help in the camp hospitals.

On the morning of May 2nd, a beautiful spring morning, I decided to go nearer the battle field with my loaded ambulance and a young assistant from the hospital as my driver.

We saw trains of army wagons heading toward the front and slightly wounded soldiers making their way back to Falmouth. We drove farther past abandoned crude houses until we came to a brick house used as a hospital. I immediately began dispensing stimulants and nourishment to the wounded. They were from our own corps and told us of what they had seen.

Later that afternoon, Dr. Paxton, who had come on the boat, asked if I would go across the Rappahannock, where the battle was raging, to care for soldiers there.

I found the same driver to take me there once I had secured a pass from the quartermaster. It was my luck that he was a soldier I had met before, and he said he would give me whatever I needed.

My helper and I loaded the wagon with medicines, stimulants, clothing, blankets, bandages, food and whatever else I could think that would be needed.

The driver and I took off on that unfamiliar terrain. We got lost, tangled in brambles, squeaked around trees, and almost mired in a mud hole. Coming down a steep hill the driver lost his balance, probably from too much milk punch, and fell from the wagon. But he picked himself up, caught up with the wagon, found the reins, and we continued on the rutted path until we got to the pontoon bridge at the U.S. Ford to cross the river.

By this time it was close to midnight, but the moon was shining and the sky clear. The sounds of artillery and exploding shells we heard until dark had become quiet. We went about three miles before we came upon a large brick house where the wounded were brought.

I shall never forget the scene. The injured lay along the fences, all over the grounds, on the piazzas, under the piazzas, in the cellar, through the halls, in the rooms above and below. I set up a storeroom in a closet not big enough for a man to lie down in and set about caring as I could. I had to shut out the cries and moans of the suffering

Officers came and talked of a victory and a great battle to be fought the next day. There was no great battle the next day. The Army of the Potomac was defeated once again. We loaded our wounded into ambulances and headed back across the river with the help of many Sanitary Commission aides and nurses.

It was shortly after Chancellorsville that the wounded were taken to Washington and the army hospitals.

Chancellorsville left 17,000 Union dead, many wounded, and Richmond still intact. The southern Generals Lee and Jackson had prevailed with a lesser force, although the noble warrior Lt. Gen Thomas Jackson was felled by friendly fire and died of pneumonia a few days later.

When I returned to Washington, I was too busy to think about anything but caring for these demoralized men. I didn't know where Daniel was. There was a letter waiting for me from Jenny saying she was ready to return. I hoped she was right. I could use her company and her help, but only if she was healthy and in a good state of mind.

After this horrific Battle of Chancellorsville, witnessing the death and dying, shattered bodies, lives altered forever, I had to wonder what state of mind I was in. I was still intact. Had I seen too much human misery?

Chapter 37

Jenny returned with her brother, Charley, as her escort. Charley was back in Washington as he had finished his week of military furlough. I was working at the hospital when she arrived at the hotel late in the afternoon.

I was happy to see my sweet cousin when I returned. There was color in her cheeks and no trace of deep dark circles under her eyes. She had also put on some weight, but not all that she had lost.

While I changed my clothes she told me of what was going on in New York. She said she faithfully followed orders for resting and taking the medicine Dr. S. had prescribed. She also had word of Ted.

"Ted is in a hospital at Fairfax Court House, not the government one where Emily is head matron," she informed.

I was in the process of settling my shawl so we could go for our evening meal. "How do you know this?"

"He sent a telegram to New York."

"How did he know you were there?"

"That's the ironic part," she said. "He saw Daniel before he left Falmouth for Chancellorsville, and Daniel said he'd had a letter from you that said I was going home for a rest."

I let out a gasp. "Daniel didn't tell him about the baby I hope."

"No, I'm sure because Ted never mentioned it."

I was relieved. "Why is Ted in the hospital? Is he sick?"

"He was wounded at Chancellorsville."

I groaned. "Oh, no, Jenny. "How bad is he injured?"

I was shocked when I saw a smile appear on her face. "Bad enough to keep him out of the war, but not bad enough to cripple him for life."

I was skeptical. "Are you sure?"

"No, only what he said in his telegram. Tomorrow, I'm going to see him."

"May I go with you?"

"I'd love to have your company. Let's go down for supper because I'm hungry."

Her mood was so upbeat I tried to keep my doubt away as to what we would find at the hospital tomorrow. Ted was always one to project an optimistic front. For Jenny's sake I prayed he was truthful in his telegram.

After a decent night's sleep and a filling breakfast of ham, potatoes and corn bread, Jenny rented a buggy. We got passes from the quartermaster after swearing we were not spies and were faithful to the Union "so help me God."

It was another pretty May day and so very nice to be in the clean air of the country instead of the grungy atmosphere in Washington.

I had to ask, "What if Ted's injuries are more serious than he has said?"

"I'm prepared for anything. The fact that he's alive and lucid enough to send a sensible telegram gives me trust in his words."

"Are you going to tell him about the baby?"

Her answer was hesitant. "I want to be sure the time is right for that. Once I see what he has to deal with I will be able to judge better." She looked over at me with the sun reflecting on her glasses. "I'll take him in any condition, Mary."

I could see she was resolved in what she said. "Jenny, you are a remarkable woman."

She smiled. "You know how you say that there is something good that comes out of something bad?"

I nodded. It was something I believed.

"Well, I think going through what I did with the baby made me a stronger person. Life has been good to me. Sometimes it takes a setback to realize what is truly important."

"I'm learning that lesson every day," I replied. "We shall meet Ted with a united spirit."

We had found the hospital of the 6th Michigan wounded and tethered the horse at a rail. A red flag had been hoisted high as the rumor was that General Lee and his Army of Northern Virginia was on the march north. A red flag meant a hospital and would be honored by the advancing army.

We walked up the brick walk and six steps to a wide porch where some injured soldiers sat in rocking chairs. Most had their eyes closed and were snoring in slumber.

One soldier was awake with a bandage over his eyes. "I can't see you young ladies but I heard your light laughter. It's good to hear. The doctor says I'm going to be able to see again. I hope he's right."

"We're Sanitary Commission nurses," I told him.

"Bless you, sister. One of the mercy ships brought me up from Chancellorsville."

"I was there," I said.

"We served our time in Hell. Didn't we, miss?"

"That we did," I agreed. Chancellorsville and all the bloody battles on the Peninsula and Antietam, I thought. I patted his arm. "Rest easily."

A smile appeared under the bandaged eyes. "Thank you, miss."

This hospital was no different from the others: soldiers with missing limbs, others in their last days, a few who could be patched up to be sent back into the military. Always the moans and groans of the suffering.

We were directed to Ted's cot where we were shocked to see his right arm missing below the elbow and a bandaged chest. His eyes were closed.

Jenny hurried to his side and gently placed her arms around her husband, kissed his cheek. He opened his eyes. "Hello, sweetheart."

"Oh, Ted. I promised myself that I wouldn't cry. But these are tears of happiness."

He tried to smile. "It's a good thing I'm left-handed," he said.

"I don't care. I wouldn't care if you lost both arms."

"Yes, you would," he replied, wiping away the tears on her cheeks with his good hand. "I wouldn't be able to put my arms around you. This way I've got an arm and a half."

Jenny leaned back and wiped her glasses and face with her handkerchief.

"Is that Mary behind you?"

Jenny took a seat next to the cot in a straight chair. I stepped forward and took his good hand. "Hello, Ted. It's good to see you. I am sorry for your injuries."

"Well, so am I, but I'm not going to pity myself. I could be a lot worse off."

I pointed to the bandage. "What about your chest?"

"That'll heal. The shell passed through a couple of ribs before it decided to rip off my arm."

He looked over at Jenny and took her hand. "It's not going to prevent me from dancing. We'll be back on the dance floor and this will all seem like a dream."

Jenny kissed his hand. "Right now I'm going to stay close until you're out of here."

"I've lucked out with a good surgeon. Not true of a lot of them I've seen. Jenny, come sit on the edge of my cot and Mary can sit in your chair.'"

"I don't want to cause you to be in more pain than you must be."

Ted gave her a loving smile. "You're no heavier than a feather. I want you at my side."

I was glad to sit. "Jenny said you had seen Daniel in Falmouth. Is he well?"

"The last time I saw him he was. It was a quick unexpected meeting. I was on my way to Chancellorsville but his corps had not been called up at that time. I don't know if they ever were. Our grand Army of the Potomac isn't proving to be so grand. They are winning in the West, I'm told."

"Let's not talk about the war," said Jenny.

The surgeon of the day was making his rounds. When he got to Ted's cot I almost fell off the chair.

"Well, well, Miss Sullivan, we meet once more."

"Dr. S.," I acknowledged.

"And, Mrs. Stevens," the surgeon said. "You're looking much improved."

I caught the confused look on Ted's face.

"How are you doing, Lieutenant Steven? I assume this is your wife," said the physician.

"She is," answered Ted.

I wondered what Ted was thinking. I knew he was going to question Jenny once the doctor left, and I didn't want to be around to hear it. I remained in my seat until Dr. S. finished his examination of Ted's wounds and then excused myself.

Dr. S. followed me. "What are you doing here, Miss Sullivan?"

The man had no thought of what he had just created between husband and wife. I was vexed. "Ted knew nothing about Jenny's miscarriage."

"That's too bad" he said, "Now he'll find out. He can handle it and they'll work it out."

I'm not sure what came over me. I looked at him and said, "There are times when I think you have no sensitivity or compassion for others."

He just gave that hint of a smile. "Sometimes I wonder myself, Miss Sullivan. Would you care for a cup of tea?"

The man was exasperating. I wanted Ted and Jenny to have their privacy so I agreed.

In the hospital's kitchen, the attendant prepared two glasses of cold tea with chips of ice. Dr. S. and I walked out the back door of the hospital to a small courtyard where we sat on a bench. I had never been in this kind of situation with this man. I wasn't sure what to say or what he was going to talk about. He was ten years my senior and I was always uptight when around him.

"It's pleasant out here," he said. "I left the city and signed on for another three months. Washington looks like a wartime fortress with the camps, forts and barricades. The soldiers are still dying from dysentery, pneumonia and all the diseases that come from being crowded together in poor sanitary conditions. Why are you back instead of staying in New York?"

"I've been working at the Patent Hospital. When Jenny went back to New York, I decided to stay in Washington. Then I got a call to help on the ships again. I believe Chancellorsville was worse than the Peninsula battles."

He shook his head. "Another senseless loss of men. What about your sensitivity, Miss Sullivan? Do you think you are losing it after all this bloodshed?"

216

"That is a question I've asked myself. But I feel for the suffering. I believe I steel myself to cope with the horrors or I couldn't stand it. In my heart I know I am meant to do what I can to alleviate the misery." Then I asked him, "What about Ted? Is he going to heal?"

"He's strong," he replied. "I see no reason why he won't heal in both mind and body. I expect he can be released in a week."

"That's good news," I said.

"What about your young man?" asked Dr. S.

"I haven't heard from Daniel. I don't know where he is."

We finished our tea and went back into the hospital. Dr. S. went on his way and I went to Ted's cot. I found them holding hands both with red eyes but big smiles.

"The surgeon thinks you might be able to leave here in a week if all goes well," I told them.

"That's good to hear," said Ted. "Jenny and I have a lot of catching up to do."

Jenny looked at me. "We've decided to go to New York once he's released."

"I'm happy to hear that. Aunt Martha will be relieved to have you both together and under her roof."

Jenny was pleased. "We've decided the rooms we can take."

It was wonderful to hear them so full of plans for the future.

Once Ted was discharged from both the hospital and the army, I knew my life would also

217

be altered. What about me? What was I going to do? I was in my twenties when women my age were settled into their way of life. What if Daniel doesn't make it through the rest of the war? What if he changes his mind about a future together? Was I going to be a spinster and become a Miss Dix? The thought did not appeal to me.

Chapter 38

General Lee did not attack Fairfax Court House nor did Mosby's Rangers raid the place as feared by rumors. Unfortunately, what was true was that the Confederate army was on the move toward Pennsylvania.

To my delight and relief I received a letter from Daniel. He was well. General Hooker was on his way to Washington and Daniel would be coming with the Army of the Potomac or what was left of it.

I was elated. Jenny and Ted had gone to New York, and I continued at the hospital with the thought that perhaps I should go back home.

However, with Daniel's news I was glad I had stayed. It was June and the weather was perfect. While Confederates were advancing toward Pennsylvania, the Army of the Potomac needed recuperation and morale building. Therefore, the army was not in pursuit of the Rebels.

I witnessed an impressive parade of troops and an artillery review for President Lincoln. It caused me to wonder where these men would next see battle and how many would survive. Those thoughts dampened my enthusiasm for the grand performance. I could not pick Daniel out of the throngs of soldiers, but I felt he was there. I didn't know when I would see him.

It was two hours after the display when I heard a knock on my hotel room door and rose to answer it. There stood my Daniel. I heard myself gasp, the door close, and I was tight in his strong arms.

Neither one of us spoke. We stood together molded in each other's grasp, neither moving to break the bond. When we did loosen, he kissed me lovingly and longingly and I returned his fervor.

"I can't believe you are here," I whispered.

"There was a moment when I almost wasn't," he replied. "But, I'm here and all in one piece."

We had so much to talk about. I didn't care that he was in my hotel room nor did I give a care to what others might think. I had seen so much loss of life I knew every moment was precious.

Dusk had not yet fallen. We ate an early supper in the hotel then went out behind the building to sit on a bench. We sat holding hands while he told me of where he had been. It was in Chancellorsville when a cannonball exploded near him and two other soldiers. Daniel escaped with a piece of shrapnel in his back, but the other two were killed instantly. "I knew then that I was meant to see you again."

"I was at Chancellorsville, Daniel. It was horrific. That's where Ted lost his arm."

I could tell from the stunned look on Daniel's face this was the first he had heard of Ted's injury. That opened up the whole conversation about Jenny and their baby and Ted's return and their decision to live in New York. By that time it was getting dark. We left the bench and went into the back entrance of the hotel. Daniel had to report back to his company by ten o'clock.

How long his corps would be in Washington neither of us knew. Regardless, this day had been heaven for me. If we were not to see each other before he was to leave, we had both had a day of sheer bliss. I went to bed feeling the happiest I had been in weeks.

We made the most of the little time we had because the army pulled out of Washington a few days later. Daniel was always proper and reserved in his behavior, but this time I saw a more serious Daniel. "I don't feel confident about where the army is headed. We have suffered too many defeats. As we must part again, I want you to know that you have brought more happiness to me than I have ever known."

Was he thinking he might not survive? Wouldn't that be a natural concern for every soldier who faced an enemy? I had never heard those words before.

By the 26th of June, General Lee had led his army through the Shenandoah Valley and was in Gettysburg, Pennsylvania. General Hooker was in pursuit. The pursuit was slow and the army was only a few miles northwest of Baltimore by June 27th. That caused President Lincoln to relieve General Hooker of command and replace him with General Meade. One more commander of the grand army.

General Meade was quick to march the army into Pennsylvania.

The Sanitary Commission prepared for the onslaught that was to come. Little was it realized his battle would leave the highest casualties of all. From July 1st through July 3rd the destruction went on.

Chapter 39

I left Washington with a group of Sanitary Commission nurses. We traveled north through Frederick, Maryland in our supply wagons. Doctors brought their medical supplies in tall cart-like conveyances outfitted for a traveling apothecary.

I prepared my own satchels with what I felt necessary to have at hand. Heaven knows I had tended enough battle-sore men, and I had trained under that capable physician, Dr. S. Without exaggeration or conceit, I was more knowledgeable than many who called themselves doctors.

One satchel I called my emergency bag, which held: extra bandages, rags, tourniquets, lint, splints, brandy, whiskey, Spirits of Ammonia, and opium compound. The second satchel I called my insurance bag. That contained: baking soda, Blue Mass, mercurial ointment, Tincture of Iodine, vinegar, salt, lye soap, corn starch, jelly, soda crackers, and wine. If I was to be on the battlefield, as in Chancellorsville, I wanted these goods at the ready. A canteen filled with water would be carried around my neck.

I might have enjoyed the sights along the way with the dense forests mixed with the rolling countryside and farm land, but my thoughts were on what lay ahead. The hard-packed road was dry making it an easier pull for the horses and mules.

We reached Gettysburg on a hot July 1st. We could hear the roar of battle with the booming cannons and sounds of musketry. The residents of Gettysburg had taken shelter in their homes and cellars.

White tent field hospitals had been set up for the different corps. We waited for orders from the Sanitary Commission agents before we women began our mission. Those of us who were battle-hardened pleaded for passage to the front. In this third year of the war, the restrictions Dorothea Dix had put on nurses were grossly ignored. Women were essential.

To this day I praise the U.S. Sanitary Commission for its constant supply of medical, clothing and food supplies, and the organization in which they dispatched empty wagons to return to Frederick to be filled again. The wagons traveled by way of the main road and Westminster.

I went into the field to help the wounded. I kept at the rear of the front lines always conscious of my position. A dead or wounded nurse was of no use.

We worked all day and into the night helping the wounded back to the field tent hospitals. The carnage went on for two more days.

Whether it was because the war had come on northern soil or not I don't know. However, the Pennsylvanians responded as did other Northern states sending supplies. Women came to the fore in force working as nurses and in the supply depots. Men enlisted in the army or came from their homes with muskets to fight along with the Union soldiers.

Many society women did their part either by physically joining the cause or raising funds. I remember meeting a woman from Maine who said she had canceled her family's plans to spend the summer at their summer home on Cape May in New Jersey. "How could I, in good conscience, go to sit idly by in my cottage by the sea while my country is at war?"

The bloodbath was declared a Union victory. Over 23,000 Union soldiers lost their lives and 28,000 Confederates. I blocked out what I could and kept my head by methodically taking care of the soldiers and surgeons' needs. It was a living nightmare.

I did not see Daniel during my time in Gettysburg, yet I knew he was there. Each dark-haired wounded soldier I came to struck a pang in my heart that it would be him.

Abby and Aunt Martha came by rail from Baltimore. They said it took twenty-four hours when it should have taken four due to some rails being ripped up. All lines of communication from Gettysburg had been destroyed by the Confederate army.

We had a short and tearful reunion. Cousin Charles was at Gettysburg and had been wounded with a slight injury.

Mr. Olmstead had come with my aunt and set up a U.S. Sanitary Commission Lodge where the workers could stay.

Edward had been sent from behind his desk, although he was not on the battlefield. There were still considerations for his stature. At that time, I thought Edward's privileged position was unfair. Then I came to realize that his behind-the-lines contributions were as important as those of the soldier on the field.

On July 4th, crowds gathered at Independence Hall in Philadelphia to honor the flag and give thanks for the victory.

In Gettysburg I did not feel like celebrating for I was taking care of the mutilation left behind, both Union and Confederate soldiers.

While I was tending a Confederate soldier, a short and bearded local came by in his boots and farm clothes. My tent was full of Confederate soldiers. The man came right into the tent and peered over my shoulder. I turned with a startle. "Are you looking for someone?" I asked.

"No," he replied. "I wanted to see what a Rebel looks like."

I grabbed him by the arm and escorted him out the open flap saying, "They look just like we do, and they have wives and children just like we do, and they feel pain just like we do. Go home and say a prayer for these brave men."

The whole town of Gettysburg became one big hospital. The homes and buildings were full of injured soldiers. Once the fighting was over the residents of the town did what they could and shared what they had. Once the telegraph lines and the railroads were repaired communication was restored.

Aunt Martha and Abby stayed on for three more weeks. I returned to Washington on a train filled with injured soldiers on their way to hospitals in the city.

Leaving the place, I could see fresh graves, dead horses, disabled cannons and caissons. I turned my back to the coldness of death and destruction.

General Meade was criticized for not pursuing the retreating Confederate army. Perhaps General Meade had good reason.

General Lee led his troops west toward Waynesboro, Pennsylvania and Hagerstown, Maryland in heavy rain. Once across the Potomac the Confederate army would be back on Virginia soil.

General Meade dispatched his troops on different routes through Emmitsburg, Maryland to eventually meet in Middletown. The Catoctin Mountains lay between Meade's army and General Lee's. Entrenched in the mountains, the Confederates might have held the advantage. Was that Meade's concern for not chasing General Lee?

However, all blood shed was not confined to the battlefield. On July 13th all hell broke loose in New York City. Because of the Enrollment Act, signed into law by President Lincoln on March 3, 1863, immigrants were eligible for the military draft but the free slaves were not. Immigrants fearing they would lose their jobs to freed slaves began to riot. For three days the unruly mobs looted, burned, plundered, brutalized, and dragged colored people from their homes. By the time the army brought order to the city 120 people were dead, homes and factories destroyed.

Aunt Martha and Abby were still in Gettysburg when the riots broke out. She later wrote that Ted and Jenny stayed in the house with all shutters locked and no lights burning, afraid for their lives while the mobs ran at will with guns and flaming torches burning and smashing anything in their path. They thought the iron fence surrounding the yard was what had saved them.

Chapter 40

After Gettysburg I remained in Washington to care for soldiers in the hospitals. Daniel was with Meade's army in Stafford County near Fredericksburg. His letters were about the day to day business of the military and, to his knowledge, there were no big conflicts planned for the Army of the Potomac. Perhaps there would be time off allowed closer to Christmas. Meanwhile, he was kept busy training the new recruits. He wrote that he missed me, so I was content.

I knew this was only a lull in the war as there was no political progress. There would surely be more battles and battered men. It wasn't only the war wounds that felled the soldiers. There were still diseases that were just as deadly. Dysentery still swept through the camps along with cholera, typhoid fever and the lung killers of pneumonia and consumption. I had seen big, robust men brought to skeletons from those wasteful diseases.

There were nurses who died from sickness as well as bullets and my friend, Annie, had died of repeated bouts with malaria. Yet, we women were a brave crew who put the needs of others before our own.

Concerns about future terrible battles led me to pay a visit to Dr. S. His housekeeper answered my knock and welcomed me with a warm smile. "Miss Sullivan. How nice to see you. The doctor is in, I'll tell him you are here."

I found Dr. S. sitting in his office on a pretty Sunday in September. He looked up but didn't rise from his chair. "Well, Miss Sullivan. What have you brought me today that is going to dampen my spirit?"

Tact was not Dr. S.'s strong point. I was used to his brash manner and emboldened in my response. "Only myself. Will that be enough to ruin what's left of your day?"

He offered that hint of a smile. I continued and came straight to the point, "Will you be signing on with the Sanitary Commission again?"

"Why do you ask?"

"Because I will continue to serve with the Commission, and I am certain there will be more horrible battles. I wish to work with a capable surgeon. If you will be signing up again, when the time comes, I will request to work with you."

He sat back in his chair and intertwined his fingers over his trim waist, sitting for a quiet moment as though his slate-blue eyes were analyzing me. I felt my face begin to blush and was unable to stop it.

Dr. S. actually smiled at my embarrassment. Should I have come?

There was some relief when he began to speak. "You want to work with me as a Sanitary Commission surgeon, yet you have not taken up my offer to work in this office."

"I see more need among the wounded in the hospitals."

He sat forward and leaned his elbows on the desk. "Do you think my work here is not important?"

"No, sir, I didn't say that. I believe I should be where the needs are greatest."

He leaned back again in his chair. "Miss Sullivan, I have questioned myself. Am I being selfish in not giving more time to the soldiers? I soothe my conscience by telling myself that the citizens are as much in need of my services. Now, here you come and put me back questioning myself."

I shook my head. "Sir, questioning yourself is not the intention of my visit. I only wish to know if you would sign on again. Perhaps it is selfish on my part, but I do not want to witness some of the inept men who pass themselves off as surgeons."

He looked at me with a wary eye. "Why, Miss Sullivan. I do believe you are becoming cynical."

I laughed. "It does sound that way, doesn't it? I want to learn all I can from you. I want to know I am doing the best I can for the sick and dying."

He rang the bell for his housekeeper. "Mrs. Miller, Miss Sullivan and I will have a cup of tea in the garden, where we are going to talk medicine."

There was not a choice and I'm glad for that because Dr. S. loved to talk about his vocation and was more than eager to impart his philosophy.

It was late afternoon when we finished our discussion. He insisted on driving me to the hotel in his dray. Any apprehensions about intruding on his day were forgotten. He gave me a couple of medical books and papers he'd written of his beliefs regarding medical practices.

I was delighted with this information and eager to absorb all I could. Dr. S. said he believed it was the teacher in me that made me so curious.

When we arrived at the hotel, I thanked him for the afternoon. I told him I would return the articles he lent me as soon as I was through with them. He still had not told me if he planned on contracting with the Sanitary Commission. That was fine with me because I knew I would press for an answer when I returned his books.

Chapter 41

I decided to visit my parents. I had not been the dutiful daughter who wrote religiously. In truth, I had only written a few times over these three years leaving it up to Aunt Martha. Of course, I didn't ask my aunt to write to my parents, but I knew she would feel it her responsibility to keep her sister informed of my welfare.

I made arrangements with the Sanitary Commission and the hotel as I planned to be absent through the month of October. I wrote to Daniel, to my cousins in New York City, and my parents to tell them of my plans.

The thought of traveling up the Hudson River Valley in the fall gave me a sense of excitement. The red, orange, yellow and rust colors of autumn would make the country come alive, heralding the quiet winter to come. Maybe it would help me forget the desolation of Antietam and Gettysburg.

On October 1st, I was sitting in Union Station, dressed in my blue dress over one petticoat, straw hat and gloves waiting for the announcement to board the train to New York. While I sat reading a book Dr. S. had lent to me, a soldier came and sat on the bench beside me.

"Good morning," he said.

I looked up from my book. "Good morning," I answered.

"I assume you're waiting to board the train for New York."

"Yes, I am."

"Where are you headed?"

"Albany," I replied as terse as possible.

"That's a coincidence," he said. "I'm going there also. Perhaps we could sit together on the train so we don't have some unwelcome passenger to contend with."

I put my book in my lap and looked straight at him. "Sir, you are a soldier so I have no problem with you sitting beside me. But I must tell you that I plan on a quiet, contemplative ride. I do not wish conversation."

The rebuff did not seem to annoy him. "I apologize for not introducing myself. I'm Major Cyrus Roberts. I promise I will button my lip."

His words did make me smile. "My name is Mary Sullivan."

Right then the conductor announced, "All aboard!"

I gathered my book and tote bag and rose from the seat where I had been waiting. When I leaned to pick up my travel satchel, Major Roberts grabbed the handle. "I'll carry it for you."

This man, perhaps a few years older than I, was handsome, taller than average, green eyes, neatly combed acorn-colored hair, and a clean-shaven face. As I looked closer, I saw he was thin and quite pale as though he had been ill.

"It isn't necessary for you to carry my satchel," I said.

"My mother always told me it was polite to carry a lady's bag," he answered.

We mounted the metal steps and walked to the middle of the train car. I entered first and sat next to the window. Major Roberts settled next to me. His slender form allowed me plenty of room to squirm around in the seat if I felt the need. Train seats were never comfortable. I knew this train would stop in Baltimore where I could get up and stretch my legs. If I was not pleased with this major sitting next to me, I could change seats when the train stopped.

True to his word, the soldier never attempted any conversation while I sat and read the medical book. I think he napped most of the way, but I didn't glance over at him to see. At least he never snored.

In Baltimore, we had a thirty minute wait. I folded up my book and put it in my tote. I needed to get off the train and walk a bit.

Major Roberts stood and stepped into the aisle so that I could get out of my seat without climbing over him. It was then he spoke, "The wait is thirty minutes. We could go for a cup of tea, Miss Sullivan."

To decline his invitation was on the tip of my tongue. However, I did not want to appear ruder than I had already been. "A cup of tea would be nice," I replied.

We walked into the station and found a refreshment stand where he purchased a cup of tea for me and coffee for himself. Then we sat on a bench as people milled around the busy station.

"It's hard to believe there's a war going on," he said.

"I noticed the same when I was last in New York City. It seems the public is merely going about its everyday business."

"Do you live in Albany?" he asked.

"No. In a small town near. Since the war started I have spent much of my time in Washington. I am a Sanitary Commission nurse and have worked on the mercy boats and in the hospitals."

He was pensive for a moment. "I know the ships," he said.

I expected more of a reply but none came. "What is your opinion of them?"

"I know they are necessary, but my knowledge comes only from being carried on one from the Peninsula Campaign. I don't remember a thing."

I came to life. "You were in the Peninsula Campaign? Oh, Major Roberts. I was there also."

"God bless you, Miss Sullivan. We have both been to Hell itself. I have been trying to recuperate ever since. The Minnie-ball wounds were not as bad as the typhoid fever and then dysentery. I'm going home to get my strength back. If I ever do."

I noticed the note of sadness in his voice and silently chastised myself for having been unkind. "You will recover. The fall season is pretty and the clean air will do you a world of good. Do you have family there?"

"In Saratoga, my parents and two sisters. I lost my brother at Chancellorsville."

My heart went out to him. "I was there, also. I am so sorry to hear of your loss. We have lost too many."

"That's true," he agreed. Within a heartbeat the tone of conversation brightened. "Let's leave that awful war behind us, and you tell me about that book you have your nose glued to."

I laughed. "It's a medical book that a surgeon has let me borrow. When we get back on the train, I will have to tell you about Dr. S."

"Does this mean I won't have to keep silent all the way to Albany?"

I liked his levity and promised myself to be a sociable companion from that moment on. I believe I must have been because, when we parted in Albany, he said my companionship made the trip most enjoyable. I wished him well.

My parents were waiting for me at the Albany station in Father's buggy. They were as overjoyed to see me as I was to see them. Mother shed a few tears at my arrival as she had done when I departed the first time. A light rain was falling but the buggy was covered.

The sight of the house where I had grown up with many happy memories welcomed me, and I felt a relief from the horror I had experienced over these past years.

It was good that I spent that time at home. I had visited the school where I had taught for three years. The one-room school was the same, but I felt as though I did not belong there. Mother continued on with her quiet way of life and worrying about nothing. Father kept busy at the bank where he had been promoted, which required longer hours. Much of my time was spent devouring the medical information Dr. S. had given me. I thought about Daniel and wondered about his last letter. He said Colonel Dowd's wife and daughter had come to stay in Fredericksburg for the winter. What made me wonder was his talk of Colonel Dowd's daughter. He said she reminded him of me with her fair face, quiet ways and chestnut-colored hair worn in a long braid. Colonel Dowd had said Daniel was like a son to him. Was there mischief afoot on the colonel's part?

Perhaps I had a twinge of jealousy. I touched the pebble I wore that Daniel had made into a necklace. Surely he wouldn't have done that if he didn't care for me. I decided to put the colonel's daughter out of my mind.

Mother made it a point to cook all my favorite foods and I couldn't resist. By the end of the month I was having difficulty buttoning my skirt and my blouse felt tight. I was more than ready to get back to the fast pace of the hospital and working with my soldiers.

Chapter 42

By the end of October, I had returned to Washington. There had been a minor skirmish in Fredericksburg in November, which resulted in no casualties and both armies retired for the winter.

I returned Dr. S.'s books on a chilly November day. We again shared tea. This time in his study, and he insisted on seeing me back to the hotel. He asked about Jenny and Daniel indicating that underneath his brash exterior there was kindness and caring.

We were in his buggy on the way to the hotel when he said, "Now, Miss Sullivan. The fact you have held onto my books for so long, I expect you to be well versed in medicine."

I remembered smiling as I said, "Sir, I understood you were in no hurry for their return."

He gave an abrupt nod of his shaggy head. "Quite right. I will expect exemplary performance from you when we work together."

I'm sure the surprise showed on my face. "Does that mean you will sign on again with the Sanitary Commission if you are needed?"

"Let's hope those idiot politicians in Washington can come to some agreement with the South before that."

"I don't see that happening. Are you going to sign on?"

"You will be notified if the time comes."

"Dr. S. that is not an answer." I pressed further, "Will you serve or not?"

He offered that hint of a smile. "You are persistent, Miss Sullivan. I will volunteer my services when I am needed."

"How will I know so that I can be assigned to where you are?"

He gave a deep sigh. "I will make arrangements with Miss Dix. The woman scares me to death."

I laughed. "She scares me, too, but so do you. I can't thank you enough for your help. Not only for me, but for Jenny, Ted, and Daniel."

"You can begin by learning how to pronounce my name, Scholkemohle." He ran the name off as though it was as easy as Smith.

I looked squarely into his face. "You will always be Dr. S. to me as I cannot pronounce it to your satisfaction nor can I spell it. I don't intend to try."

He shook his head. "Shameful words from a teacher, Miss Sullivan, I believe you have a bit of a stubborn streak."

"I have been accused of that," I answered. "Thank you for driving me. It would have been a cold walk."

"You should be more careful walking around in this city full of soldiers."

"I thank you for your concern. If I am ever accosted I will tell them they will have to deal with you."

This time he laughed aloud and tapped the reins. I waved to him before I turned and walked up the steps of the hotel.

That night I slept well. I had the answer I hoped for from the surgeon, and I was satisfied to have returned the articles in the same condition in which he had lent them.

The next day I received a letter from Daniel that he had ten days off for the holidays. Ten glorious days, I thought. I made arrangements with Miss Dix to be absent from hospital duty for those ten days so that Daniel and I could spend the time together.

Miss Dix was a tall, stately, slender woman. She came into the hospital and that's where I asked for the time off. "You have had the whole month of October from your duties. Why is it that you are requesting more free time?"

I explained. Her response was, "I don't see the need, but as you have been one of my dependable nurses, I will grant you the time. At least there are no battles going on."

Daniel arrived in Washington on December 23rd. The day was cool but dry with only a trace of a past snowfall a few days ago. I was warm in my wool coat, bonnet and the muff I carried over my gloved hands.

He looked healthy, rested and impeccable in his blue uniform. His shoes were polished and his belt buckle and buttons glinted in the sunlight. His face clean shaven, dark hair neat, and his beautiful smile was broad as he hurried to where I stood waiting.

"Mary, I am so happy to see you."

I know I was beaming. "I decided to meet your train," I said. He held my elbow as he escorted me from the throng of people. Daniel was too proper to be demonstrative in public, but as soon as he found a private spot he pulled me into his arms and held me close. Neither of us spoke. We stood there wrapped in each other's arms and then he kissed me with fervor. I melted at his touch that told me I had no worries about Colonel Dowd's daughter.

We walked arm in arm back to my hotel and chatted all along the way. In my hotel room we sat on the edge of the bed and caught up with all the hugs and kisses we'd missed.

A friend of Colonel Dowd had graciously offered a room for Daniel to use while he was in Washington. He did not wish to appear rude and arrive at that home late in the evening. We had an early meal at the hotel and he left to make his acquaintance with the promise of seeing me in the morning the next day.

We spent ten wonderful days together. Christmas was quiet and we spent the day in the hotel which had lovely greenery; bows of red, silver, green and gold; and plenty of lighted candles.

I bought Daniel a deck of playing cards, chocolates and hard candies. He gave me a blue folding fan with a panoramic picture of Washington painted on it, which I have to this day.

Ted and Jenny surprised and delighted us by coming to Washington after Christmas. Ted had not been discharged from the military so we were all invited to a New Year's Eve party for the officers.

Abby would have been proud of me and Jenny because we both wore hoops and the lovely gowns we had worn to the Christmas Ball the year before. True to his word, Ted could still dance the night away even with his half arm.

We talked as we sat at the table and the orchestra took a short break.

"I may be coming back to my regiment if the war sparks up," said Ted. "I still have an arm from the elbow up. I may not be able to reload a musket but there are plenty of things I can do."

I watched Jenny's reaction to what Ted had said and saw no sign of disdain or alarm. Apparently, they had discussed the possibility.

They told Daniel of the riots in New York and how they had hid in the cellar when they thought the unruly mob might overtake the house.

"I was deathly afraid," admitted Jenny, "but Ted said we were safer there and we could go out the back way if they broke in, or, God help us, if they had burned the place."

They said there was a big Manhattan Fair planned to benefit the Sanitary Commission in April. "The public is not donating and the stores are low."

"Of course Abby is energized and making elaborate plans. She and Florence are going to have a garden booth," said Jenny.

"I don't see Abby as a gardener," I remarked.

Ted laughed. "I don't believe she plans on getting her hands soiled."

"Ted, that isn't kind," admonished Jenny.

He patted Jenny's hand. "Maybe not, but it's true, love."

I said, "I think a Sanitary Commission fair sounds like a grand time. I'm afraid we are in for some terrible times once this winter is over. We will need all the supplies we can get."

Daniel reached over and placed his hand over mine. "Let's not talk about the war, Mary. We're ringing in a new year and with the help of Providence, I pray 1864 will see the end of it."

I was sorry for putting a damper on this evening. The worries of war were always in the back of my mind. It was then the orchestra decided to play a waltz.

Daniel took my hand. "That sounds like our kind of music, Mary. May I have this dance?"

"I'll have to see if my dance card is open," I replied.

He grinned and pulled me to my feet. I was lost in the smoothness of his moves as we glided about the floor. The subject of war forgotten as we became one.

The New Year's Eve party of 1863 was another to remember fondly. Ted and Jenny left the next day. Daniel and I saw them off at Union Station and spent the rest of the day together. He would be leaving the next morning.

The ten days passed quickly. I was so alone when I waved my farewell.

Chapter 43

On March 9, 1864, Ulysses S. Grant became General-in-charge of the Union Army. He had been successful in the West and hopes were high that he would put an end to the war. General Meade was still commander of the Army of the Potomac, General Sherman was in charge of the Western portion.

I received a letter from Daniel:

Dearest Mary,

I pray you are doing well and not over-working in the hospital. Here in our camp, where winter will soon be over, we are invigorated by the news of General Grant in charge. This seems to be a good move on the part of President Lincoln. General Grant has proven to be a man who likes to get the job done as evidenced in the West.

Could it be there is an end in sight? I don't see the Rebels surrendering easily and, even though I am a Union man, I must admire R. E. Lee for his military ingenuity. The South has been scraping for provisions for two years.

Mary, once the war is over I have plans. I hope you are in agreement. When Ted and Jenny were married, I thought they had made a mistake and should have waited. However, they have proved me wrong as they seem very happy.

I do have concerns about Ted returning to the army. A one-armed soldier is a handicap. Perhaps

Jenny can talk him out of it. Or, the army can find a spot for him safely behind the lines where he can work up to his ability.

I noticed at Christmastime you are still wearing the pebble necklace. I'm glad because it is a symbol that bonds us together. How I wish I could come to Washington. With this new shake-up of leaders, it is possible that Colonel Dowd will be called up there. If he does, he will need my services. That is something we can both offer up. Two prayers must be stronger than one.

I must close, dear one. Please know that I miss you on a daily basis.

Affectionately,
Daniel

I read the letter again as I usually did with all his letters. Daniel had never professed love or marriage to me, although he has strongly hinted at it. We were both reserved in that regard. His words made me conjure up all sorts of good things to come. Yet, I knew General Grant was in charge in Vicksburg and Shiloh, the bloodiest of the Western campaigns, causing me to shudder.

Abby wrote and said I must come to New York for the Manhattan Fair. She had worked very hard at organizing and she desperately needed my help at her garden booth. As Abby was one to exaggerate, I wasn't sure of her desperation. However, the invitation was tempting.

I was skeptical of Miss Dix allowing me the time off, but Aunt Martha had influence and on April 14, 1864, I found myself smiling and trying to drum up business for Abby's booth at the Great Manhattan Fair of the U. S. Sanitary Commission. It was held in a large wooden building in Union Square. Even the women of society had prepared with gusto to enrich funds for the Commission. The fair ran for three weeks.

Abby insisted that Jenny and I wear huge name pins that she had made to identify us as Sanitary Commission nurses. It did no good to protest. "This will bring in more money," she insisted.

There was a booth of every description. It seemed the women tried to outdo one another with their ingenuity in decorations. Abby, Florence and Jenny had made dried flower wreaths and delicate flower adornments for little girls to wear on their heads. In the garden booth they sold gloves, hand spades, seeds, gardening hats, pocketed aprons and baskets. There were ribbons, bows, and large urns of various dried flowers so people could make their own bouquets. Abby raffled off a lovely navy blue straw gardening hat decorated with flowers, lace and ribbons. For one dollar each a person could take a chance on winning the exquisite hat. After three weeks the hat alone brought in over four hundred dollars. And, a farmer from upstate brought fifty, three-year-old saplings of Northern Spy apples. He called them war apples although he didn't know any Northern spies. Abby laughed heartily at his pun and made a big show over his contribution, which made the man go away with a happy countenance. I was less than amused. Had I lost my sense of humor?

247

There was a trophy room with flags and military articles, even some that had been taken from Confederate soldiers. One day a volunteer from a convalescent hospital brought wounded soldiers to the fair to enjoy the sights and raise some money for themselves. There was a refined young man who had lost an arm at the shoulder, another man who had lost his hands, and an entertaining pair who were inseparable. One had lost both his legs and was carried around on the shoulders of the other stocky soldier who had lost both arms. In spite of their handicaps they were a cheerful pair. They helped each other as what one couldn't do the other could. After taking in the fair, the maimed soldiers stayed in the trophy room where a donation box was set up. At the end of the day, the proceeds were distributed among them. Each received over two hundred dollars.

Ted helped at our booth and I marveled at how he had learned to use his half arm. He went to the restaurant booth and brought Jenny and me a tray of sandwiches, cookies, and a pot of cold tea. "They were selling the tea pots," he said, "but when they saw my sleeve folded up and pinned to my shoulder they gave everything to me. It seems it pays to be an injured Union man," he said without sadness or regret.

I did enjoy the fair even though it ended on a sour note. Mesdames Grant and McClellan had spent their time soliciting votes for the favorite general.

Julia Grant was cordial and quietly reserved as she graciously accepted votes. The vivacious and outgoing Mary McClellan was easily outdistancing with garnering votes for her husband. General McClellan was clearly ahead.

Five minutes before the voting ended, a Philadelphia relief group telegraphed five hundred votes for General Grant. The coveted sword was awarded to Julia Grant for her husband. Mary McClellan was unforgiving. Who could blame her?

The fair brought in thousands of dollars to resupply the Sanitary Commission stores. At that time we did not realize how much they would be needed.

Before I left to return to Washington, we sat around the large dining room table at the Morgan house and talked and reminisced about how successful the fair had been. Abby was ecstatic. Not only were the proceeds greater than expectations, she had met many influential ladies from Philadelphia, which would put her in high standing once she and Edward were married. I was happy for her.

Ted said he was determined not to sit idly by if the war heated up. He planned on joining the Sanitary Commission as an agent and Jenny would help again as a nurse. "In that way, we can be together and still do our part for the war effort," said Ted.

I had to admire their spirit.

We were all exhausted and exhilarated from the three weeks of the fair. Abby said the fairs were beginning to catch on in the smaller communities. Those proceeds could only mean boosting the supplies of the Sanitary Commission.

Chapter 44

The fair and reuniting with my cousins was a rejuvenation. I was ready to tackle the chores of the hospital. The day I arrived in Washington was a pretty spring day in May with the dogwoods and redbuds in full bloom. I enjoyed the walk to the hotel even with the clatter of vehicles, clopping of horses, and the smell of dung in the streets.

There was a note waiting for me at the hotel. I opened it in the lobby and almost shouted for joy. Daniel was coming. It would only be for one day. I didn't care as long as I got to see him.

I laid out my prettiest day dress, pleased to see that it wasn't badly wrinkled. I shook it out and hung it on a hanger. Yes, it looked suitable.

Daniel had army business during the day and arrived late afternoon. I knew his knock and hurried to open the door. He looked so fine in his uniform. With a big smile, he closed the door behind him and pulled me into his arms. "You feel so good. Let's just stand like this for the next few hours," he murmured.

I chuckled. "I just finished standing for hours for three weeks at the New York Fair. I'd rather sit."

He kissed me soundly which always sent a pleasant rush through my being. His warm brown eyes took me in. "Then we shall sit. I have found a nice place for supper. We have a lot to talk about."

Indeed we did, and it wasn't all good news. He said Grant was determined to end the war, but he knew there would be fierce opposition from the Confederates. Exactly what that meant Daniel wasn't sure or maybe not privy to repeat.

The small restaurant was run by Asian immigrants. I'm not sure their heritage, but the food was delicious. They were quiet and respectful and we had a cozy spot.

"Mary, what do you plan to do once the war is over?" His question took me by surprise.

"I haven't thought much about it. Dr. S. has offered me a position in his clinic. I find I like nursing as well as teaching. Maybe one day I can combine them both."

"Have you thought about marriage?"

I smiled. "What young woman hasn't?"

He smiled back. "I'm sure. I have been giving it a lot of thought since I found you."

I felt my heart race. Was he going to propose?

He reached over and covered my hand with his. "I have given it a lot of thought. The odds are too high for me not to survive or to become a cripple, and I wouldn't put that burden on anyone. I will never propose until the war is ended nor will I ask you to wait for me."

It was clear to me then that Daniel had serious plans for both of us. I should have been pleased but I was uneasy. "I have never heard you talk like this, Daniel. Your ominous tone makes me shiver. Have you learned of more horrible conflicts coming?"

He did not answer that question. 'Mary, I want you to think seriously about your plans. I look at the little pebble you wear as a bond between us and it gives me much comfort. Providence has answered our prayers to be together once again, so let's pray He sees us through the rest of this tumultuous time."

Our walk back to the hotel was arm in arm, and I cherished every minute we spent. We had a few short hours as Daniel was due back at the base at eight o'clock that evening. We sadly parted with a warm hug and loving kiss. We had parted before. The problem now was that each parting was getting more difficult to endure.

Chapter 45

It was one week after Daniel left when I was tired from a long day at the hospital. My hotel room felt stuffy, so I opened the window to let in the pleasant evening air and heard the newsboy shout, "Battle of the Wilderness! Many Union dead! Come get your evening paper!"

My heart skipped a beat. I rushed from my room to the street to buy the paper then hurried back to read the full story. According to the paper, Lt. Gen. Ulysses S. Grant had begun his Overland Campaign, which would be an intent to end the war. I had witnessed the carnage left from McClellan's attempt during the Peninsula debacle. I knew first-hand what campaigns meant.

The reporter wrote that the fighting had gone on from May 5th-7th. Both Union and Confederate armies suffered heavy losses leaving over five thousand dead men.

I packed up my travel bags because I knew the boats of the Sanitary Commission would be put in use. I wanted to run to Dr. S. to ask if he was going, then thought better of it thinking he might just close the door in my face. He told me he would contact Miss Dix to see that we could be working together. I had to be patient.

I don't think I rested that night. The images of the horrible cases I had seen flooded my dreams:

heaps of amputated limbs, grotesque saber slashes, disfigured faces and bodies. I knew what lay ahead and I had to prepare myself to go through the Peninsula, Antietam, and Gettysburg once more. What about Daniel? He must have known about this plan of Grant's when he was here. Could that have been the reason for his serious tone and sadness on parting?

The next day I reported to the U.S. Sanitary Commission headquarters where I was assigned to a boat. It was May 9, 1864 when we left Alexandria with a ship filled with supplies and Sanitary Commission agents and volunteers. Two doctors were aboard but neither one of them was Dr. S.

We reached Belle Plain on the Potomac creek southeast of Fredericksburg next to a government flatboat containing horses and cavalry recruits. There were no docks so supplies were landed over pontoons. We set up a feeding station near the shore and two miles farther out. The mud was frightful as much as the rain coming on. I cannot explain the scene. It was worse than Harrison's Landing, White House and Gettysburg. The ambulance trains were a mile long. The men had been on the train for two or three days without food. There were thirty-five dead on the first train and five died on the stretchers being loaded onto the boat. Soldiers with arms gone to the shoulder, head and face injuries to disfigure them for life. Death would have been more merciful.

The men were packed onto the boats headed for the hospitals in Washington. As we finished feeding one train, another ambulance train arrived. The exhausted horses and mules pulling the ambulances were standing in a quagmire almost up to their knees. There was grain and hay to feed them that had come on the cavalry boat. The weary overworked animals ate right there in the mud.

I was assigned to a distributing area, which was filthy, but so was I from the foul weather. There were so many wounded it became necessary to load them according to their need. I had good male assistants who helped me feed and do what we could. There was a special room of soldiers of which three had died during the night. But, our diligence and hard work paid off as four boats of wounded had gotten off that day heading for the hospitals in Washington.

Then I was ordered to take the next ambulance train to Fredericksburg a few miles away as the conditions were worse there. I couldn't imagine anything worse. The ambulances moved at a slow pace over corduroy roads where every jolt was felt and many a man called out, "God have mercy!"

My assistants and I fed as we could. There were no government provisions except hard bread. When we reached Fredericksburg, I prepared for over nine hundred patient suffering men. We served eggnog, tea, coffee and a hearty soup made with chicken, turkey and beef. To this day I thank the Sanitary Commission and other relief organizations for their rations.

By May 22nd Fredericksburg was in a state of confusion. Hospital tents had been set up and orders came from Washington not to fill them. Then orders said to remove the guard from the road and take the wounded to the railroad as it would be repaired. But, the surgeons refused to send injured men over an unguarded road. Then another order came to cancel the first as the railroad would not be ready. Therefore, the hospital tents were filled.

By that time the government had sent provisions. However, getting them to the men was time consuming as the requests went through four chains of command before they could be filled.

The townspeople refused to give us anything, so we took to stealing whatever we could find: straw, hay, cornshucks, wood, cotton, etc.

Four of us nurses were housed in an older lady's home where we boarded ourselves with crackers, bread, beef and sometimes a slice of ham. The old woman had a beautiful backyard full of roses. The town would soon be deserted by the troops that were moving to the front, so we begged the old woman for the roses and she granted permission. With happy hearts we took them to the departing troops who wanted them for their bridles or saddles, lapels or wherever. A lieutenant called to me, "Give me one, miss and I'll bring it back to you." I gave him a small bouquet tied with a ribbon.

Three days later many of those soldiers returned on an ambulance train. We waited with pails of soup and milk punch. Some of the soldiers recognized us and one soldier called to me. "The Lieutenant's here and he brought your flower back as he said he would."

I rushed to his side hoping to help a wounded man. There lay the dead lieutenant with my small bouquet of roses tucked in the breast of his coat. This brave lieutenant could have been Daniel. With tears in my eyes, I lifted the crushed roses and threw them to the wind.

Chapter 46

Fredericksburg was worse than Belle Plain. The trains of wounded kept coming and we fed, bandaged, cleaned, and did our part to keep filling the boats to Washington, each sent with a silent prayer that the men would survive.

I received a letter from Jenny:

May 20, 1864

Dear Cousin Mary,

I trust this letter will reach you. Ted and I are at Port Royal on the Rappahannock and will soon be leaving for White House on the Pamunkey with seventy boats in our flotilla. This is a big campaign to end this war, but the mutilation continues.

I know that you are in Fredericksburg as Mother had news of such from Miss Dix. You may be transferred to White House, so I want you to be aware that Ted and I will both be there. The army has put him to work helping with the guarding of prisoners and supplies and transferring of prisoners. We care for the Union and Confederate wounded alike as I'm sure you do, also. It is so sad.

White House is a big Union base of operations. We have one hundred and fifty Sanitary Commission volunteers who are making the trip with us. There are also the slaves who come carrying their feather mattresses, bags of grain, pork barrels and frying pans. Some of them are dressed in what appears to be looting of their former master's home: outdated stovepipe hats, fancy umbrellas, young boys dressed in frock coats that drag to the ground, girls dressed in flowered silk dresses. They say they are coming with us and what else can we do but take them. Mr. Lincoln should have made better plans.

Anyway, dear cousin, I will close and pray we will meet at White House Landing.

Sincerely,
Jenny

Her letter cheered me. I had received a message that I was to leave for White House Landing. I needed to see some friendly faces, someone from home. Someone I could sit and talk to who knew and understood what we were going through.

Anyone who has not witnessed war first hand cannot even imagine what we in the Sanitary Commission and other helping agencies has endured.

I prepared to go to White House Landing where I had been once before during the Peninsula Campaign. The place the Confederates had chased us from in a hasty retreat.

At the dock all boats looked alike. I was alone with no one to guide me so I went aboard a boat others were boarding. It was early morning and misty. I went inside the cabin where a bearded soldier sat reading a newspaper. I sat in the first chair I saw empty when I heard the grinding of the ship as it headed south.

While I sat as quiet as a mouse, a soldier came into the cabin, walked straight to me and said, "What are you doing on the General's boat?"

He startled me. With a hasty reply and probably a weak voice, I replied, "I am with the Sanitary Commission and was told to go to White House Landing. I thought this was one of our boats."

At that point the bearded soldier put the newspaper away and said to the young soldier questioning me, "Give the lady whatever she wants." Then he went out on the deck.

"Who was that?" I asked the soldier.

"That was General Grant and this is his boat."

I was not chagrined at my mistake. Instead, I felt rather proud to be in the company of the man our country was depending on.

When we landed at White House, it was the same scene of wounded and dying men lying all over the grounds. I tried to picture a grand white house, the very place where George Washington came to court Martha Custis, but I could not.

Tents covered acres of ground with a few wooden buildings hastily erected. There were more relief agencies and nurses than I had seen before. Although Miss Dix was still called the Superintendent of Nurses, the Surgeon General had usurped some of her authority by adding a clause that allowed women to apply directly to him. Thus, many women were given the go ahead who would not have passed Miss Dix's criteria.

I found the place designated for the Sanitary Commission agents and was assigned to a tent near one of the field hospitals where I inquired about Ted and Jenny. The agent checked his list and said he had no word of their arrival.

It was June and the heat of summer was beginning. My tent was shared with two other older nurses who had come through the permission of Miss Dix. For that I was gratified as I had heard stories about unsavory conduct of other women who called themselves nurses.

Our tent was under a large tree, which was a blessing as it provided shade from the west sun. I was the last one to leave the tent that early morning and was met by an injured soldier assisted by his comrade.

"Would you take care of my arm?" he asked.

It was clear the filthy bandage had not been changed since he left the field of battle. He was ragged and dirty. I took clean bandages, lint, soap, and ointment from my bag. When I unwrapped the bandage I felt myself gag as the wound was full of creepy things, like raw meat covered with maggots. But, I persevered cleaning first with lye soap and water. I wanted to use alcohol but knew it would burn the raw flesh unmercifully. The wiggly things didn't like the lye soap and I was able to scrape them out. Then I cleaned it out with mercurial solution, applied ointment and packed the wound with lint before I wrapped clean bandages around it. An orderly was passing by. I called to him to get a clean shirt for the soldier. I cut the ragged shirt off him and cleaned and put ointment on smaller cuts and scratches covering his chest and upper arm.

When the orderly returned with the flannel shirt, the soldier gave a big smile. "It sure feels better. Thank you, sister." Off he went with the help of his buddy. I don't know what became of that soldier but I was glad I was there to help, although I had lost my appetite for breakfast.

Two days later I was standing over the cooking pot when I heard my name, "Mary?" I turned and there stood my sweet Jenny, all five feet of her with glasses reflecting the sun under the wide brim of her straw hat. I laid the long wooden stirring spoon on the table and went to her with a big hug. "Jenny! You don't know how happy I am to see you."

She stepped back and gave me a long look. "I wasn't sure it was you from the back. All these plain dresses and wide-brimmed hats make most of the women look the same."

I laughed. "And, with all the dust and grit, one has to look hard to get under the first layer."

"I didn't expect all this dust."

"Everything is thick with it. It even gets into your teeth. General Grant has ordered the grounds wet each day to reduce the grit and ease the extra burden on his injured men. He said he didn't care if it took a regiment the whole day. They are pumping water from the river. Where's Ted?"

"We have a tent with a Michigan regiment. The Sanitary agent told me where you were."

"We're stationed with a New York corps. I have two older tent mates, both from Auburn. One of them is a spinster and the other has a husband in the army. Can we get together this evening? We usually finish feeding around seven o'clock."

"Let's meet at the Sanitary Commission headquarters. It's about half way for each of us. I have so much news from home, Mary."

"And, I am dying to hear it. I'll meet you at seven-thirty." We hugged once more and I watched as she gaily bounced away before I turned back to the chore of cooking for the one hundred men under our care.

That evening Ted came with Jenny. We were a happy trio as we sat at a large wooden table outside the Commission's small frame building. Ted had no word of Daniel but assured me that he had his eye out for any soldier who may have been in his regiment. That was no easy task as there were wounded men at every step over acres of ground.

Jenny said that Emily was still in Washington and serving as a director at a hospital in Alexandria. Aunt Martha continued at supervising the New York Relief Association. The surprising news was that Abby and Florence were asked to organize a ward at Beverly Hospital in New Jersey, about fifteen miles outside of Philadelphia.

"Abby working at organizing a hospital?" I asked. "That doesn't sound like our Abby."

"I didn't think so either, but Miss Dix has given them high points. I guess she still thinks she's in charge."

263

"Did Miss Dix appoint them Sanitary Commission nurses?"

Jenny snickered. "No. I don't even think she knows who they are, but she toured the hospital and was satisfied with the way they had set up their ward of one hundred men. It wasn't without frustration as their ward surgeon was absent more than he attended and supplies were short. The surgeon ordered milk and eggs but there were no eggs. And, milk was in short supply. Abby and Florence went to the village store and made an agreement to pay for butter, eggs, milk and bread for their patients. Then they contacted Mr. Hodge for rocking chairs as the government had made no provisions for the men to sit."

"I guess Abby's winning ways came in handy," said Ted.

"It seems that way," said Jenny. "They will be leaving at the end of June because the agreement was only to organize that one ward. Abby said she will be glad to leave because old people, calling themselves philanthropic Christians, had a habit of coming through and preaching to the wounded. She said the men suffered enough without hearing a sermon. If she ran the hospital nosy do-gooders would be barred at the door."

I laughed aloud, "That sounds like Abby. What of Charley?"

Ted answered, "He's still in Washington and working as an aide to the men who think they are running the war."

"Think they are running it?" I asked.

"They're sending down orders but I think General Grant is doing as he sees fit." Ted gave a deep sigh. "I'd like to be marching along with him."

Jenny touched his good arm. "I want our baby to have a father."

My ears perked up. "Are you expecting, Jenny?"

"It's early but all signs point to it. I've been there once before if you recall."

I reached over and took her hand. "How could I forget? I'm happy for you. Shouldn't you be back in New York with Aunt Martha?"

"We're leaving at the end of the month before the really hot weather sets in. Have you run into Dr. S. again?

"No," I replied in a sad tone. "I had hoped he would contract but there has been no word if he has."

"He may seem brash to some, but I appreciated his honesty," said Jenny.

"He is cautious of letting his caring for others show. I am still in awe of him, however."

Jenny laughed. "He made me nervous."

"We need to liven this place up," Ted said. "I learned to play the fiddle, Mary. These men could use a little music."

"Ted. That's an inspiration. Come and play for my men."

"I'm still a little scratchy but no one seems to complain. When do you want me to come?"

I was elated. "How about this same time tomorrow evening?"

"We'll be there at seven-thirty."

We hugged all around before we returned to our quarters.

It was past nine o'clock and time for milk punch for our soldiers when I returned. The milk punch helped them sleep. We just had to be careful not to put too much whiskey in it.

Chapter 47

In July, Ted sent Jenny to New York. He said it was too hot and he didn't want her to take any chances of losing this baby. She protested because she did not want to separate from him. Sensible heads prevailed and she made plans to go home to the Morgan house in New York City. A part of me wanted to go along with her.

Ted and I walked her to the boat that was leaving for Washington. At least Ted was still here. We waved at the small figure dressed in a yellow dress with a wide-brimmed hat and glasses reflecting the sun. The boat pulled away from the wharf and we watched it go down the Pamunkey until it was out of sight.

"Mary, do you think she's going to be all right?"

I gave Ted the most assuring smile I could conjure up. "I think our Jenny is going to be just fine."

We walked back to our duties of the day, which were almost intolerable with the heat, swarming insects, and smells of sickness.

I insisted that the water our men were to drink was boiled first. Dr. S. had taught me the importance of clean water. It required more hauling, filling and carrying of pails. It was the assistants who balked at the extra work, "That ain't the way they do it over in the other tents."

"Well, we ain't in the other tents and this is the way we do it here." Then they'd mumble to themselves and do as I asked. Ordering others around made me feel ten years older than my twenty-three years. Even my nurse tent mates followed my instructions. Was it because I had trained with Dr. S. and learned from the medical books and papers he had given me? Did I appear more confident in caring for the sick?

Ted came over as often as he could and the soldiers loved to see him. He'd fiddle their favorite hymns and ditties and dance around the tent. One of the soldiers, who had lost both legs, had a harmonica and they would play duets. Not only was Ted's outgoing personality a lift, but here was a soldier with half an arm gone. He was one with them and had gone through their battles.

In August the White House headquarters and field hospitals were shut down. Many of us went to City Point, where the James and Appomattox Rivers meet. This had become the headquarters of the Union army. General Grant was housed in a small house where an American flag was installed on the roof.

The shabby appearance of City Point was discouraging. It was barren, almost treeless with small wooden buildings, Negro cabins, large tents. Soldiers and guards could be seen running from one tent to another.

When I arrived at the U.S. Sanitary Commission quarters, I was told that the Masonic

Mission had requested a volunteer to fill in for a nurse who was absent from the Point of Rocks Hospital, six miles up the Appomattox. It would only be for a short time, I was told. In my third year of caring for the wounded one hospital was like another to me. I agreed to go as City Point didn't look all that inviting.

Taking my traveling bags with me, I boarded a smaller boat and found a place to sit on the deck. The day was hot and muggy. I had no desire to go into an enclosed area where I would no doubt get seasick from the smell of bilge water.

I knew nothing about the hospital I was going to. I had heard stories of medical officers not behaving as gentlemen should, which caused me to question my hasty agreement to go. We steamed up the monotonous river past small bluffs and scant foliage. The hospital was set up on the bank of this narrow river. I was told Point of Rocks had been a plantation abandoned by its owner when he saw the "boys in blue".

I was apprehensive about this hospital set out by itself. A group of soldiers came out onto the deck as we were landing. I saw a refined looking major, I could tell by his shoulder straps, and decided to approach him. To my absolute delight, it was Major Cyrus Roberts whom I had ridden with on the train to Albany over a year ago.

"Why Miss Sullivan, how nice to see you again."

"Thank you, Major Roberts. I am relieved to see an acquaintance and more pleased that you recognized me. Do you know the surgeon in charge here? I would like to be assured that he is a gentleman."

He smiled and said, "It so happens that I do, and I am sure you will find him a gentleman."

When the ship docked, he said, "I will send an ambulance to take you to the general's quarters."

The ambulance arrived and I rode to General Butler's headquarters where I showed my pass and was directed to the medical man in charge. I entered the small wooden building into a dim but cozy room. There at a desk sat Major Roberts. He rose from his chair. "Miss Sullivan, I hope you will always find me a gentleman."

I know my face reddened to the roots of my hair. It was not the first time I was embarrassed, but this time I was dumbstruck.

"I'll summon an orderly to take you to your tent. You will be taking Miss Barton's place until she returns."

Miss Barton? Clara Barton was the champion of battlefield nurses. It wasn't possible I would be replacing her. "Miss Clara Barton?" I asked in a tentative voice.

"The very same," he replied. "Would you care for a cup of tea once you are settled?"

I offered a relieved smile. "At this point, Major, I can't think of anything I would like better."

"Good. I shall come by your tent in a half hour." He rang a bell on his desk and a young orderly appeared in an instant. "You are to take Miss Sullivan to Miss Barton's tent."

The major and I shared tea in the officers' dining hall, which was not more than two wooden tables with benches shrouded by mosquito netting. We talked about what had transpired since our last chance meeting. He told me he had become engaged and was planning to be married once the war was over. I told him about Daniel and showed him the pebble I wore. "We are not officially engaged, but this is our bond until the war ends."

He smiled and said he hoped it would work out for both of us. He then bolstered my courage by saying that he was sure I was capable of standing in for Miss Barton. I wish I'd had shared his confidence.

I was at Point of Rocks for two weeks overseeing and taking care of our injured men. The major and I shared a cup of tea every evening. I did not like the setup of this camp that seemed out in the middle of nowhere yet, I thanked the good Lord that he had placed Major Cyrus Roberts in my path. It seemed that at the most depressing times Providence would set me straight.

Each night I prayed for Daniel. "Where was he? Was he well? Was he out of harm's way? Why hadn't I received any news of his whereabouts?

From all reports the Union was gaining ground. Still the wounded masses continued to come. On the six mile trip back to City Point, I was wrestling with myself as to whether I had seen enough of this killing. Should I return home, secure a teaching position in a small community far away from this bloodshed?

As I stood on the deck of the boat overlooking the narrow river, thoughts of my mother popped into my head. Unlike Aunt Martha, she had shielded herself from the country's trials. She was content in her solitary way of life by keeping busy with all kinds of handwork during the winter months and vegetable gardening during the summer. I wanted to think she was sewing for our troops and maybe she was.

Then I felt a pang of guilt that I should have been a more understanding daughter. Should I have stayed close to her and continued on safe and secure? Those thoughts vanished as City Point came into view with its large tents of wounded. I knew my calling was here right where God wanted me to be.

Chapter 48

City Point was a big operating base. I was housed with another nurse about my age. Grace was a farm girl from near Syracuse, New York. In her looks, there was nothing attractive about her. She was average in height and squarely built. Her facial skin was rough and oily as was her light brown hair. With close set eyes, large nose, overweight, lumber gait, Grace was anything but comely. The one good thing, I thought, was that she and I were both from the same state.

I set my bags next to my cot and held out my hand. "I'm Mary Sullivan," I said.

"I'm Grace Fitch. It looks like they've given us the President's suite."

I looked around the tent and laughed. The tent had patches where it had been ripped, an uneven dirt floor, two narrow cots with mattresses filled with corn shucks.

I pointed to the back of the tent. "We do have a flap to let the air in."

"If you like the bugs." She pointed to the front of the tent. "There's no netting."

I laughed again. "Grace, I think you and I are going to get along just fine. Tomorrow, we'll see about having netting put up."

We did get along fine. I found her to be bright, laid back, and always with a dry sense of

273

humor. Even though she worked at a slower pace, she was methodical and I could count on her whenever the need arose.

It was in October when Sheridan's forces drove the Confederate army from the Shenandoah Valley. The Army of the Potomac was on the rise.

Two of the Northern nurses that came to City Point said they had come by way of Harper's Ferry, Virginia because they thought there would be wounded there to care for. However, they were sent south to Winchester. It wasn't an easy trip. At one point, their train was stopped because the Rebels had torn up tracks thinking the train ahead of them contained payroll cash. One of the nurses said it was unfortunate for the Confederates as the payroll was on their train along with General Custer and his men.

It was unfortunate for them, also. They left the train where all passengers, soldiers, horses, and supplies were unloaded in a torrential rain. They rode in a wagon on to Winchester after stopping for the night in Bunker Hill, which to her seemed a scruffy little place. When they stopped, wood fires were started and two soldiers rode off. They heard a shot, expecting they ran into Confederates, but the soldiers came back with a pig to roast. Those men didn't even scald it like the farmers do. In no time at all it was cut up and cooking over the fires. The only way the women got a taste of the pig was to trade it for a can of beans and tin of crackers.

The nurses said they worked a couple weeks in Sheridan's Hospital in Winchester until they were sent to City Point.

I had never seen so many volunteers before. Some of the behavior of the women was not to my liking, especially those who got into the stimulants meant for the injured men. For the most part I was proud of the work the women were doing. Those who acted otherwise were sent back to Washington, if they were caught.

I was there at City Point for almost a month when one morning I was out walking and saw a surgeon standing at his medical wagon. There was something familiar about him, so I walked to get a closer look.

I thought it was Dr. S. because he was always trim and fit like this man, but where was the unruly hair and beard?

With a brave carriage, I walked to him. "Dr. S.?"

He turned with a frown that turned into his half smile. "Well, Miss Sullivan, where have you been?"

His words did not please me in the least. "When we last met, sir, you informed me that you would let me know if you were to contract."

"No. I told you I would inform Miss Dix."

"I disagree," I said, becoming bolder by the minute. "You said you would inform Miss Dix and see that I would be assigned to work with you."

This time he actually smiled. "She's a strong-willed old lady. She said it was at her discretion as to where her nurses were placed, and she would take my request under advisement."

I simmered down a bit. "I like your hair instead of the shaggy stuff. You look much younger without the beard. Is there a young miss who's caught your eye?"

He stopped what he was doing and looked straight at me, which gave me pause. "No, Miss Sullivan. Not at this time," he answered.

"I apologize. That was unkind of me."

He didn't respond but turned back to his medicines. "Are you of a mind to work with me?" he questioned.

"Certainly. It will be up to the surgeon in charge," I replied.

Without looking at me, he said, "I am the surgeon in charge of this unit."

"Then why didn't you come looking for me before?"

He turned with an exasperated sigh. "I was told you were at the Point of Rocks Hospital. Now, I have duties to attend. I will expect to see you here after the second feeding of your men."

My insides bubbled with joy, but I kept my composure. "Thank you, sir. I shall be here."

"Be on your way, Miss Sullivan. I will take care of the matter."

"Could my friend, Grace, also be assigned to your unit?"

"You are trying, Miss Sullivan. There is only so much within my power."

"I'm sorry," I said and left before I further irritated him.

Back at our station Grace was bending over the big pot of farina she was cooking for our soldiers.

"Grace, you'll never guess my good news," was my enthusiastic greeting.

"The war is over and we're all going home."

"No. It's not that good. I stumbled onto Dr. S. Remember me telling you about him?"

"How could I forget? You hold him higher than the president. Not quite next to God, but close."

"He's an excellent surgeon. Anyway, he told me to report to his tent after our second feeding. I asked if you could be assigned there, also."

Grace continued stirring the farina. "Scoop out a couple of these flies while you're standing there. What makes you think I want to go work with him?"

"Because you're smart and he appreciates intelligence."

"You're just trying that to butter me up so you don't have to go alone."

I stuck up my nose. "That's not true, I do many things by myself."

"All right then, from what you've told me about him, if something goes wrong you don't want to be the one who catches the devil for it."

I was chagrined. "I thought you would be pleased. We work well together."

She turned her wide frame and smiled. "I wanted to get you riled up so you have extra energy to feed these one hundred men. The farina's about ready."

"I can feed five men to your one."

"That's the idea." She grinned from ear to ear.

Chapter 49

Jenny wrote:

Dear Mary,

I trust this letter will reach you at City Point. I hope you are still doing well. As for me, I am growing by the day along with the baby. My appetite is enormous.

Have you worked with Dr. S. once more? I know you hoped for that. And, what about Daniel? Ted has had no word.

Ted is back in Washington. He is discharged from the army. However, he has signed on as an agent with the Sanitary Commission.

The newspapers call General Grant a butcher, but I believe he is doing what is needed to get our beloved country back together. I earnestly pray that the politicians in Washington have the country foremost as they seem to be consumed with the coming election.

After the first of the year there will be a new baby Stevens. The doctor says I am in good health and there should be no complications. Won't it be wonderful when we are all together again?

Until that time Mother, Abby, and Florence keep busy boosting the stores of the Sanitary Commission. The Metropolitan Fair will be held soon with each society woman trying to outdo the other. It tickles me to see the quiet competition. It is for a good cause.

Our men in the military, Johnathan and Charley, are also stationed in Washington, along with Abby's Edward. Ted said the four of them get together as often as they can. He says because they enjoy each other's company. As Ted is not of the station as the other three, I was not sure how he would be accepted. I know you will understand.

If Johnathan ever gets settled with an appointment, Florence says she and Baby Johnathan will join him. We cannot call him Baby Johnathan much longer because he is trying his best to walk. He does brighten the house.

With colder temperatures coming on and General Grant seeming to be bogged down in Petersburg, we are hoping that furloughs will be granted and we can all spend another Christmas together?

Do you have any thoughts about returning? You rate right up there with the other notable women of the Northern nurses.

I must close, dear Mary, for I have rambled on enough.

May God's peace be with you,
Jenny

I tucked the letter into my apron pocket. I was pleased to hear that Jenny was doing well. It was good that she had left this hot, muggy place before the onslaught of gnats, flies, mosquitos, fleas and lice that plagued the sick men and the rest of us.

We could walk or wave them away, which was not true of many of our injured.

Had I thoughts of returning? Frequently. Every time the desire hit me, I would be confronted by more wounded. I knew I should do my part.

Grace and I were both assigned to Dr. S. He secured a rather comfortable building for us near the field hospital he overlooked. We had two cots with feathered mattresses, two small windows, a wood floor and a door. Outside the officer's dining hall we found two apple crates to use any way we pleased. Small luxuries.

"I wonder how we rate this grand hotel," Grace mused.

"I'm sure our benefactor will make us pay for it in one way or another," I replied.

And he did. The medical wagon contained about seventy different medicines. Dr. S. expected us to know their names and what they were used for. If he called for a certain medicine we were to procure it for him, which saved him valuable time in treating the men.

Grace and I took our free time to study the drugs, learn all we could about them, and then test each other as to our knowledge. The surgeon in charge should have been pleased, but the surgeon in charge was Dr. S. and he expected proficiency.

Most disconcerting was when he would come into the ward unexpectedly, and he'd call out for a medicine. Either Grace or I would have to stop what we were doing and hurry to the medicine wagon. I was usually the one to do his bidding because I was faster on my feet than Grace.

One day he asked me to spell the name of the medicine that was written in Latin, which I did.

"Why is it that you can name and spell this word but you cannot pronounce my last name properly?"

I found the man irksome. "I am well versed in Latin," I replied. "I can spell your name, S-c-h-o-c-k-e-m-o-h-l-e, I just cannot pronounce it to your satisfaction."

"My first name is Karl, the German spelling with a K. Is that easier for you?"

"Yes and also for a five-year-old," came my sarcastic reply.

He was treating the stump of a soldier's leg. "Hold up his leg so I can wrap this," he said.

I gently lifted the injured part while he sprinkled alum on the healing stump, then skillfully wrapped the wounded part.

We left the bedside. Out of earshot I asked, "Dr. S. Do you ever say please or thank you?"

He hesitated. "Will you please call me, Karl?"

I was taken aback. "If you prefer that, I will call you Dr. Karl."

"Thank you," he said and walked away.

I went to where Grace was giving a patient some apple juice. "Grace, I do not understand that man. He now wants to be called Dr. Karl."

Grace finished with the soldier and turned to me. "What's the matter with that?"

We started to walk to the Diet Kitchen. I shrugged. "I guess nothing, but if he didn't like me calling him Dr. S. why didn't he tell me before this? He certainly let me know he didn't like me mispronouncing his last name."

"Maybe shaving his beard and changing his hair style gives him a softer edge. Dr. Karl sounds more human. I like him. He wants what's best for the men."

I considered what she said. "I like him too. I just wish he wasn't so crusty."

Grace stopped walking and looked at me. "Do you think it is to keep from getting too close? Every time he has to dismember a limb from these young men, barely out of childhood, it has to tear at his heart."

Her words were like a snap of lightning. "Grace, that possibility never entered my mind."

We continued on to gather up jelly and crackers to give our soldiers, a small boost for the day.

After the afternoon feeding I went outside to enjoy breathing some cooler October air. All of a sudden there was a large boom. I looked toward the dock to see an ordinance ship had exploded. I watched it rain muskets, shells, cannon balls, splintered wood, and every kind of debris before it burst into flames. It was far more impressive than any Fourth of July fireworks show I had ever seen. Grace came running out of the hospital tent.

"I've never seen you hurry so fast," I teased.

"Holy mackerel!" she exclaimed. "I thought the Rebels were at the door."

"I've never seen anything like it," I said. "We'd better get back inside and let our boys know that all is well.'

When we went back into the hospital I saw Ben, one of my favorite soldiers, who couldn't have been more than eighteen. He was sick with the fever and dysentery. Ben had crawled from his cot and was in the rocking chair next to the pot-bellied stove. I went to him and tucked a blanket around his frail shoulders. "Are you feeling bad, Ben? Do you want some water? Some jelly?"

He tried to smile. "No, ma'am. I just want to sit here and rock."

We were saddened by the loss of the few soldiers on the ordinance ship, but I was feeling numb to death. I worked with it each day when I went into our unit to find we had lost another of our brave men. That same morning I found that Ben had died.

The camp diseases continued. Dr. Karl, I got used to his name, was a stickler for cleanliness and more than once I watched as he reprimanded a nurse or assistant for sloppy work. Our patients were segregated as to their medical conditions, which made our unit one of the healthiest at City Point.

Grace and Dr. Karl worked well together, although he always requested me for surgery.

We were working on a patient when I said, "You seem to always choose me for surgery. Why not Grace?"

Dr. Karl replied, "Miss Fitch has a quick mind, but a slow pace. Would you rather not be my assistant?" he asked.

"Of course not."

He looked at me. "Then why do you ask. Idle conversation, Miss Sullivan. Put your nose to the grindstone."

Chapter 50

Clashes of the two armies slowed, but still the wounded came and the mutilation continued. The race against time to save a man's life was ever present.

While working one morning with a fresh batch of wounded, I was startled when a soldier walked to my side and took my arm. He was filthy, bearded, dusty and almost black from the battle. I started to pull away.

"Mary," he said.

I looked closely and there saw the kind, brown eyes of Daniel Phillips.

"My God, Daniel! I didn't recognize you."

"Can you come outside?"

I called to Grace to finish my work of cleaning up the soldier I was attending and walked outside with my battle-scarred Daniel.

In a private spot he took me into his arms and we stood there neither saying a word, relishing the feeling of being back together. I didn't mind his haggard, rough and smelly condition. He was Daniel and he was in one piece.

"I have been so worried about you. It has been months," I murmured into his shoulder.

"We're almost there. Mary. We are gaining ground and the Rebels cannot supply their troops."

We finally separated and sat on the ground under one of the few trees on that bleak barren shore.

"Have you been well?" he asked.

"Yes. Some of the nurses grew ill and had to go home. A few have not made it home."

We sat holding hands. His were calloused and mine chafed from the work.

"What happens next, Daniel? Will you be staying here at headquarters?"

"For the time being, anyway. I want to get cleaned up. Where's your tent?"

I smiled. "My nurse friend and I have a small building near our unit, thanks to Dr. Karl."

"And, who is Dr. Karl?" inquired Daniel.

I laughed. "I used to call him Dr. S. He signed on again with the Sanitary Commission and I've been working with him."

A smile appeared on Daniel's face. "The same man who treated me."

"Yes it is. He'll remember you, Daniel."

He kissed my hand. "We are going to eat in the officers' quarters for supper. I'm sure the food is better than what you've been eating."

I laughed and kissed his cheek. "What time?"

"Six-thirty," he said as he helped me to my feet. "It'll take me that long to look presentable." He grabbed me into a bear hug. "I'm so glad to see you."

We parted and I went back to help in the hospital tent. I could hardly wait to tell Grace.

"Ah, Daniel, the mystery man," she said. "I knew you wouldn't leave without a good reason. Does that mean I'm going to have to serve the milk punch by myself tonight?"

"I should be back by then, besides you have two helpers."

"When do I get to meet this man of yours?" Grace asked.

"I'll see if he can come by after supper."

Dr. Karl was standing outside the Diet Kitchen.

I was in a chirpy mood. "Daniel is here, Dr. Karl. We're having supper in the officers' hall."

"Your young man is back," he said. He looked at me for a long moment. "How is he?"

"He seems to be fine. I shall tell him you inquired."

I almost danced away as I went to put on the only suitable dress I had, the blue cotton I used for travel.

Daniel came at six-thirty looking clean in a new uniform with lighter skin where his beard had been. The summer Virginia sun had browned and leathered his face. When I answered his knock, he stepped inside and kissed me soundly. "Why don't we stay here?"

I sighed. "Two reasons. I have a roommate and I'm starved."

"My practical Mary," he replied.

This officers' dining hall held tables and chairs. There were a few other women there, so I did not feel out of place. Many wives followed their men during the war. Officers' wives had better accommodations than those of the enlisted men, but this dining hall was not lavish. It was in a building instead of a tent. The individual tables held a white candle in a tin candleholder placed on what had been a white doily.

We sat at a small table. Daniel walked to the serving counter and brought back two plates of food. "Anybody's guess," he said as he laid them on the table. I wasn't sure what was on the plate as the interior of the building was shadowy and lit by lanterns. There was a pot of tea on the table so I poured each of us a cup.

Before we began eating he held up his cup. "May we share many more evenings together."

I touched my cup to his and smiled at him across the table. "I can't believe you are here, Daniel. I feel almost as if I am living in a dream."

"Then let us dream on, Miss Mary. There is no war and we are the only two in our own little world."

We ate our dinners, which was far better than our usual rations. There were beef ribs, mashed potatoes, gravy, beans and a piece of fresh bread with butter. Then came the big surprise, a slice of apple pie was delivered to the tables by one of the cooks.

I looked across at Daniel. "I am living in a dream. I haven't had apple pie since I left New York."

We laughed together and relished each bite of that slightly sour pie. Sugar was a guarded commodity.

"Do you think they might have an extra piece I can take back to Grace?" I asked Daniel.

"I can ask." In a matter of minutes he came back with half a pie in a cardboard box. "The cook's from Vermont," he beamed.

Back at our place, Grace was getting milk punch ready for the evening feeding.

"Look what Daniel's brought us," I said as I proudly sat down the box.

She leaned over the box. "Do I smell apple pie?" She raised her hands toward heaven. "Thank you, Lord."

I laughed as I grabbed her hand and turned to Daniel. "Daniel, this is my friend, Grace."

He gave a slight bow. "I am most pleased to meet you, Miss Grace."

She shook his hand with a hearty grip. "I'm always proud to meet one of our brave souls," she answered. "Mary, here, has been dancing on air all afternoon."

"Grace, you're embarrassing me," I told her.

"What is there to be embarrassed about? You've worried over him for a long time and he's finally here." She stepped back and took him in. "And, in mighty fine shape, I might add."

"We've got half a pie," I told her. "Do you think we should invite Dr. Karl for a bite? He might like to say hello, Daniel."

"By all means," agreed Daniel. "If anyone deserves a piece, he does."

"Don't be discouraged if he refuses," warned Grace. "He keeps himself in trim shape."

Daniel and I walked hand in hand to his tent where the surgeon was reading by lantern light.

I made a rustling sound outside before I went around the open flap of the tent. "Dr. Karl?" He looked up from the page. "Would you like to come over for a piece of apple pie?"

Daniel stepped beside me.

"Lieutenant Phillips. It's good to see you in one piece." Dr. Karl rose from his chair and came to shake Daniel's hand. "Are you doing well?"

"Yes, sir," Daniel answered, "thanks to your skills."

"What's this about apple pie?"

"The cook at the officers' dining hall gave Daniel half a pie and we'd like to share it with you," I said.

"That's the best news I've heard in a long time. Let me get my hat."

Back at the site, Grace had brewed a pot of coffee, and the four of us sat together eating apple pie and laughing till tears ran down. Grace was full of stories about her farm life. The funniest was when the pigs got out and she chased them down the road for a mile. Another farmer came out to the road, fired a gun, and the pigs all turned around and squealed all the way back home almost trampling her in the process.

"I moved as fast as I did that day the ordinance ship blew up."

Even Dr. Karl laughed. I was glad we had invited him to share the pie. Before he went back to his tent, he said, "Lieutenant Phillips, I wish you well. To you ladies, thank you all for a respite from our trying work."

Was this the Dr. Karl I knew?

Grace cleaned up from our impromptu party while I said good night to Daniel. I watched as he walked away to join his regiment. For once, I looked forward to tomorrow.

Chapter 51

In October of 1864, Dr. Henry Bellows of the Sanitary Commission sent a letter to General Grant. The letter was sent with five copies of the report of the "Commission of Inquiry" appointed by the U.S. Sanitary Commission. There were grave concerns regarding the treatment of prisoners held in Rebel hands. The intent of the letter was to forge an agreement with the Confederates to allow the U.S. Sanitary Commission to aid the Union prisoners.

The bulk of the Union army was fronted between Petersburg and Richmond, a distance of about twenty-five miles.

Daniel came whenever he had free time. We walked and talked and many times sat silently as the watch fires up and down the James and Appomattox glowed in the fall evening air. Perhaps it was a false feeling of comfort for the enemy was still out there.

One morning, I woke with an excruciating headache. Grace went for Dr. Karl.

He came and after examining me, he held a concerned look, which for Dr. Karl was rare. I could not bend my head or neck and my head throbbed with a vengeance.

"Miss Fitch, find two orderlies to erect a tent next to mine. Miss Sullivan will have to be moved from here and away from the hospital."

Grace and Dr. Karl moved outdoors where I could hear mumbling, but I could not understand what they were saying. Not long after that, I was carried on my cot to a small tent with only a stove in the interior. I did hear Dr. Karl order the inside of the building where Grace would remain to be scoured with a mixture of baking soda and vinegar and the floor sprinkled with lime. Windows and the door were left open to let in fresh air. Even in my sad state I knew Dr. Karl suspected my condition was contagious.

Once inside the tent was better as the sun did not penetrate to hurt my eyes. I lay straight as an arrow with my eyes closed.

I felt a warm hand in mine before I heard his soft voice, "Mary." Dr. Karl had never called me by my first name. I tried to open my eyes, and, when I did, I saw he was wearing a mask. "I suspect you have meningitis, although I am not sure of the source. However, I am taking precautions."

The news was blunt. I know I gripped his hand as I knew what meningitis meant and I knew the outcome was most times fatal. At that moment I was so miserable anything to relieve the god-awful throbbing would have been a blessing. I was burning with fever and my whole body hurt.

Dr. Karl brought a basin of cool water with a mixture of alcohol and placed a soaked rag on my forehead, bathed my face and neck. "I am going to give you some opium to address the pain. Then I am going to mix my own remedy. It will have a bitter taste, but it is the best I know how."

I wasn't sure if he was talking to me or assuring himself. The opium put me in a hazy state and dulled some of the pain. I knew Grace had come at some time. I recognized her voice as my mind was in and out of the real world.

For a whole week I remained in that state. The bitterness of the medicine Dr. Karl concocted, even though it was disguised in honey or apple sauce, caused nausea. I had to fight to keep it down. I relished the drugs to relieve the pain. By the seventh day I was able to sit on the edge of the cot. Never had I felt so weak.

Dr. Karl came into the tent. "You are back with us, Miss Sullivan."

I looked up under hooded lids. "I will have to tell my body that. What day is this?"

"This is your seventh day since you became ill. You are to continue with the medicine, drink plenty of water and eat crackers and broth. As you tolerate those, you will be able to get into more solid foods."

"What is wrong with me?"

"You are recovering from a serious infection I believe was caused by the bite of some bug. Maybe a mosquito, even at this time of year. I think the toxin entered your blood stream."

"How much longer must I take that nasty tasting medicine?"

Dr. Karl smiled. "You have been my guinea pig. I am pleased to see that it helped or it appears it did. I want you to take it four more days."

I wrinkled my nose at him.

"Do you think you can stand? The quicker you can be on your feet the better it will be for you. You know that."

I wasn't sure I could stand but I had to try. I reached my hands toward him. He put his arms around me and pulled me to my feet. "How do you feel now?"

If someone had told me that one day I would be standing in Dr. Karl's arms, I would have told them they had lost their mind. But, there I was.

"I need to lie down. I feel dizzy."

He sat me back on the cot. "I will have Miss Fitch assist you four times a day until you are steady on your feet. Are you ready to see your young man? I have not allowed anyone into this tent except Miss Fitch and myself."

"Did Daniel come by?" I asked.

"Too often," he replied and left the tent.

It was after supper when Daniel arrived. A lantern lighted my cozy tent and a fire crackled in the stove. Grace had found a kettle and kept water and tea leaves to brew a cup for me whenever I wanted it.

I was so happy to see Daniel. I could sit on the edge of the cot for a short time, so he helped me to a sitting position. "Come sit next to me, Daniel. I think I'm good for a few minutes."

He smiled and kissed my forehead before he sat next to me taking my hand in his. "You scared all of us, Mary."

"Including me," I replied. "Dr. Karl assures me I will recover with time."

"He told me I was not to stay long and to be gentle in my affections."

I laughed. "That sounds like him. I'm not sure I would still be here if not for him."

"Are you going home? He thinks it best if you do."

I looked over at him. "It seems you and Dr. Karl have had conversations regarding my recovery."

He kissed my hand. "Don't be offended. It's only because we both want what's best for you."

I laid my head on his shoulder. "I'm sorry. Does it seem fair after these weeks of worry that you are here and I should leave?"

He put his arm around me. "Let's not talk about it now. Once you have had more time to heal, you will know what you have to do."

That was my sensible Daniel. We sat together for fifteen minutes before I had to lie back down, drained of energy.

It took two weeks before I felt strong enough to take short walks around the camp. Daniel came as often as he could. He and Grace were pleased with my progress.

Dr. Karl was not. He called me into his tent. "Miss Sullivan, I believe you should prepare to go home." Never did he beat around the bush.

"I don't think so. I am much stronger. I should be able to work in the hospital in another week."

"Sit down," he ordered, which I did in a chair beside his desk.

"What makes you think that?" he asked.

"As I said, I am stronger."

Looking straight at me, he said, "I am the surgeon in charge and I say you need full rest or you will wear yourself out and be right back on the cot."

I knew he was right. I was pale, had lost weight, and was always tired. I didn't want to leave Daniel.

Dr. Karl held up a paper. "My contract is up in three days and I am not extending it. The Commission is aware and has secured a replacement. The volunteers are coming in droves, which means there are others to take your place. Go home and get your health back."

His words sent me into a spin. I did not want to work with another surgeon. "You're needed here."

"I'm tired, Mary." It was the second time he had called me by my first name. "I can make arrangements for you to leave with me, so I can see you safely back. Once you are well, you can do as you please."

I didn't respond immediately, although I could see his reasoning. "I will think about it," I said.

"You have until tomorrow morning," he replied.

That night Daniel and I discussed the matter. With reluctance, we came to the conclusion that Dr. Karl was right. It would be the smart move to make. In my weakened condition I was of no use to anyone.

Grace said she was leaving after Christmas. She was needed on the farm and had done her part. "I'll go home, fatten up those animals and grow crops to feed our boys."

The day before I left Daniel and I spent the whole day together. He said Dr. Karl had promised him that he would stay with me until I was safely settled.

He could not come when the boat was to leave, and for that I was relieved. Too many times we had to part on a sad note. I didn't want to see him waving from the shore.

It was cold on the boat. The water was choppy, which didn't agree with my stomach. I could have gone into the large cabin where stoves gave out warmth, but I preferred to stay on the deck. There were many wounded making the trip with Dr. Karl and me. As much as I wanted to help, I could barely help myself. Dr. Karl was called upon when the need arose. I sat in a sheltered spot he found for me, which was comfortable enough. He brought two wool blankets. "You need to stay warm if you insist on staying here," he said.

I thanked him with a smile. Was my welfare his concern or was it that he didn't want me to decline and become a bigger burden? It wouldn't do to lapse back into a weaker state.

City Point, the bustling Union headquarters, drifted from view as the ship pushed out into the ocean heading north for the Chesapeake Bay and the Potomac River.

Dr. Karl brought hot coffee and a sandwich for lunch, which I devoured. I hadn't eaten much for breakfast. My stomach had been in knots anticipating the trip ahead. Now that we were underway a peaceful calm had settled over me.

At suppertime Dr. Karl appeared and insisted I go to the dining area to eat. We ate in a room with the few officers aboard. It was good to listen to their good-natured bantering. We had stew, fresh bread and plain cake.

Dr. Karl sat across from me. "How are you doing?"

I looked across the table that doubled as a checkerboard. "Fine. I'm glad I'm going home. Are you going to your private office or work in the hospitals?"

I noticed his slate-blue eyes were without the tiredness I had seen so often. Perhaps it was because we were away from City Point and he was going back to Washington, I don't know. On this evening he was the kind person who had lent me his medical books after we shared tea in his garden. I liked his neat hair and clean-shaven face. He was always in trim shape.

"I need away from this insane butchery, Miss Sullivan. At this time I am unsure of what I will do, I know that I need a respite from our wounded and so do you."

I grew bold. "I would like it if you called me Mary. I remember hearing you say my name when I was ill. Too often I feel like I'm walking on egg shells in your presence."

He set his coffee cup on the table before a half smile appeared. "I know I have that effect on people. I'm sorry if you're uncomfortable." He changed the subject. "Are you going to stay with your relatives in New York City or going to your parents?"

I took a bite of my cake before I answered him. "Do you plan on going with me?"

"I promised Lieutenant Phillips that I would see you safely home."

It surprised me he remembered it was my relatives who lived in the city, not my parents. It was clear he planned to see me home so I told him I would stay in the hotel in Washington, where I'd stayed before. I figured I could go on to Albany by myself.

"That is not acceptable. You should go to your cousins where you are among relatives. Healing the whole person is necessary."

He was good at changing a subject before I could disagree. "How is Mrs. Stevens?" So, he did remember Jenny and me talking about Jenny and my New York City relatives.

"She says she is doing well. There will be a baby Stevens after the first of the year."

He nodded. "Good news. One miscarriage does not mean all is lost. " He buttered another piece of bread. "How did your parents accept your decision to leave teaching?"

I shrugged. "About the way anyone would, I guess. They thought I was making a big mistake. Father thought I was out of my mind and Mother worried about the pension I would lose."

He said, with a serious tone, "I might have agreed with them. One thing this war has taught me is that tomorrow is never sure. Have you had regrets?"

I shook my head. "I have learned much. I like medicine, and I thank you for sharing your knowledge. If I had stayed teaching I would not have met Daniel, or enjoyed the time with my cousins, or signed on with the Sanitary Commission. I have gained ten years of knowledge in three."

He cocked his head to the side, "Have you? What about Lieutenant Phillips? Do you have plans?"

I showed him the pebble I wore. "This is what keeps him uppermost in my mind. He hints that he has plans for us after the war ends."

"But, no formal commitment?"

I shook my head. "No. Daniel is very sensible."

Dr. Karl shook his head. "No, Mary. If he were sensible you would have a ring on your finger and follow your soldier like many of the army wives do."

That ended the conversation for he pushed his chair back from the table before he came around to where I sat mulling over his words. "Now, you have been up far too long. There is a cot in the cabin you may use for the night."

"It is not necessary for you to watch over me like a mother hen," I told him.

"I am watching over you as a surgeon in charge."

"In charge of what? I am not a patient." I said.

"I made a promise to Lieutenant Phillips," he answered.

The cot in the cabin was among other female volunteers with the Sanitary Commission. Men sleeping on cots were not too far away from the women so I slept in my clothes. It was good to lie down. I don't think I slept well as many times Dr. Karl's words popped into my mind. What did he mean by saying Daniel wasn't sensible? Of course he was. I did not want to become a widow at twenty-three.

One more day and we would be in Washington. I hoped for a hot bath and clean change of clothing before taking the train to New York. I knew there would likely be an overnight in Washington, and I could get a room for the night in the same hotel where I had stayed so often. If Dr. Karl was determined to see me to the Morgan house in New York City, he would just have to work out the details himself.

Chapter 52

The boat docked at dank, shabby Alexandria where a soldier drove us across the bridge into Washington. I planned on going to the hotel. However, Dr. Karl had other plans. "You are to come stay at my place overnight. The housekeeper will provide whatever you need."

"I planned on going to the hotel."

"Miss Sullivan I promised to see you safely settled and that is what I intend to do."

He was back to Miss Sullivan. "Sir, you have seen me safely from City Point to here. I am perfectly capable of taking the train to New York. You have fulfilled your promise to Daniel."

He ignored me and gave the directions to the driver once we crossed into the city.

The rest of the way was in silence. Washington still looked like a city caught in a war. Here in late November it appeared bleak with the leaves gone and the putrid smells of unsanitary conditions. Lots of freed slaves had been sent here, but to what? The government was slow at providing what was needed. Did those men running the country ever think ahead?

The housekeeper answered Dr. Karl's knock with a questioning look, but no exclamation of surprise.

"We're back, Mrs. Miller. You remember Miss Sullivan."

It was then she smiled. "Of course, welcome, Miss Sullivan." It may have been Dr. Karl's house but Mrs. Miller was the housekeeper. She quietly reprimanded him. "I received no word you were coming. Guests take preparation."

"Nonsense," he said as he set our trappings on the wood floor. "You always have the house in shape. Miss Sullivan is on her way to her relatives. You can set her up in the guest room. I expect supper at six as usual. I'll be in my study."

He left the housekeeper and me standing in the foyer. She shook her head with a big sigh. "The doctor can be exasperating," she said. "Come along, dear, I'll show you to your room."

I started to pick up my case but she held up her hand. "I'll have Tim bring them up. He's our man who takes care of everything I can't."

I followed her up the curved stairs. "I'm sorry to be so much trouble."

"You are no trouble. It's good to have another woman in the house."

The guest room was straight ahead at the top of the stairs. She opened the door and I was pleased to see a flowered spread on the twin bed. There were curtains to match at the window that overlooked the garden. There was nothing pretty about a garden in November, but I liked looking down at it.

"I'll have Tim fill the tub with hot water for a bath. I'm sure you are weary from your trip." She

305

was kind not to mention that I looked worn out, which I felt. I also felt I needed to explain what I was doing there with Dr. Karl so I told her the whole story.

"You don't have to explain, Miss Sullivan. The doctor is a gentleman. I'm sorry to hear you were so ill, and I'm pleased you are on the mend."

There was a full-length mirror in the bathroom. After removing my dress, petticoat and underpinnings, I was shocked to see how much weight I had lost. There were dark circles under my eyes. I believe I looked as haggard as some of our wounded. It was no wonder Dr. Karl insisted on seeing me to a safe place.

I sat at the dining table in my blue dress that Mrs. Miller had washed and ironed while I napped after my bath. I hadn't felt this clean in a long time. The camps were always dirty, the stench of animals ever present, and the awful foul smell of our sick men permeated the air. I had dealt with all kinds of mice, rats, lice, worms, and bugs. My hands were still red and chafed from the hard work.

"You look very nice, Miss Sullivan," said Dr. Karl. "Did you get a restful nap?"

"Yes, thank you. The warm bath was heavenly. It has been a long time since I've enjoyed such a comfortable mattress."

"Better than the hotel?" he asked.

I had to smile. "You know it was."

"I'm happy to be back, Miss Sullivan. I believe we both needed to leave to keep our sanity. It is no wonder some of our young men will never regain their senses."

"Let's not talk about the war," I said. "What time will the train leave tomorrow?"

"Are you getting anxious to leave?"

I shook my head. "It's not that I am anxious, but I would like to feel settled. I saw my reflection in the mirror upstairs. No one told me I looked so bad."

"That would serve no purpose. You don't look bad, you look like someone who has come through a serious illness. Bad is some of those women who followed the army camps. Their behavior is going to haunt them in the days ahead."

I knew what he meant, although I felt sorry for many of them.

"The train leaves from Union Station at six-forty. Are your relatives aware you are coming?"

Did my relatives know I was coming? Of course they didn't. I had no excuse. "No."

"Then I shall send Tim to the telegraph office and have him wait for a reply."

"That could take hours," I protested.

"Not if I request an immediate reply. Do you expect no one is at home?"

I shook my head. "The maid is always there, and I suspect Jenny is confined until the baby comes."

"Then Tim will be compensated for his time, and we shall have your answer before going off on a wild goose chase."

Those words brought me out of any guilt I may have felt. "I am no more at fault for not contacting my aunt than you for not letting Mrs.

Miller know you were coming home and bringing a guest."

"You do speak your mind, Miss Sullivan."

Mrs. Miller had baked a pineapple cake for dessert as it was one of Dr. Karl's favorites. I had eaten my fill of lamb chops, baked beans and fried apples, but I could not refuse the cake.

Dr. Karl did not seem bothered by my admonishment. He enjoyed the cake and took a second piece. "It's been a long time since I've tasted Mrs. Miller's cake," he said.

At eight-fifteen Tim returned with a reply telegram from New York: Mary…welcome…anytime…we are joyous.

At six-forty the next morning Dr. Karl and I left the Union Station on the train headed for New York City. I was glad to leave Washington behind. It was a quiet ride as I spent the time looking out the grimy window, often thinking of Daniel, and the doctor spent his time reading. In my heart, I was glad he was with me as I still tired easily, and I knew my mind was fuzzy at times. I had to wonder if it was Providence at work to make me leave the sad conditions I faced each day at City Point.

Dr. Karl left the train at the Baltimore stop and returned with an egg sandwich wrapped in wax paper and a pint jar of tea.

"How did you manage that?" I asked.

"Much is available if one is willing to pay for it," was his answer.

"I am able to pay for my food."

"Certainly you are. Accept it as a gift. Are you so difficult with everyone who tries their best to become a friend?"

I knew I had offended him, which I seemed to have a habit of doing. "I'm sorry. It was kind of you and I thank you."

He took his seat beside me. "Miss Sullivan, you can be difficult."

"I guess that makes us even," came my sharp reply. Then I was sorry I had said it, but I didn't apologize. I knew my irritation stemmed from my illness. I did not like to depend on anyone.

He gave a deep sigh. "We have a trip ahead of us. I suggest we call a truce. From now on, we will ride as friends. I will call you Mary, which you seem to prefer, and you will call me Karl, which I prefer. I am not your doctor and you are not my patient. We are two close acquaintances going to New York." He pulled out his book and began reading.

"I don't feel right calling you by your first name."

He didn't look up from his book. "Why not?"

"Because you must be ten years older than me. I was taught to call my elders with a polite address."

This time he looked over at me. "You have chided me for being tactless."

"I wasn't being tactless, I was stating a fact."

"Do as you wish," he said and continued reading.

I sat and replayed this conversation over in my mind. He meant to try to be genuinely friendly, and I was beginning to sound like a shrew. "I am sorry. I will call you Karl." He kept his nose in the book he was reading.

I napped some of the time, although each jolt of the train woke me up. There were stops along the way with the loading and unloading of passengers. It was a long tiring trip.

The train stopped at the New York Central station. We left the passenger car and found a bench to sit on until our cases were placed on the luggage platform.

I looked around. It seemed nothing had changed since I had last been here. How could that be when I had seen so much death and destruction? Were these people going about their daily lives oblivious to what was going on in this country? This nonchalance annoyed me and I felt myself grow tense.

Then there was a warm hand on mine. "You'll get used to it, Mary. It will take time."

As if he sensed my feelings, I relaxed. "I've never questioned a person's way of life before. I don't like feeling like this. It's as though I'm on edge all the time."

"It will pass. You need to be back where there is some normalcy. Good food, plenty of rest, close friends and you will be back to your former health."

"I hope so. I do understand now why you refused to let me make this trip by myself. I may not have lasted past Baltimore."

"If that far," he replied.

The touch of his hand gave me solace. "I've decided it is all right for me to call you Karl."

A half smile appeared. "I heard you on the train. That's one thing settled."

I nodded. "I'm not sure I'm up to walking too far. My body still thinks it's riding on the rumbling train tracks."

He took his hand from mine. "Sit a while longer while I arrange for the luggage and transportation. We have rooms at the Fifth Avenue Hotel for the rest of the night. I will see you to your relatives in the morning." Off he went.

It was close to one o'clock in the morning when we reached the hotel, but New Yorkers never seem to pay attention to the clock. People were coming and going. We followed a bellboy up the stairs to the second floor. He unlocked both doors and set our cases inside the rooms.

I waited until he was gone before I turned and said, "Karl, if I don't appear to be grateful, I do thank you for all you have done for me."

His smile was my reward. "You are welcome, Mary."

I didn't have the energy left to open my case and pull out my nightgown. I slept in my chemise and pantaloons. Morning would come too soon.

And the morning did come early. I was up and eager to see my cousins when Karl tapped on my door. He looked refreshed in a brown suit, high-collared white shirt and natty tie. Stately and trim, he was a fine looking figure.

311

"We will have breakfast before we go on to your relatives."

I wore a white blouse, heavy sweater, long navy skirt and navy felt hat. New York was cold in November. "I'm all set to go. A cup of hot tea should get me fully awake."

He took the key from my hand and locked the door behind me before he took my arm and escorted me down the stairs and into the dining room.

We sat near a window where I could see the city waking up. In less than a week I had come far away from City Point, away from Daniel.

A white tablecloth covered the table for two. There were chandeliers hanging from the tall ceiling and caramel-colored velvet drapes at the long windows. I loved sitting in such an inviting room. The menus were on the table so I began perusing the bill of fare.

Karl sat across from me. "What do you fancy?"

"Poached eggs on toast and tea."

"A good choice," he replied. "Did you sleep well?"

"Yes, I did. It seems I sleep too much."

He looked over at me. "You have been seriously ill. A person doesn't bounce back quickly from a serious illness. You should realize that."

The waiter came to the table and took our orders.

A question had been gnawing at me since I left Virginia. "Karl, why did you come with me?

Was it only because you promised Daniel you would see me safely home?"

He didn't hesitate. "I did promise your young man, and I keep my word. I was also concerned for you because you have a streak of stubbornness about not admitting you are not ready to be on your own. It was a coincidence I was leaving City Point and it was time you left, also."

"I could have stayed in Washington until I was back on my feet."

He cocked his head to one side. "Would you have stayed?"

I shook my head and smiled. "No. I would have taken the first train to New York once you thought I was settled in the hotel."

The waiter poured our drinks.

"Tea in a china cup," he said. "We're back in civilization."

I raised my cup to him. "My thanks to you. When does your train leave for Washington?"

"As soon as I deliver you."

Maybe it was the hot tea or the fact that I was within reach of my cousins, either way or both, I had a lighthearted moment. "Are you ready to get rid of your burden so quickly?"

"No, Mary. I do not find you a burden. I have responsibilities in Washington."

"I shouldn't have been so flippant. When I am completely back in good health, do you still want me to work with you? I could come to Washington and work until Daniel returns. That might be some payment for the trouble you've gone through."

He leaned in toward me. "And then what? If Lieutenant Phillips has plans for the two of you, you will leave and I will be without an assistant."

I thought about what he said. I knew most nurses he found unsatisfactory. Most did not want to put up with his guff. Except for Grace, I had always been the one who he called upon. I had learned to accept his brash manner and appreciate his knowledge and skills as a physician.

"You must have had a helper before the war."

"I've tried a few and ended up carrying on by myself."

"I'm not surprised," I said.

Karl just shook his head.

"Karl, for the first time, since I saw you going up the steps to the U. S. Patent Hospital, I feel I can talk freely to you. I apologize for my last remark, although it was honest."

He smiled. "So, we part on a friendly basis?"

I nodded, "I would say we do."

It was a short ride to the Morgan house in a horse-drawn taxi where Jenny was at home when we arrived. The front door flew open and there she was. She looked so glowing and healthy my spirits were lifted. I hurried up the walk to her welcoming arms.

"Mary! I've been waiting for you." Then she saw Karl bringing my case. "Dr. S.?" She whispered. It was a question and exclamation in one.

314

He set down the case and doffed his hat. "Good morning, Mrs. Stevens. It is nice to see you again."

"Please come in," she said as she backed from the open door.

"No, thank you," he replied. "I promised Miss Sullivan's young man that I would see her safely back. My mission is complete and my train leaves for Washington within the hour."

I was cordial. "Karl, I can never repay you for your kindness. May you have a safe trip home."

"Drop me a letter to let me know how you are doing." He touched a finger to his hat, turned and left.

The maid appeared to take my case and closed the door. Jenny hooked her arm through mine and led me to the parlor where we sat together on a settee. Behind the glasses, Jenny's eyes appeared as saucers. "You called him Karl."

"He asked to be called by his first name. Don't ask me why, Jenny. The man baffles me. Ever since I took sick, he has acted as if I was his sole responsibility."

"He probably thought you weren't going to make it and didn't want it on his conscience. You won't like me saying this, Mary, but I must say it. You look like a wilted flower."

"A black-eyed Susan," I said.

Jenny laughed. "At least you haven't lost your sense of humor."

I smiled at my sweet cousin. "I know what I look like. I saw myself in a full-length mirror. I planned on going on to Albany, but I knew Karl would insist on going all the way, so I decided to stay here for a while. Only until I'm stronger."

"When we received the telegram you would be coming we were all pleased. Mother and Abby are at the warehouse and Florence has taken the toddler for a walk in the fresh air. Once we are all together, you must tell us what you have been through. The newspapers are optimistic the war is nearly over."

"At City Point the sick and wounded keep coming. It is a disheartening scene, Jenny."

"I can picture it. Right now you need to get settled in your room. I am so glad to have company. Mother has me confined to the house until the baby comes. I feel like I'm in jail."

"What about Ted?" I asked.

"He is helping on the Commission boats. I expect he will be home for Christmas. You wrote that Daniel was at City Point. Is he well?"

I offered a weak smile. "He was well when I left. I was the one who looked like I'd been through the battles."

"You have, Mary. It is so good to have you here."

I went up to the cozy room I had occupied before and lay my tired body on the soft bed. It was good to be back.

At the large dining table that evening I told them what I had seen and done and about getting sick. Aunt Martha, Abby, Florence. Jenny and I ate a meal of ham, carrots, cabbage and potatoes with sourdough bread. It tasted so good. Little Johnathan sat at the table in a high chair and we laughed at his antics. Little children have a way of bringing smiles even in the darkest of times, which unknown to us, were yet to come.

Chapter 53

I stayed with my cousins for three weeks. As Jenny was home all day by herself, I stayed with her. She was doing a lot of handwork getting a layette ready for the baby coming. I did my part by knitting a sweater and bonnet. I used peach-colored yarn with cream ribbon for the bonnet ties. Jenny was delighted. We played cards and checkers. Most times we talked and ate and laughed. For exercise we strolled around the back yard.

I wrote to Daniel. His return letter said he was in good health and he was kept busy. He said he missed me but did not elaborate further. The tone of his letter was upbeat even though he would have no free time during the holidays.

I wrote to Karl as he had requested and told him I was doing much better. I had color in my cheeks, was gaining weight, and the raccoon eyes were gone. I told him I was going to Albany. I was not sure of what I planned after that. He wrote back:

Dear Mary,

I am pleased to hear that you are strong enough to go on to your parents. It will give you quiet time to sort out your thoughts. With your improved well-being I trust it has brought with it your cheery smile. It always pleased the wounded as it did me.

I am doing some work in my private practice and helping out at the hospitals, but I do not do it on a contractual basis. I do it on my own schedule. The hospitals can always use a helping hand. I do my best to keep a low profile and hold my tongue at the inadequacies of others.

I have told Mrs. Miller of your progress as she was concerned about you when you were here. To put it in her words, 'the poor dear looked awful'. I had to agree. We both send good wishes that you continue to do well.

Sincerely,
Karl

The letter made me smile. Mrs. Miller would undoubtedly blush if she knew what he had written, but that was Karl. Diplomacy was not his strong suit. His letter brought to mind the soldiers in the hospitals. Help was always needed. Would I go back? I didn't think so. I had seen enough.

Aunt Martha and Abby took me in a carriage to catch the train to Albany on a cold December morning. Aunt Martha had sent a lovely shawl for Mother and two pairs of socks for Father along with jars of strawberry jam, pickled pears, and molasses cookies. They had been so good to me I wanted to repay their kindness in some way. Aunt Martha said being Jenny's company through her long days and seeing me back in good health was payment enough.

As the train moved northward, I liked looking out at the Hudson River Valley even in the winter. There was a light covering of snow which gave the countryside a calm serene appearance. I didn't want to think of City Point, the faces of the anguished men, or the peaceful countenance of those who had died. However, I couldn't put them out of my mind no matter how hard I tried to concentrate on joyful things.

Father was waiting in the buggy when I arrived at the station. He loaded my belongings in the back before he gave me a hug. "We're glad to have you back, Mary. Mother stayed home to prepare a welcome home supper," Father said. We had five miles to go in the cold air, but he had brought a fur lap robe and I was toasty warm sitting under it. I held a wool scarf to my face at intervals to relieve the sting of the cold.

Father looked much the same. There was a little more silver hair at his temples, but he looked as pleasant as he usually did. He tapped the reins and we were on our way.

"Martha wrote that you have been in poor health."

"I would rather she hadn't. I know how Mother worries. The doctor who treated me thought I had a bad infection from a bug bite of some kind. That is the reason I'm back or I would have stayed at the headquarters." I let out a big sigh. "But, I think it was time for me to leave."

We turned off the main road toward the village where we lived. It was some time before Father said, "I realize what you've been through, Mary. I believe it is best if you keep it from your mother."

I nodded. "Yes, I know."

"Do you plan on staying?" he asked.

"I am not sure. For now, it's good to be back. I do like working in medicine, which I never would have known if I hadn't left and joined the Sanitary Commission."

He looked over at me and smiled. "That has been a blessing for your mother. The church has formed a relief organization where the ladies all get together to work on whatever the current need is. She says they ask about you. As your infrequent notes are in the positive vein, she can report how grateful the nurses are for the supplies they receive."

"I didn't need to write about the horrors I saw every day, and it was the goods provided by the relief organizations that many times saved our soldiers. The government wasn't prepared. Father, the men would have been in dire straits without the Sanitary Commission."

The modest white Cape Cod house with blue shutters I grew up in came into view. I looked up at the dormer on the left where my room had always been. A flood of memories washed over me. I felt a lump in my throat as I fought back tears. Could it be I wasn't as strong as I thought I was?

Chapter 54

It was January 27th when we received a telegram that Jenny had delivered an eight-pound baby girl. Both mother and baby were doing well. It was welcome news to all of us.

Later, I received a letter from Jenny asking me to come to New York for the christening. Would I like to be Elaine Martha's godmother? Elaine Martha was named for her two grandmothers. The christening would take place on February 28th.

I was thrilled not only for being asked to be the godmother, but because it meant a good excuse to leave. After being at home for two months, I was getting antsy to leave.

Christmas had been Father, Mother and me attending church services. Mother spent the whole afternoon preparing a chicken dinner. Father read a magazine. I played solitaire.

Mother and I had made fruitcakes, sweet-breads and cookies the week before. That didn't seem enough sweets for Mother because she baked a pumpkin cake and an apple pie. I was not allowed in the kitchen on Christmas Day. It was her special dinner, and I smiled to myself when I heard her humming.

She did let me set the walnut dining table with her prized china, crystal water glasses, and silver.

After dinner we opened presents. I gave Mother a set of soap, toilet water and bath powder.

Father received a smart-looking tie. He had a respectable position at the bank, and I thought he should brighten up a bit with his clothing. He gave Mother a box of chocolates. She gave him a sleepshirt she had sewn. I received a lovely Cameo necklace.

"You needed something pretty to wear, Mary. That white stone around your neck is not much to please the eye." At times Mother could be as blunt as Karl.

"I wear that for a soldier," I replied.

Her eyebrows flew up. "A soldier? You must tell us about him."

I shrugged, trying to appear nonchalant. "There isn't much to tell. We met three years ago at Christmas. He is from Vermont, and we have seen each other sporadically since. The pebble is one I had found on the beach in Long Island. I have always considered it a good luck charm, so I gave it to Daniel. He had it made into a necklace."

Father looked over at me. "That's quite personal."

Those words aggravated me. "Father, Daniel and I have both seen the terrible disasters of war. If wearing a pebble around my neck gives both of us a promise of hope, then I shall continue to wear it with honor."

"I'm sorry, Mary. I didn't mean to upset you."

I simmered down as quickly as I had flared up. "I shouldn't have been offended so easily. Daniel is frequently in harm's way, and I have much concern for his welfare."

Mother sighed. "Vermont is not that far away. When I was young, my parents took me to visit a lady who lived there. I remember it as a quiet place much like it is here."

Here? Where the Town Hall is the center that holds town meetings, local theatrical productions, wedding receptions, and dances every Saturday night? Was that to be my destiny? I had sat in the sewing circles with the church ladies discussing children and home life. Would I still be doing that twenty-five years from now? Mother didn't know it, but she had planted a seed. I knew what I was going to do.

Chapter 55

On February 28th I was holding Elaine Martha in my arms and listening to the Episcopal minister pronounce the christening words. The sweet cherub was dressed in a long white gown of silk and lace. The godfather was Ted's brother, who was as stocky and jovial as Ted.

I looked over at the parents who were beaming with pride. Daniel said it was a mistake to wed before the war was over. It had worked for Ted and Jenny. I wondered if it would have worked for Daniel and me. I wasn't sure.

At the Morgan house there was a crowd of people to celebrate the christening of the new baby. It seemed all was right with the world, but it wasn't.

Wilmington, North Carolina was now in Union hands. Johnathan was appointed to Brigadier General and was in charge of that section of North Carolina. Florence and little Johnathan had joined him.

Two days ago a letter arrived from her, which was disturbing:

Dear Mother and Sisters,

This is a most distressing time. Nine thousand prisoners have arrived from the Georgia prisons of Andersonville and Florence with three thousand of them in need of hospital care.

As if that wasn't enough to overload the place, Sherman sent nine thousand refugees: men, women, and children. Both white and black, they came ragged, helpless and hungry.

The condition of the prisoners is beyond description. They appear as skeletons, they are so emaciated. Many have lived in such cramped conditions they cannot straighten their limbs. Forty men have all or portions of their feet rotted off. They are full of vermin and some are reduced to imbeciles. Along with them came camp fever and smallpox.

I know many will die before they reach the North. The boats are coming to transport them to Washington for the northern hospitals. In the meantime, Johnathan is overwhelmed at trying to provide for all the needs. Houses and buildings are turned into shelters. Many of the helpers, enlisted men, nurses and doctors alike have taken sick. Even the chaplains are not immune.

Thanks to one of our tireless Commission ladies back home, we have received nine thousand shirts and drawers. Our men came in rags and are so thankful for what they receive. We do what we can for the refugees, but our supplies are short for so many.

I have a nanny for Johnny. We have a nice back yard and I have instructed her that he is not to leave the house or yard without my permission. I want to keep him away from the sick.

I am not sorry I came. I have put some of the willing refugees, to work: cleaning, washing, cooking, and any chore I find where they can be useful.

Mother, when you see Mrs. Schuyler, Mr. Olmstead, or Dr. Bellows, you must tell them what marvels they have performed in starting this Sanitary Commission and the relief organizations.

I know the country is tiring of this war, but the needs are great and maybe even greater than they were in the beginning. In all honesty, I did not realize the gravity of it all. It is one thing to read about it and another to live it.

Please tell Cousin Mary that I appreciate what she has done for our soldiers. It was wise of her to take a respite, one cannot do this day after day without some relief from the sorrow.

And, dear Jenny, she did her part also. I am happy she is home and has presented our family with a new baby to fill the void of Johnny's absence. One day we will all be together again.

Until that time, I beg you to continue singing the praises for the relief organizations. We need those supplies!

It may be a few weeks before I can write again. I have written without glossing over the conditions for I felt the need to be truthful.

Our love to all,
Florence

After the christening guests had left, I told Aunt Martha that I was going to resume my position with the Sanitary Commission to work on the boats. They would be bringing the men from Wilmington back to the northern hospitals.

She cautioned me as I had been ill, but I was healthy and ready to take on the sick men once again. These prisoners would be different as they weren't coming from the battlefield. I would be prepared.

Once I had made the decision, I wrote to Daniel and Karl. Karl sent a telegram which read... arrival time?... He knew the Sanitary Commission ships would leave from Alexandria.

I had received a letter from Daniel the week before. City Point was still the headquarters. He said he thought they would take Petersburg in the spring. He gave no explanation as to why. I knew Colonel Dowd attended meetings with General Grant. As Daniel was an aide to Colonel Dowd he was privy to undisclosed plans. He was well and that gladdened me.

Chapter 56

I had fifty dollars that Father had given me. He said it was a gift to start the year of 1865 on the right foot. Aunt Martha gave me a pair of shoes and two pairs of cotton stockings. She called them going away presents. With money in my pocket and new shoes, the world looked rosier.

I took the taxi to the train station by myself and bought my ticket for Washington. Karl had insisted on a reply to his telegram, so I sent back: unsure…arrival…leave...Thursday.

On the train my mind was on Wilmington. I did not bring the valises with supplies I carried on the battlefields as there should be enough supplies on the hospital ship. I had informed Miss Dix that I only wanted to work on the boats.

She wrote back saying she was pleased I was fully recovered. She said I was already on the roster of nurses working on the *Wilson-Small*. It was a comfort to know where I was assigned as I could go directly to the ship based in Alexandria.

It was evening when I arrived at Union Station. I was uneasy. It was early evening and already dark. I walked to the luggage platform and reached for my case when a hand reached from behind me and grasped my suitcase. I let out an exclamation of alarm drawing the attention of others nearby.

"Mary, I had to hurry to get here on time."

My heart was fluttering like a hummingbird. "Karl! You scared me to death!"

"I'm sorry. I didn't see you get off the train before I spied you going for your luggage."

"How did you know I would arrive at this time?"

He picked up my case, slid his other arm through mine and escorted me toward the exit. "I had the stationmaster check the passenger lists. There were only two trains from New York and you weren't on the earlier one."

"I can't say I'm not happy to see you. I don't like the streets of Washington once the sun goes down."

"You will spend the night with us again. I want to talk to you."

There was his buggy waiting. He gave me a hand up, stashed my case in the back, unhitched the horse, and took his place beside me. Immediately, we were on our way.

"You have certainly taken liberties with making decisions for me," I said. "You are very good at giving orders. What if I said I had reservations at my usual hotel?"

"You could cancel them."

"What if I said I preferred to stay in the hotel?"

"You'd be telling a fib and that is unlike you."

I chuckled. "I am glad you came. You aren't going to try to talk me out of going on the ships, are you?"

He didn't answer as he guided the horse onto a side street where men were playing dice on the sidewalk under the gas light, and young women walked the streets.

"I don't like this area. It makes me nervous."

"It's a shortcut. After all you've been through I would think you could handle any situation." He slapped the reins and the horse went into a brisk trot.

When we reached his house, Tim came out to put the horse and buggy away. "Tim, take Miss Sullivan's suitcase up to the guest room after you're through here."

"Yes, sir," responded Tim and climbed into the driver's seat.

We walked up the short brick walk. Karl opened the door and Mrs. Miller appeared from the kitchen.

"You're back in good time," she said to Karl. "I have dinner ready." To Mary she gave a big smile. "Miss Sullivan, it is good to see you looking well. Go ahead up to the guest room, dear, and freshen up. I have a lovely pork roast for supper."

In the bedroom, I poured water into the white porcelain bowl, sloshed the wash cloth in it and washed my face and hands. I no longer wore the long braid. I wore my hair in two braids, crossed them at the back and pinned them together with hairpins, which had a tendency to work their way out. I tightened the pins and smoothed the sides of my hair before I went down to the dining room.

Karl was waiting. He pulled out a chair for me to sit and took a chair across from me. Globe oil lamps lit the room giving it a dim glow. Mrs. Miller put the roast, baked potatoes and green beans on the table. Karl carved the roast then filled our plates with the meat and vegetables. I had to pace myself as I hadn't eaten since breakfast. Second helpings are not always polite, but when one is hungry one doesn't care. I ate my fill and a large portion of the bread pudding for dessert. We continued to sit at the table with our tea after Mrs. Miller cleared away the dishes.

"What is it you wanted to talk to me about?" I asked.

"First, I wanted to be satisfied you are as well as you say, and it appears you are."

I shrugged. "Did you doubt my word?"

"I had to see for myself. I am wondering if you have thought this through. These men coming out of those deplorable prisons are going to be in a much different state than the soldiers from the battlefields."

"How do you mean?"

He took a sip of tea. "Many are going to be crazy as bed bugs."

I smiled. "Is that your medical diagnosis?"

"You understand what I mean. They cannot help but be emotionally warped. Along with their physical disabilities it is going to be a daunting task."

"That's why I'm going, Karl. They need care. Why don't you sign on again?"

332

He shook his head. "Not this time." He changed the subject, "What do you hear from Lieutenant Phillips?"

"He's optimistic that the Union will take Petersburg in the spring."

"What's his reasoning for that? They've been bogged down for almost a year."

I don't know why his words annoyed me, but they did. "How should I know? He is in on private meetings with the generals. I assume they have some kind of military strategy planned."

"More loss of life and limbs no doubt. Do you have to be on the ship at a certain time?"

"My information says the ship leaves the dock at eight in the morning."

"Then we should leave here by seven. You are to be up by six and have breakfast." He said.

I cocked my head, "Still giving orders? If you have nothing else to say, I shall say goodnight. Please thank Mrs. Miller for such a luscious supper."

Karl came around and held the chair as I rose to leave. "Mary, you must promise to send me notice if you feel the need to come back. This time is going to be an emotional drain."

"I am prepared for what I will find. As you said, I have been through so many terrible conditions I should be able to shoulder anything." Karl had been very good to me, but not good enough that I was going to change my mind.

Karl stood looking at me. "I hope you are right. Sleep well."

333

"Good night, Karl, and thank you for meeting me at the station."

Chapter 57

Karl took me to Alexandria the next morning. The *Wilson-Small* sat bouncing with the waves at the dock.

"This is a good boat, at least there's no butcher shop on it," Karl said as we stood looking at the tall ship. "The captain is a good sailor."

"I wish you wouldn't describe an operating room in those terms. I served on it once before. Usually, I was on the *Daniel Webster*. It's much smaller than this one, but I feel a kinship to it. The *Daniel Webster* is considered the most efficient of the fleet."

"You're in good hands," he said. "I wish you well."

"Thank you. We've come a long way, haven't we? I am sorry you're not coming. I know you have much to give."

He shook his head. "Not this time, Mary. My heart isn't in it."

We shook hands and I walked up the gangplank to stand at the rail until the boat backed out of the dock.

Karl stood and watched until I could see him no more.

I made my way to the cabin where I was introduced to the matron, who was an army nurse.

She was hefty and unsmiling. In her forties the woman was all business. "You are to wait here until the rest arrive."

I stood in the large cabin as there were no chairs in which to sit. Within ten minutes, fifteen Sanitary Commission nurses had gathered. We were taken on a tour of the ship to familiarize ourselves to the Diet Kitchen, the apothecary, area reserved for the seriously ill, and the supply room. The quartermaster was a young soldier I had met at White House Landing.

We were shown to our crowded quarters below deck. I had a tendency to get sea sick in the hull of the ship, so after we were dismissed, I looked for a place I might sleep that was closer to the outside air. My search took me past the supply room.

"Miss Sullivan," the young soldier called. "Is that you?"

I tried to think of his name, although that wasn't necessary because he said, "It's Howie Robinson. Remember me from White House Landing?"

I walked to the counter. "I recognized you, Howie, but it took me a minute to remember your name."

"I didn't forget you, Miss Sullivan. How about Miss Annie?"

"Miss Annie died almost two years ago." I had not thought of Annie in months. Her image popped into my mind and I had to smile to myself.

"I sure am sorry to hear that. Miss Annie was one of a kind."

"She was that," I said.

In a confidential voice, he said, "Now, Miss Sullivan, if there's anything you need, anything at all, you just tell me and I'll see you get it."

"Howie that would be wonderful. I don't know what to expect from the patients we're going to load on board."

"I hear they're in right bad shape."

"We'll know soon enough. By the way, I'm looking for a place to sleep that isn't below deck. I get sick."

He was quick with an answer. "In the big cabin, where the bunks are for the patients, I've got an extra storage room. It ain't too big and you'd have to sleep with crates of supplies, but I think it could work. I can move a couple of crates…"

"I've slept on crates before," I interrupted him. "Have you got a mattress?"

"I'll fix it up for you and give you an extra key."

"Thank you, Howie, you have saved the day. I knew I couldn't stay below, and the only other choice was out on the cold deck."

"I'm glad I can do it. You probably only need it for two nights. On the way back, it's always so busy for the nurses, they don't get time to sleep. They catch a nap in a chair if they can."

I slept two nights in the extra storeroom. Howie had given me the softest mattress he could find, two pillows, sheets and two blankets. I opened the port hole in the back to let in the cool air. As we went south the cold March air wasn't as biting.

We reached Wilmington in late afternoon. The matron in charge told us we would be taken to a house where there would be food and lodging for the Sanitary Commission nurses. I hoped to see Florence, but time was regimented, which gave me no free time. We would be taken back to the boat at five o'clock the next morning. There would be two hundred and fifty soldiers taken aboard beginning at six o'clock.

Chapter 58

Karl had said I should be ready for anything after what I had been through, but I wasn't. When the former prisoners were brought to the dock to be loaded onto the boat I almost threw up. I had never seen such emaciated men or the conditions of their bodies. Florence had said they looked like skeletons and they did. The skin was drawn so tight I couldn't believe they were still alive.

Those who needed it were loaded onto stretchers and drawn by pulleys to be deposited in the waiting cots and bunks. There was the smell of rotting flesh, the grotesque positions of those who couldn't straighten their arms and legs. Some men were in a fetal position.

As Karl had suspected there were many with emotional wounds. Young men who sat in a catatonic state, others who screamed out reliving the horrors they had endured, and those with darting eyes of mistrust and fists raised when they were approached. Young men still in their teens who looked forty. What could we do for them? How could they be brought back into a sane world? Or was the world sane to allow such treatment? There were some who wouldn't make it back to the hospitals of the North. For them, death was a blessing.

I was assigned to the seriously ill ward with two other nurses. We had fifty patients in our care with conditions that ranged from smallpox to tuberculosis to gangrene. I wore a mask as Karl had suggested when working around the chest cases. I wore rubber gloves when changing linens and staying clear of the bubbling rotting flesh of gangrene. I washed my hands as often as I could before and after giving nourishment, which meant spoon feeding some of the patients. Most feeds were soft or ground up in an attempt to get their stomachs back into working order.

The other two nurses and I worked around the clock. The *Wilson-Small* sailed directly to Annapolis, Maryland, where the soldiers that successfully made the trip were taken to the Naval Academy Hospital. Alongside the army nurses were the volunteers. I had heard that so many women volunteers came from Maine, they were called the "Maine stay".

I was happy when our sad cargo was unloaded for I knew they were home and would be given the proper care they needed. It was the end of March when our fleet delivered the former prisoners to the hospitals in the North.

On my last trip, the *Wilson-Small* docked in Alexandria. I had gone to my usual hotel when I left the ship on the last day of March. I wanted some time to myself. I had survived four years of destruction of human life. The war was almost over and I had to make plans for what I was going to do. I had no teaching position to go back to. Did I want to go back to the small quiet town? What if I went to New York City? I couldn't stay with my cousins forever. What if Daniel returns and asks me to marry him? What if Daniel returns and doesn't ask me to marry him? There were so many questions for which I didn't have an answer.

On April 2, 1865, I heard the newsboy calling, "Petersburg falls! Come get your evening edition!"

It seemed the city of Washington came alive. I heard the firing of cannons and muskets and loud shouts of "God bless Grant". Church bells rang with deafening clangs.

I wanted to share the good news, but I had no one to share it with. I was alone.

The next day I found myself knocking on Karl's door. Mrs. Miller answered it. "Miss Sullivan, this is a pleasure."

"Hello, Mrs. Miller is the doctor in?"

"No, dear, I'm sorry. I believe he went to help in the hospital. Is there something I can do for you?"

"No, thank you. Do you know when he will return?"

"He never misses supper. Do you want to wait?"

"No, that's all right. Please tell him I stopped by."

"Isn't it wonderful news that the war is almost at an end? Are you on your way home?"

"It is wonderful news. I believe I will be leaving in a day or so. It was nice talking with

341

you, Mrs. Miller. You have been kind to me and I appreciate that."

"I do admire what you have done for our soldiers, Miss Sullivan. If I brought some kindness into your life, I'm glad."

I turned to leave and waved to her when I reached the street as she watched me go. I went straight back to my hotel room and took a nap. I napped later than I had planned. The hotel dining room closed at seven, so I hurried to freshen up before I went down. There were a few other diners still there. I ordered the special of the day as I thought it would be the fastest way for the cook and hoped there was some left. I sat near a window, but it was getting dusk outside and there wasn't much to see. There was one good note for the day. I had decided to return to my parents' home. I guess it was still mine, also, but it didn't feel that way when I had left in January.

I finished my food, paid the bill and went out to the foyer. There stood Karl. "What are you doing here?" came my startled welcome.

"And, it's nice to see you, too," he said. "Come have a seat. Mrs. Miller told me you had stopped by. How long have you been back?"

"We docked on the last day of March. I have decided to go home to Albany."

"Why did you decide to come and see me?" he asked.

"I wanted you to help me make that decision. From the news, the war is almost over, and I have to think of my future."

"It looks that way. Have you heard from your young man?"

I shook my head. "Not since I told you, he thought the siege of Petersburg was near an end." Then I grasped his hand, "Karl, you were so right not to sign up to care for the prisoners. I thought I was prepared, but no one could prepare for such a pitiful sight. How could others be so cruel to their fellow man? At least they are back and being cared for."

He placed his other hand over mine. "I'm grateful you returned with your full faculties. Go home, Mary. Take your time in deciding what you want to do."

He rose from his seat and gave me a hand up. "Lieutenant Phillips should be home soon. Write and let me know of your plans."

"Karl, I have to thank you for all you've done for me. At times, I think you understand me better than I do myself."

He gave a quiet laugh. "That is the role of a well-trained physician. We are taught to heal others but not ourselves."

His words confused me and that wasn't unusual.

"Thank you for coming. You have a habit of showing up at the right time. Goodbye. I promise to write and I always keep my promises."

He leaned down and gave me a kiss on the cheek. "Goodbye, Mary. You have brought some sunshine into my life."

I smiled to myself on the way to my room. Tomorrow, I would send a telegram to my parents and buy a ticket for home.

Chapter 59

Four days after I returned home, April 9, 1865, General R.E. Lee surrendered to General Ulysses S. Grant at Appomattox Courthouse. The North went wild with joy.

A week later I received a letter from Daniel, which was forwarded from the Morgan house in New York City. Daniel was sure Aunt Martha knew where I was. He would be arriving in Washington and would be mustered out of the army. I sent a letter to the army base in Washington telling him I was in Albany.

Finally, in early May he arrived at my parents' house. I ran out to meet him. We wrapped in each other's arms right there in the street. The guest room was ready for him, and Mother had prepared her favorite fried chicken dinner.

In the living room, I introduced him to Father and Mother. "We are proud to have you here," said Father. "Thank God this awful war is behind us."

"Yes, sir. May we learn from this and never allow it to happen again. It will take a long time for us to heal."

"I hope you like chicken, Daniel," said Mother. "This is one of Mary's favorites. We are so happy to have her back home."

"I'm sure you are, Mrs. Sullivan. The odor of your dinner makes my mouth water. Mary tells me you are an excellent cook."

Daniel knew how to flatter, and I could see it pleased Mother to the tips of her toes.

Later that evening, Daniel and I sat holding hands on the porch swing. "What are you going to do, Mary? Do you plan to go back to teaching?"

"I haven't made any firm plans."

His next words were like a dagger in my heart. "I'm going to stay in the army. There's a lot of work to be done, and I want to be a part of it."

I don't know why his plan to reenlist hit me so hard, but it did. "I thought you wanted out of the military way of life. Army officers don't stay in one place. They have to relocate at the whim of the army."

He kissed my hand. "There'd be promise for us. You could teach in the schools or work in the hospitals. An army base takes care of its own. You would have privileges as an officer's wife."

I thought this decision very unlike Daniel. "What has made you change your mind?"

"I've changed," he said. "I don't want to go back to Vermont. I find I like the pace of the military life. I can move up in rank and one day be in charge of my own base."

I shook my head. "I don't know, Daniel."

"Think it over, Mary. We could do it all together."

He kissed me in a loving way. I hadn't felt his lips on mine since we were in City Point. Those were gentle kisses when I was so weak. His touch still sent a thrill through my very being. "I will think it over, Daniel," I whispered.

All that night I couldn't get his decision out of my head. Did I want to be an army wife? I had seen enough to know what was expected. It seemed to me that officers' wives were to be proper at all times and never make a misstep. They arranged teas for other wives, arranged for dinners, dances, concerts and plays. The types of social displays that Abby could do to perfection. And, when the soldier got an order to move, it was the wives who made the arrangements.

The next morning we had breakfast after which Daniel and I went for a walk. I did the most difficult thing I have ever done. I took the pebble from around my neck and handed it to him.

"Daniel, I can't be an officer's wife. I thought about it all night. I don't fit into that way of life, and I'm rather surprised you think I would. That little piece of stone has seen us both through the perils of war, and that's what it was meant to do. As much as I have dreamed of being your wife, I realize that war has changed us both. I hope you reach your dream. I am going to go to Washington and work with Karl. I want to live in the city, and I want to work in medicine."

"When did he become Karl?" he asked.

"When he promised you to see me home safely. He is an excellent physician, Daniel. I can learn so much more."

"Is there anything I can do to make you change your mind?"

347

"No. Not anymore than I can do anything to make you change yours."

He pulled me to him and hugged me tight. "I love you, Mary."

I cried on his shoulder. "You don't know how many times I've wanted to hear those words."

He stroked my hair. "Let's give it some more time."

"What good will that do?"

"We will be separated and know exactly what we should do."

I stood back, wiped my teary eyes, and nodded. "All right, but we've been separated before."

"And always came back together." He smiled at me and the world was right again. He stayed that night. When he left in the morning, I told him we would both be in Washington. I planned on staying at my usual hotel where he could find me.

Chapter 60

I sent a letter to Karl to tell him I wanted to work with him. He wrote back that was better news than hearing war was over. He even enclosed a train ticket and said he would meet me at Union Station. I was to use the guest room.

He met me at the station, but I told him I was going to stay at the hotel as Daniel and I had to iron out our problems.

He didn't protest. Karl took me to the hotel and told me to contact him when I was ready.

Daniel and I saw each other once more in Washington. We knew that a marriage between us would not work. I cried for a week. We deeply cared for each other, but the war had changed us both. Daniel said he wanted to keep the little stone I had given to him as a good luck charm. "Perhaps it will get me where I feel I have to go."

I was glad to leave it with him. I would never wear it around my neck again. And, if he carried it, I would always be a part of his life.

Daniel married a woman who cherishes the role of an officer's wife and is behind him every step of the way on his climb to the top.

Two years after working with Karl, he and I were married. We are the proud parents of four children (who all know how to spell and pronounce their last name, thanks to Karl). To their friends I am Mrs. S.

My cousin Abby is the queen of the social set in Philadelphia after her marriage to Edward. Jenny and Ted have three children and have stayed with Aunt Martha. Florence is a military wife as Johnathan remained in the army. Emily is director of a soldiers' hospital. Charley is vice president of a shipping company. Aunt Martha is a pillar of the American Red Cross started by Clara Barton a few years after the U.S. Sanitary Commission was disbanded. Father and Mother are still in their quiet little town near Albany.

When our first daughter was born, I received the good luck pebble I had given Daniel. He wrote:

Dearest Mary,

May your little girl wear this charm and may it keep her safe as it did me through those terrible years. It pleases me to know that you and Karl are happy. He is a good man.

Do you think it was Providence that brought us together during those years so that we could keep our sanity? You will always hold a special place in my heart.

May God continue to bless you.

Sincerely,
Daniel

Karl was sitting in his office when I showed him the necklace and Daniel's note.

"Think, Mary. Someday we'll read he's a general and you'll still be stuck with me." He raised the necklace and gave it a gentle swing. "Put it in a safe place. One day you can tell our daughter the whole story."

I took it from him and dropped it in my pocket. "Do you think Daniel will ever make it to the rank of general?"

"A general with no sense," Karl said.

"Karl, that's unkind. Daniel is a bright man."

He shook his head. "No, Mary, if he had any sense, he would have snagged you when he had the chance." Karl reached out and grabbed me around the waist, pulled me into his lap, and kissed me with passion. "The best man won."

My husband never ceased to amaze me, and still does.

As I put an end to this memoir, I give thanks for the U.S. Sanitary Commission: to Dr. Elizabeth Blackwell, who saw the need for female nurses, for the forward thinking of Frederick Olmstead, Henry Bellows, Louisa Lee Schuyler, and all the dedicated women of the relief organizations for their selfless and tireless efforts to provide for our soldiers.

I am proud of the noble work we nurses performed for our men who fought so gallantly. Truly, we earned the right to call ourselves the Sisters of Mercy.

About the Author

Millie Curtis makes her home in
Clarke County, Virginia.

Other Books by Millie Curtis

Beyond the Red Gate
The Milliner
The Newcomer
Window of Hope
Of Course She Knew!
Never a Sure Thing
Roseville's Blooming Lilly
English Lessons
The Itchy Foot

Available on Amazon and Barnes & Noble

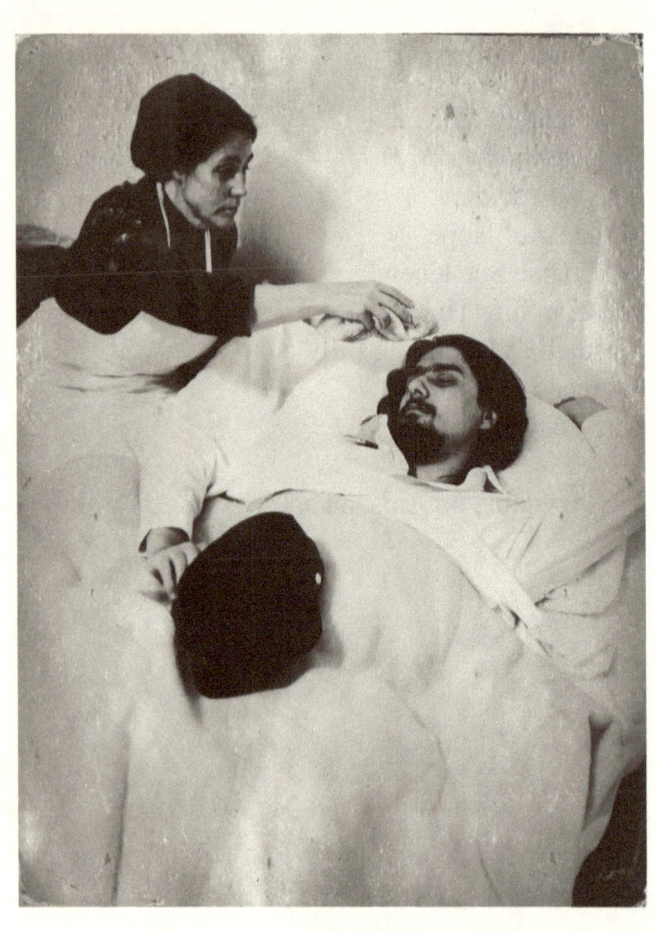

www.ingramcontent.com/pod-product-compliance
Lightning Source LLC
Chambersburg PA
CBHW05091525O626
47155CB00001B/238